HOLDING OUT
FOR A
COWBOY

A. J. PINE

Published by Sourcebooks Casablanca, an imprint of Sourcebooks
P.O. Box 4410, Naperville, Illinois 60567-4410
(630) 961-3900
sourcebooks.com

Printed and bound in Canada.
MBP 10 9 8 7 6 5 4 3 2 1

To second chances.
It's not too late.

Chapter 1

CASEY WALSH SWORE SHE HEARD THE SWEET melodic sound of harp strings, as if heaven were opening its gates to welcome her—or more like the serene reception area of one of those fancy Chico spas she'd been to once, but that was a lifetime ago.

She hummed out a soft sigh and pulled her quilt tight over her shoulder, snuggling deeper into her pillow as whatever dream she was having played out in her subconscious. Heaven or spa, it didn't matter. She'd wake to the same reality either way.

Again, the soft refrain chimed, a sound so familiar she could almost hum it, yet it still felt out of reach.

Over and over, the same few notes twinkled, pulsing like a wave.

"Casey," it cooed softly. "Casey. Casey. Casey."

"*Casey!*"

Her eyes flew open, and Casey bolted upright only to knock her forehead against what felt like a boulder, but she had zero recollection of a boulder dangling over her bed.

"Ow! Jesus, Case. If that was my nose, you would have broken it!"

Ivy Serrano, Casey's best friend since childhood, rubbed her temple, her lips pursed in a pout.

The harp from Casey's dream was still there, playing on repeat just off to the right.

Her *phone* alarm.

"Oh my god!" Casey cried. "What time is it? How much did I oversleep? Why the hell did I say yes to shooting whiskey with Pearl right before closing?"

Pearl Sweeney—Meadow Valley matriarch and owner of the Meadow Valley Inn—had popped into Midtown Tavern just as Casey was closing up the night before.

"You didn't think I was letting you off the hook without a shot for luck, did you?" Pearl had asked. "It's not every day a girl gets a second chance at her dream."

Only one shot had turned into two, maybe three, which was fine because Casey's interview wasn't until 1:00 p.m. Only now it was…it was…

"Ivy," Casey croaked, her voice not yet caught up to the fact that it and *she* were awake. "What time is?"

"Eleven fifteen," Ivy said. "You told me you were leaving at 11:30, so of course I came to see you off, but when you didn't answer, I used my key, and—long story short—I think we might both be concussed."

"Shit," Casey swore, scrambling out of bed. "Ives, what am I gonna do?"

Ivy tossed her bright yellow scarf over her shoulder and brushed off her navy wool coat. "Give me your keys. I'll warm up your car while you get ready. Your good-luck pumpkin spice latte is on the counter in the kitchen."

Casey grabbed her keys off the dresser and tossed them to Ivy with a snarl. "There had better not be pumpkin spice *anything* in my kitchen, and you know it," she said with half a sneer.

Ivy snorted. "It's black coffee with a dusting of cinnamon, the same way you've had it since high school. But I do adore how much you hate autumn's most beloved fruit."

"Are you gonna start my car or what? I haven't driven Adeline all week, so she's gonna need some extra love." She patted her head, feeling a knotted tuft of what needed to be her perfectly beach-waved silver balayage.

Ugh. What had possessed her to grow her hair out when she'd been doing the wash-and-go pixie for years?

This morning had. Today. This interview. After twelve years, she was going to reclaim part of what she'd lost all those years ago. But that meant wowing the board of directors at the prestigious Salon and Cosmetology Institute in Reno, Nevada. The same Salon and Cosmetology Institute she dropped out of over a decade ago. The *same* Salon and Cosmetology Institute that needed to readmit her with the credit hours she'd already completed so she could finally put her tavern apron to rest and open her own salon.

But if she was late for her interview, there would be no wowing of any board, no matter how fabulous a specimen her hair was.

She stumbled out of her room and into the bathroom where she plugged in her hot iron, threw her hair in a shower cap, and hopped in the shower to rinse the late night at the tavern from her body.

Two minutes later, she stood wrapped in a towel as she sprayed her homemade detangler—a mix of water, her favorite conditioner, and a few drops of rosemary and peppermint essential oils—in her hair, brushed away her bedhead, and then reached for her waving iron.

She wound the first lock of hair around the barrel of the wand and squinted at herself in the mirror.

"Is that a...?"

She leaned closer to the reflective glass, rolling her eyes at herself as she confirmed that—*yes*—that certainly was a bruise forming above her left eyebrow from coldcocking Ivy as she flew out of bed. Nothing a little concealer couldn't take care of.

But wait... Did she smell smoke?

Casey sniffed, looking to her left and then to her right. Something definitely smelled like it was burning. Like burning—*hair*.

"Shit!" she yelled, practically ripping the wand from her hair.

Her *smoking* hair.

"Do I smell burning?" Ivy called as Casey heard the front door slam. "Because this is some *really* bad déjà vu, Case. Are you okay?"

Casey didn't have time to ruminate on how Ivy had almost burned her clothing boutique down just days before her grand opening. Because—her *hair*!

"Um…Ives?" she asked quietly at first, too nervous for her friend to see what she'd done.

"Case?" Ivy called, louder and a bit frantic.

"In the bathroom!" Casey called back, but the words came out as more of a whimper.

Ivy stopped short in the doorframe, a hint of smoke still wafting in the air.

"Oh, Casey," she said, the corners of her mouth turning down. "What happened, sweetie?"

Casey's eyes burned, but she swallowed the threat of tears. She'd been putting on a brave face for twelve years now. She'd played the long game, trained for the marathon when it came to caging her emotions. Because the alternative was what? To let everyone know that she might be broken—might have been broken ever since the day…

Nope. She wasn't going there, not now when she had burnt hair, a bruised eyebrow, and mere minutes to get on the road.

"I can fix it!" she exclaimed, pulling a pair of salon shears from one of the bathroom drawers.

And she did. Because if there was one place where Casey Walsh didn't falter—even if it meant recovering from a monstrous blunder like singeing a lock of hair—it was hair.

"You always did want bangs," Ivy said with a forced smile.

Because Casey had *never* wanted bangs. Every time she thought she did, she'd cut them, hate them, and then grow them out. It became a running joke. Every time Casey needed to change something in her life, especially when it was one of the pesky external factors over which she had no control, Ivy would say, "You always did want bangs," and Casey would grab her shears.

Ninety seconds later, Casey Walsh had blunt silver bangs that fell just below her eyebrows.

"It's a win-win!" she admitted as realization set in. "Covers my bruise from our unfortunate headbutting."

Ivy pouted and rubbed her temple. "I'm sure I'm bruised too," she insisted. "Just because you can't see it doesn't mean it isn't there."

Casey laughed. The morning started out as a disaster, but she'd turned it around. After a quick change from her towel to the denim jumpsuit Ivy had insisted she borrow from her boutique, she dabbed some gloss on her lips and gave her on-the-fly haircut another look of approval.

"How do I look?" she asked Ivy as she slid her arms into her red puffer coat and slung her bag over her shoulder.

"You look like my gorgeous, take-no-prisoners friend who is going to knock the socks off that board of directors and get all her credits reinstated. But you don't want to forget this." She handed Casey the travel mug of coffee that otherwise would have tragically been left behind.

Casey blew out a long breath. "And Addy?"

Ivy winked. "Only a couple of mild coughs before she purred to life. I can't believe you're still driving that thing."

Casey scoffed, then shushed her friend. "That car was bequeathed to me by my great-grandma Adeline when she passed. It's all I have left of the woman I barely knew, and it was *free*. No car payment. Just insurance. Plus, I've barely driven it since we graduated high school. And she was given a full Boo—" She stopped herself before completing the thought.

A full Boone Murphy tune-up before she'd ever been allowed to take it on the road.

Because besides Boone Murphy being—or having been—Meadow Valley's best and only mechanic, he was also Casey's ex, a man whose name went more the way of Voldemort in Casey's presence—*he who shall not be named*.

"You think," Ivy started hesitantly, "that maybe

your oversleeping and being a little scattered this morning have something to do with Boo—"

"Nope!" Casey interrupted.

It had nothing to do with today—the day Casey Walsh finally got her life back—also being the day that Boone Murphy was getting married. And leaving Meadow Valley for good.

No possible way all the setbacks that happened this morning had *anything* to do with that. Not when Casey had some rocking new bangs and Great-Granny Adeline's car purring in front of her building.

"This is *my* day," she added, ignoring the slight tremor in her voice.

"Right. The day of Casey," Ivy said. "You got this!"

Chapter 2

BOONE MURPHY STOOD FROM WHERE HE WAS sitting on the edge of the bed, brushed nonexistent lint from the jacket of his rented tux, and strode toward the hotel room cabinet that housed a mini fridge—and miniature bottles of liquor.

He wasn't usually one to crack open a bottle before noon, but today called for—celebration? Liquid courage?

He already had a tiny bottle of rum in his hand when a knock sounded on the door.

"Just a sec," he called, then grabbed the bottle of vodka as well.

He checked his watch, the timer set to go off fifteen minutes before he actually had to leave for the ceremony. He still had plenty of time. So who was already checking up on him, making sure he didn't mess up like he'd done so many times before?

"Keep yourself on a schedule," his therapist had told him. "But one that always puts you *ahead* of schedule. You'll never be penalized for being early."

Setting timers and reminders hadn't been easy at first. He was a small-town man used to the way time flowed in small-town life. Folks in Meadow

Valley didn't live by the clock. They lived by a certain rhythm only they knew. But Boone Murphy had never been able to sync to that rhythm. And it had taken him years to figure out why.

Another knock, this one louder than before.

"All right already!" he called out, irritation evident in his tone. "I said I was coming."

Boone finally opened the door to find a slightly older version of himself—his brother Eli—staring back at him. The same light-blue eyes and dark-brown hair, but Eli's already had a few strands of silver here and there, despite him being barely thirty-five. Boone guessed being a widower could do that to a man. He'd experienced loss himself, but nothing the likes of what Eli had gone through. Yet here was his big brother, wearing a tux and smiling back at Boone with that knowing look.

"Is one of those for me?" Eli asked. "Or does the groom need extra courage?"

"Sorry," Boone told him. "I thought you were… I don't know. Old habits, I guess." He held up both the bottles. "Take your pick. There's more in the cabinet."

Eli grabbed the vodka. "Since I'm not a pirate," he said, then made his way into the room, letting the door close behind him.

Boone chuckled, and the two brothers sat down side by side on the foot of the hotel bed.

"Cheers." Eli held up his tiny bottle, and Boone

clinked his own against it. "Should I make a toast or save that for the reception?"

Boone had already twisted the cap off his bottle and pressed it to his lips, but he paused.

"Depends," he mused. "Would you say the same thing now that you're planning on saying then?"

Eli scrubbed a hand across his clean-shaven jaw. Boone thought it was good to see his brother like this—smiling and making small jokes. If this weekend proved anything, it was that getting Eli Murphy out of Meadow Valley—even if only for a day or two—was good for the man's soul. On that much, Boone could relate. For the last twelve years, he'd been unable to separate his present from the past. That was what happened when you lived your whole life in one place with the same people, day in and day out. The past was always there, reminding him. Haunting him.

So he was getting out for good.

"How about I give you the abbreviated version of both?" Eli replied but didn't wait for Boone to respond. He held his bottle up high and proceeded. "To Boone and Elizabeth. I wish you both a lifetime of love and happiness, to remember that even when you might not like each other, the love that lies beneath it all should remind you of what you have—what you're lucky enough to have found while so many are still looking." He raised his brows. "Eh? What do you think?"

Boone swallowed, unprepared for how his brother's words would hit him. Not because he didn't like—or even *love*—Elizabeth. But because those words made him think of someone else entirely instead of the woman he was hours away from marrying.

He cleared his throat. "That was…um…really good."

"Thanks," Eli said, a seldom seen grin on his face. "Want to know what I'd say now?"

Boone wasn't so sure anymore, but he nodded once.

Again, Eli lifted his miniature bottle. "To my brother Boone. I wish you a lifetime of love and happiness. But sometimes that whole life part has other plans. And when those other plans unfold… shit. I don't know what you're supposed to do. But I do know this. Whoever you choose as your partner through all of it—especially if you're a lucky enough son of a bitch for her to choose you right back—make sure it's someone who not only loves you at your best but can also still find that hidden ray of light when you're at your worst. That's when you know, you know?"

This time, there was no brow raise or smug grin. Eli simply twisted the cap off his bottle of vodka and swallowed it all in two long swigs, not bothering to make eye contact with his brother. Eli was somewhere else now, thinking about Tess, he was sure. But Boone was right here, hours outside Meadow Valley, yet his present still collided with the past.

His throat burned, and his palms began to sweat. So he followed his brother's lead, downing his tiny bottle of rum and running through all the decisions he'd made in his life that had brought him to this point.

"I love her," Boone told him. "Elizabeth, I mean." Though he wasn't sure who he was trying to convince now, Eli or himself.

"I know," Eli said. The two men stared straight ahead rather than looking at one another. "And I'm not saying that we only get one great love, even if that might be what it was for me." He paused for a beat. "But does she love you at your highest high? And your lowest low? Is that how you love her?"

He tipped the bottle to his lips again, even though it was empty. It was a sign that the conversation was over, that Eli wasn't looking for Boone to answer him out loud.

But Boone had to answer to someone, even if it was only himself.

"Did you at least talk to her before leaving town?" Eli asked, surprising Boone by not only continuing their conversation but by butting up against the one topic Boone wasn't willing to approach.

"Eli, you promised…" Boone started.

But Eli shook his head. "I did no such thing.

Maybe you thought we had some sort of silent agreement, but on that front, Little Brother, you are sorely mistaken. If you wanted someone here who would simply toast your good cheer and call it a day, you'd have invited Ash."

Boone let out a bitter laugh. "The guy hasn't had a permanent address in years. Wasn't like I could send him an invitation. Sent him plenty of texts, though. No reply, of course."

Eli sighed. Their youngest brother, Ashton, had been the pride and joy of Meadow Valley when his country music career took off not too long after high school. Now he was more infamous than famous, constantly showing up on tabloid websites in one scandal after another. It had been at least a year since Eli or Boone had heard from him directly, but despite the strain on their relationship with him, Boone had wanted *both* his brothers here today.

"You gonna answer the question?" Eli asked. "Or should I take your silence as a no?"

Boone stood and headed for the minibar again. This time, he grabbed the tiny tequila and Jack Daniel's, tossing his brother the former. Eli caught it in one hand.

"She knows, okay?" Boone insisted, opening his bottle where he stood. "There's nothing that happens in Meadow Valley that Casey Walsh doesn't know. That's the beauty of being everyone's favorite barkeep. You don't miss a beat when it comes to the happenings of small-town life."

So no, he hadn't told Casey Walsh, the onetime love of his life turned what? Enemy? Acquaintance? He'd have preferred the former. Then at least there would still be something between them. But Casey's animosity for him had simmered years ago so that now she barely gave him a glance, and that stung more than her hating him.

"She's not going to burst onto the scene and object to the wedding if that's what you're hoping," Eli said, unscrewing his second small bottle and downing its contents in one swift gulp.

"I wasn't—I mean, I know she's not going to… I don't know what you're talking about," Boone stammered. But hell, had his brother hit the nail on the head?

Boone hadn't thought that was his grand plan, but was it? Was this all one big bluff to reopen the wounds of the past and finally put things right?

He huffed out a laugh, opened his own bottle, and emptied it into his mouth. Warmth spread through him, as did an unexpected calm.

"I'm getting married," he affirmed with renewed certainty. "I'm getting married and starting over, something I should have done years ago."

Years ago when he'd still hoped—when he'd still believed that eventually, if he waited long enough, Casey would come around. But he was done waiting for a life that would never happen and instead grabbing hold of a new beginning. Boone Murphy had punished himself long enough. Didn't he deserve some semblance of happiness by now?

Eli looked at his watch, then back up at Boone where he still stood by the minibar.

"Then why are we emptying the minibar before we're even close to seeing a p.m. on the clock?"

Boone's head swam as he stood on the sun-washed hill overlooking Carson City, Nevada. He should have been cold in nothing but his tux in the crisp November air, but instead he felt sort of…numb. He was happy for the small ceremony and reception, that his bride-to-be had been more about getting married as soon as he put a ring on her finger than she was about planning a big, fancy affair. Yet he couldn't look out at the guests. Not yet. Instead, he set his sights on the other side of the hill—the snowy land sprawling out before him, a reminder of the horse ranch where he, Eli, and Ash grew up.

But the ranch was no more. Nor was the reputation he'd built as Plumas County's best mechanic. He wasn't that far from Meadow Valley. Not yet. But from here, he and Elizabeth would travel south to Los Angeles. *Los. Angeles.* She'd just been offered a great position at a high-profile real estate firm, and after their honeymoon in Hawaii—he'd have preferred camping in Yosemite, but camping wasn't Elizabeth's thing—they'd be relocating to the City of Angels.

"It's starting," Eli said, striding up beside his brother. As if that was the string quartet's cue, Canon in D rang out through the crisp late-autumn air. When Boone turned to face their guests and caught a glimpse of the bride on the other end of the snow-sprinkled aisle, everything shifted into place, and he *knew*.

Chapter 3

CASEY COULDN'T BELIEVE IT. SHE WAS MAKING amazing time. At this rate, she'd get to Reno with ten minutes to spare!

Ha! Take that, stupid alarm that didn't do the thing that it was supposed to do!

"This is *my* day!" she exclaimed, echoing the words she'd proclaimed to Ivy half an hour prior. She hadn't felt the conviction she wanted to project *then*. But now, with everything happening the way it should—hell, even her new bangs looked pretty fantastic—Casey was surer than sure that today would change her life.

No sooner had the thought entered her mind than she felt *and* heard the pop, sending good ole Addy careening onto the shoulder.

Casey gritted her teeth and slammed on the brakes, not realizing she'd hit a thin patch of ice—the rarest of rare occurrences even in Northern California.

Her careening turned into what felt like a slow-motion glide headed straight for the metal pole of the approaching speed limit sign. Or rather *she* was approaching *it*.

"No, no, no, no, no!" she called out, but there was no one there to listen.

Casey wasn't sure what scared her more, the impending impact in a car that was manufactured long before airbags were a thing *or* the interview she was surely going to miss. Either way, one thing still held true. Casey Walsh's life *was* going to change today. She just—ya know—hoped she still *had* a life to change when all was said and done.

She braced for impact, even though in the back of her mind she heard a familiar yet forgotten voice telling her *not* to tense up all her muscles, that she'd regret it in the end. But instinct won out, and she white knuckled the steering wheel in one final attempt to change course.

She heard the crunch of metal before she felt the jolt. And then her hands flew back toward her face, and she narrowly missed punching herself in the nose.

Except something *did* hit her in the face, which freaking *hurt*, but it didn't feel so much like she imagined a steering wheel to the face would feel. Not that she daydreamed about taking a steering wheel to the face.

Speaking of faces, Casey's throbbed. But that meant she was still alive, didn't it? She'd probably have to open her eyes and assess the damage to be sure.

She coughed, and her throat burned.

Here went nothing.

She counted herself down. *Three…two…one.*

Casey opened her eyes, blinking away an odd dust that was settling in the air before the sight before her came into focus.

A deflated airbag.

"But…" she said out loud before being overtaken by another fit of coughing.

She patted herself down—arms, torso, legs. She wiggled her feet. Everything felt like it was in working order, even if it was a little worse for the wear.

Finally, she tilted the rearview mirror in her direction and gasped.

Right in the center of her forehead, where her new curtain bangs parted, sat what looked like a curling iron burn but must have been from the airbag. And blood slowly trickled from her right nostril.

She touched the side of her nose and winced. It was tender, but she didn't think it was broken. Not that she *knew* what a broken nose felt like, but Casey was going to go with the belief that it was only bruised, which would therefore send out into the universe that it was only bruised, and then the universe would provide. Or something.

She should exit the vehicle, call 911, or—or call the Salon and Cosmetology Institute of Reno and reschedule. Certainly they'd understand this was an emergency situation.

She reached for her phone, which had been

sitting on the passenger seat beside her, but it wasn't there. Luckily, she quickly found it on the floor—its screen shattered and the home screen black.

Casey Walsh was not a public crier—unless it was in the collective comfort and anonymity of a crowded movie theater during any number of Pixar movies—so she swallowed the lump in her throat, found a napkin in the glove box to stuff in her nostril, and exited poor, poor Adeline.

Her knees buckled as she stood, but she caught herself against the car's frame.

It's just nerves, she told herself. *You've never been in a car accident before, so you're just a little freaked out.*

She left the door wide open and—after finding her footing—trudged out onto the road. She'd expected some Good Samaritan to be waiting for her on the side of the road, having already called whoever needed to be called and ready to lend Casey their phone.

But the road was empty. Not another vehicle in sight. Because of *course* she was stranded now.

She shivered, then rubbed her hands together, blowing hot air between them.

Someone would drive by eventually, right?

Casey turned back toward her car and gasped. She hadn't fully grasped how badly Adeline was damaged—or how much worse it could have been—until now. For one, the vehicle's bumper was no longer attached but sat dented on the cold ground. Smoke rose from the hood. Or maybe it was steam. Casey couldn't tell. She was too scared now to get close enough to smell the foggy air.

So she had no phone, no ride, a throbbing face, and a soon-to-be-missed interview. The day that was supposed to be *her* day would now go down as the worst day in the history of Casey Walsh's life.

Fine. The *second*-worst day. But just because she'd maybe weathered worse one time in her life didn't mean she wanted to weather *this*.

She shivered, and tears once again pricked at her eyes, but she was *not* going to give in to the wave of emotion bubbling beneath the surface. That wasn't going to fix the situation.

The faint sound of a motor rumbled in the distance.

"Yes!" Casey yelled, standing on her tiptoes and squinting into the sun as she tried to make out the approaching car on the other side of the road. When it finally came into clear view, she could see *and* hear that it was so not a car but a vehicle that ran on *two* wheels instead.

Great. Beggars couldn't be choosers, but she hadn't ridden on or driven a motorcycle in over a decade, and she'd vowed she never would again. But Casey needed to get somewhere—*anywhere*—fast. Somewhere with a phone and heat and maybe a tow truck that wouldn't mind towing her all the way back to Meadow Valley.

"Okay, then," she began out loud. "Here goes nothing!"

She marched out to the middle of the road, jumping and waving her hands above her head to flag the driver down.

"Hey!" she yelled as the two-wheeler drove right up to her…and *past* her as it sailed on down the road.

"Asshole!" she called, unable to believe the nerve of whoever it was underneath the black helmet.

No sooner was the word out of her mouth than the aforementioned asshole skidded to a stop not twenty feet beyond her. The rider's boot toed out the kickstand, and then he spun to face her, striding in her direction with such purpose that she didn't have time to think—to register the familiarity in the man's gait, because it was definitely a man. Her brain didn't make the connection between the gold horseshoe decal on the front of the helmet and the now defunct horse ranch the logo used to represent. And she certainly didn't realize that the still helmeted man was wearing a tux, as if he'd just hopped on his bike in the middle of a formal affair.

All she could think was that she was safe now. She could sense it, could feel it in her bones.

As he walked, his pace quickening with each step, he placed his hands under his chin, lifting off the helmet and tossing it to the ground when he was only three feet away.

She knew those blue eyes. That dark-brown hair that looked almost black when the sun hit it right.

"Goddammit, Casey!" he yelled, but his words were laced with worry rather than anger. "What the hell did you do?"

Nooooo. This wasn't happening.

Casey squared her shoulders and jutted out her chin.

"Boone," she acknowledged matter-of-factly, despite there not being one single matter-of-fact bone in her body. "Everything's fine. I just need to borrow your phone."

A muscle ticked in his jaw as he glanced over her shoulder at the car and then set his gaze back on her.

"Casey," he said, his tone softer this time. "You're hurt. You need to go to a hospital. You could have other injuries, and—"

"It's a couple of bumps and bruises," she interrupted, waving him off, hoping if she said it out loud, she'd believe her own lie. "What I *need* is to borrow your phone so I can call the Salon and Cosmetology Institute, tell them what happened, and see if they'll have mercy on me and hold my interview spot. *Then* I need to call Ivy to see if she can close the shop and *get* me to Reno for my interview. And then I need to get Adeline towed."

She swallowed, her throat tight. "Is that too much to ask?"

Recognition bloomed in Boone's bright blue eyes—eyes Casey did *not* want to be fixed on her like they were.

"You're going back to school. God, Casey... That's great."

She rubbed her hands together and bounced on her toes, her jacket doing nothing to calm her nervous bones or protect her from the elements— from Boone Murphy's stare.

"Not if I miss this interview," she informed him. "So please, Boone." She squeezed her eyes shut, hating that she had to beg. "*Please* let me use your phone."

"No," he replied without even a second of hesitation.

"*No?*" Casey echoed. "You're not even going to consider helping me? Then why the hell did you even stop, to lecture me on my winter driving skills? Wow. You have got a *lot* of nerve, mister. I can't even believe you're going to leave me stranded when I just told you—"

"I'll take you to Reno," he said, letting out a bitter laugh. "Even though I just came from Carson City." He muttered the second part under his breath, as if it was just for him, but it was enough to remind Casey of what today was—aside from her interview day.

"Wait," she began. "Weren't you getting"—she cleared her suddenly dry throat—"married today?"

Boone sighed and scrubbed a hand across his jaw. He looked tired. Not sleepy tired but simply tired of it all. But what that *all* was, Casey had no idea.

"Do you want the ride or not?" he asked.

She stared long and hard at the two-seater bike, several steps up from the one he used to ride when they were teens. It was still a motorcycle. But somehow it looked made for a grown-up—for a man who knew what he wanted, who knew what he was doing.

"Still no covered vehicle for you, huh?" she asked, swallowing back the memories.

He cleared his throat. "I'm not—Casey, I don't ride like that anymore. You'll be safe with me."

She closed her eyes and inhaled a steadying breath. It wasn't like she had much of a choice. And it wasn't as if Boone was *always* reckless on the back of a bike. When she'd ridden behind him, she'd always known she was safe. It was when Boone Murphy rode alone that self-preservation seemed to take a back seat to the rush of adrenaline.

Casey finally nodded. Despite not having been on a bike in years, she hadn't forgotten how good Boone was at the helm when it mattered. Fast. Precise. She might even make the interview on time.

"Good. But I have *one* condition," he noted.

"Fine," she replied. It wasn't like she expected him to make this easy for her.

"After you're done, I take you to the closest ER to get your injuries checked out and make sure they're only superficial."

Casey rolled her eyes and sighed, but she nodded once more.

The corner of his mouth quirked up, offering her a quick ghost of a smile before he couched his expression again.

"I just need to get my stuff from the car." She pouted. "Poor Adeline."

"She'll be okay," he said. "I've seen worse. But shit, Casey. I can tell those tires are bald from thirty feet away. You had no business driving on black ice like that. When was the last time—"

"Black ice?" she asked, incredulous. "Black ice? That's not even a *thing* in California, so how would I even have the forethought?" She let out an exasperated groan. "I have a napkin stuffed up my bloody nose like a damned tampon and what looks like a rug burn on my forehead. Can we just say I learned my lesson without you lecturing me and saying 'I told you so'?"

He crossed his arms and nodded once. "I'll call Eli when we get to Reno and have him fix Addy up with a tow. But I'm guessing we should get on the road."

"Right. Thank you." She spun to head back to

the car to grab her bag but saw the rising smoke or steam still emanating from the hood and pivoted back to face him. "Is it...safe? Approaching the vehicle, I mean?"

"Come on," he said, wrapping his hand around her wrist and giving her a gentle tug. "We'll go together."

Chapter 4

Twelve Years Ago

Boone paced the length of Ivy's bedroom while Ivy and Casey locked themselves away in the bathroom. He was sure he'd wear a hole in the damned carpet once the eternal one to three minutes were up.

They'd been careful. *So* freaking careful. He'd worn a condom, and she'd been on the pill. With that combination, how could—

Okay, fine. He knew *how* it could happen. Nothing other than abstinence was foolproof. But how could he abstain from Casey Walsh? He'd had a crush on the girl since they were nine years old and her parents had signed her up for riding lessons at the Murphy Horse Ranch.

He remembered his dad waking him at the crack of dawn on a Saturday morning.

"Rise and shine, kid! We've got the Walsh girl from your class coming for her first lesson today. Figured you could show her the ropes, make her feel more comfortable."

Boone had pulled the covers over his eyes and whined.

"Make *Eli* do it. He's a better rider than me."

It was bullshit, of course. All three of the Murphy brothers were expert riders soon after they'd learned to walk. But nine-year-old Boone Murphy was *not* a morning person. Neither was eighteen-year-old Boone, but at least he'd learned not to whine about it. Mostly.

It might have been Casey's first ride, but she'd taken to their mare, Sundance, like a duck to water and had proven so by smoking Boone in a race around the arena. In his defense, he hadn't *known* she was going to race him until she'd called, "Ready…set…go!" and taken off. But still. What a rider she was then and even to this day. That was when he fell for her, but it had taken until freshman year of high school for her finally to reciprocate.

And now the girl he'd loved for nine years was in the bathroom with her best friend, peeing on a stick to see if the decision they'd made the night of the homecoming dance had irrevocably changed both of their lives.

What the hell would they do? Casey was six months away from completing her dual-credit courses at the Salon and Cosmetology Institute in Reno. She'd been driving Adeline, her late great-grandmother's hand-me-down sedan that Boone fixed up for her—thanks to their school offering an autos class—ninety minutes each way, three days a week, since the beginning of their junior year. Come spring, she'd have her associate's degree and would be off to who knows where for her first job in what she promised would be nothing more than a stepping-stone to her someday opening her own salon in Meadow Valley.

"I won't go that far. I promise," she'd told him that night in the barn where he'd set up a picnic dinner for just the two of them after the dance. "Meadow Valley will *always* be home. Because *you're* here. Because you'll always be here when I need you."

"Because I'm stuck here running a ranch that wasn't supposed to be my responsibility for another few years," he'd mumbled. "If my father hadn't gotten injured, we could have—I don't know—had this adventure together." He shook his head. "Forget it. I'm an asshole for even thinking it."

Instead of calling him out for being selfish, she'd kissed him instead. "The ranch was always going to be your future," she reminded him. "But you're allowed to mourn the loss of the time you were supposed to have *before* having to grow up. But I promise"—she kissed him again—"no matter what happens for either of our futures, that it *will* be an adventure we'll go on together."

He swallowed a lump in his throat at the memory. Boone had always been impulsive, spontaneous. Part of it was his defense mechanism. Maybe he couldn't be the smart guy, but he could be the fun guy. But his life—and the level of responsibility that went with it—changed before he was mentally equipped to deal with it.

What would his reaction be now if Casey walked in and told him the test was positive—or that it wasn't? What was the right answer to show that he loved her and could be there for her like she believed he always would be when lately he'd started feeling like he was losing his grip on keeping all the pieces of his life in their proper place?

The bedroom door opened, and Boone froze mid pace.

Casey's eyes were red-rimmed, and she sniffled. "I'm pregnant," she said, then let out a hiccupping sob.

Boone didn't give himself a chance to think. He simply strode toward her and dropped down to his knees, wrapping his arms around her waist.

"Marry me, Case. Please say yes."

She stared down at him for several long moments, silent tears running in rivulets over her cheeks.

"Okay," she finally replied. "Let's get married."

She didn't smile, but she knelt down along with him, wrapping her arms around him and burying her face in his neck.

"I love you, Walsh," he said.

"Love you, Murph," she said right back, and then he held her while she cried.

Boone wasn't sure where Ivy went. All he knew was that he and Casey were the only people in the room, the bedroom door having quietly closed them inside while he'd held Casey as she wept. He realized it was the first time he'd ever seen Casey Walsh cry—including the time when she was twelve and fell off the horse during a barrel-jumping lesson. She'd broken her damned collar-bone and hadn't shed a single tear.

"You're like a superhero," Boone had told her, and the realization of her strength and stoicism had turned into one of his nicknames—Supergirl.

"I hate that you're seeing me like this," Casey said as if she'd read his mind, sniffling against his neck.

"Why?" he asked, leaning back and tilting her chin up so her eyes met his. "It just means you're even stronger than I knew, which is dumb as hell because—hello?—you're Supergirl."

She scoffed, then swiped her forearm under her runny nose. "Right. It's real strong to burst into tears in front of my boyfriend because we got the whole safe sex thing wrong the *one* time we did it."

He kissed her on the forehead, letting his lips linger for several long moments before pulling away.

"It takes strength to be vulnerable, Case. Don't you get that?"

Casey huffed out a laugh. "Since when is an eighteen-year-old boy so damned wise?"

Boone shrugged. "Maybe I'm not the best at showing it, but I know a little more than horses and cars."

This time, she smiled for real, and hell if Boone Murphy didn't fall in love with her all over again.

"You *know* I think you're smart as hell," she declared, giving him a playful push on the shoulder. "That wasn't what I meant."

"I know," he agreed softly. And he did. Even if Casey never said it, Boone knew that despite his grades not being the best, she didn't think of him like everyone else did—as the dumbass cowboy who really only needed his diploma as a formality. Eli was already small-town famous for running the ranch while also taking premed college courses at night.

"If I get a degree as an equine veterinarian, won't that just make me better equipped to run the ranch?" he'd explained to his parents before their father had the stroke. It also helped that Eli had already won scholarship money to Meadow Valley State College, which made the decision to let him go a no-brainer. Even now—with their father unable to be at the helm—Eli still managed to do it all.

Then there was Ash, scrawny first year as he was, already wooing the senior girls—and most of his teachers—with his guitar and original country tunes. The guy could sweet-talk his way straight to the top of the honor roll. As if he needed to.

But Boone was the odd man out. They'd tested him for dyslexia more than once, but he'd always passed with flying colors. Yet when it came to his reading scores, Boone Murphy always sat at the bottom of the ladder. He *tried*. God knows he tried for years. But effort never seemed to bring him success. Now that he was a senior, he'd pretty much given up. Principal Wilkes knew he was going straight on to help his brother run the ranch after graduation and had all but told him that if he kept his head down and his attendance up, Boone Murphy would walk out of Meadow Valley High School with a diploma no matter what his reading scores were.

Casey Walsh was the only one who insisted on reminding him that *he* was not his grades.

"You're *more* than what a stupid report card says, okay?" she'd told him time and again.

And because he loved her, he believed her. She wouldn't lie to him.

Her smile fell, and she worried her bottom lip between her teeth.

The air pressure seemed to change in the room, pulling Boone from his daydream and back to the reality that would change both their lives.

"Whatever you need to say, Walsh, it's okay," he told her. Though he'd never seen her look so scared, which—truthfully—scared *him*. "You can tell me anything."

She nodded slowly, then sucked in a breath. "We don't *have* to do this," she explained. "We have… options."

Boone swallowed. "You mean an abortion." It wasn't a question.

Casey nodded again. "We can still have the lives we planned on having after graduation. I could go to school. Get my experience. And eventually open a salon right here in Meadow Valley. And you—you don't need this kind of responsibility on your plate right now. This doesn't have to change things."

It wouldn't change things—not for him. Boone Murphy was going to marry Casey Walsh one day, whether it was tomorrow or ten years from tomorrow. But he wasn't so sure she felt the same anymore. He wasn't sure she trusted him to be the father of her kid—now or somewhere down the line. *You don't need this kind of responsibility* sounded an awful lot like *You* can't handle *this kind of responsibility*. And the sad thing was that he didn't blame her for thinking this.

"You're right," he said, not sure if he should be relieved or worried that this option was on the table. "I support whatever you decide."

She shook her head. "It's not *my* decision. But it's also not yours. It's *ours*, Boone. I think—I think I need some time to figure out what I really want.

What's best for us, you know?" She kissed him once but let her lips linger on his for a beat before she pulled away. "Ivy's gonna walk me home. I'll call you tomorrow, okay?"

———

Casey couldn't sleep that night, even with Ivy curled up in the bed next to her. Her parents were still downstairs at the tavern when they arrived back at the apartment, which meant avoiding the third degree of why her eyes were pink and swollen.

Once Ivy dozed off, Casey padded into the bathroom in a daze, mixing color and testing it on patches of her natural blond hair. Her final salon class—which would certify her as a colorist as well as a stylist—would finish in the spring. All she had to do was pass the written exam and demonstration, and she'd be on her way to achieving her dream. Her parents had been so supportive, despite knowing she wouldn't continue on at Midtown Tavern, the family-run business.

What would they say if they saw her now, the bottom half of her shoulder-length hair a jumble of browns, reds, and even a couple of blues? The mess on her head didn't begin to describe the chaos in both her head and her heart.

She loved Boone Murphy. There was no question about that. But they were *kids*. Who'd had sex *once* and now had to make one of the biggest decisions of their lives.

"Wow," Casey heard from over her shoulder as she pivoted to see Ivy standing in the doorway. "What happened here?"

Casey glanced at the hair color stains on the counter she hoped would disappear with a magic eraser sponge. She ran her fingers through her damp, multicolored hair and let out a mirthless laugh.

"I don't know," she admitted. "Shit, Ivy. I don't *know*."

Her friend didn't say anything, only pulled her into a hug and held her tight until Casey was ready to let go.

Finally, when they were standing face-to-face once more, Ivy spoke.

"There is no *one* right answer, Case. You know that, don't you? And there is still time before you and Boone have to make any final decisions."

Casey shrugged. "He asked me to *marry* him. Isn't that answer enough as far as what *he* wants?"

Ivy raised her brows. "Maybe. But you and he are in this together. So explore your options. But the key word is *options*."

Casey nodded.

"But first," Ivy added, "we do have to make at least *one* decision right now." She gave Casey a once-over and winced. "You have to pick a color—*one* color—and fix what's going on here." She waved her hands in an arc around Casey's head.

Casey laughed, the tiniest weight lifting from her chest. "I'm thinking blue. But first…" She opened a drawer and pulled out a pair of salon shears. "I need to give myself a trim. Can you help me with the back?"

Ivy grinned. "How short are we going?"

Casey coiled a thick lock of red around her finger. "All the way," she said.

No matter what decision she and Boone made, everything was about to change. Maybe starting fresh with the girl looking back at her from the mirror would give her the perspective she needed to figure out the right path.

Chapter 5

BOONE SWORE HE COULD STILL FEEL CASEY'S arms wrapped around him even though she'd been inside the cosmetology school's admissions office for the past forty-five minutes.

What was he even doing here? He and Casey had barely spoken in over a decade, which was no small feat when they both lived and worked—across the street from one another, no less—in the same small town. Or *used* to work across the street from one another. Boone had sold his shop and thought he'd put Meadow Valley and Casey Walsh in his rear-view mirror. Now he was driving *back* to Nevada after having left the state that very same morning, not knowing what his next step was going to be other than deciding whether to deal with the consequences of stealing his rental tux or boxing it up and shipping it back to Carson City.

It's simple, idiot, he told himself. *Picking up stranded drivers on the side of the road and towing their broken-down vehicles is your job.* Or *was* his job before he chucked it all to marry a woman who wound up chucking *him*.

Okay, so maybe the story he was telling himself

about how the day went down wasn't entirely true, but it was true enough, as was the fact that up until a week ago, Boone Murphy was the proud owner of Meadow Valley Motors, the one and only auto shop for miles. For more than a decade, he'd been in the business of towing, repairing, and rebuilding everything from two-wheelers to tractors.

That was why he stopped when he saw a woman flagging him down in the middle of the open road. He hadn't *known* it was Casey Walsh.

I'd have towed anyone back to Meadow Valley—or wherever it was they were going—if they needed it.

A gust of wind ripped through the air, stinging the skin on the tops of his ears. Boone rubbed his hands together, trying to lessen the numbness in his fingertips.

"You can't be out in weather like this without gloves, Walsh," he'd admonished as they'd approached Casey's broken-down car so she could grab her things.

"I wasn't supposed to be *out* here," she'd reminded him. "I was supposed to be in *there*." She pointed to the sedan, the hood still steaming.

"Fair enough," Boone relented. "But you won't last five minutes on the bike. Here. Wear these." He pulled off his leather gloves and handed them to her after she'd safely removed her bag from Adeline's passenger seat.

"You can't be out in weather like this without

gloves, Murph," she'd mimicked, using the nick-name she hadn't uttered since they were teens. "Murphy, I mean." Then she'd cleared her throat, realizing her blunder.

"I work with my hands all day long," he told her. "They're rough and calloused enough. I'll survive a ride without gloves. If you get frostbite and lose a finger, then what's the point of the interview? Those hands are your moneymakers, aren't they?"

She'd finally relented. And Boone *had* survived the ride without them. Had even successfully helped clean Casey up before she went inside.

"You travel with baby wipes?" she'd asked with a chuckle when he pulled the package out of his tank bag.

"I have antibacterial wipes too, but I don't want to use those harsh chemicals on your face."

"Make a list," his therapist had told him. "Every night before bed, make a list of what you need for the next day. Of course, this will only work if you're putting everything in your calendar app, because you need to know what you're doing the next day to know what you'll need."

It hadn't been easy in the beginning—remembering to pause before hitting the pillow each night to check his calendar and make his list. But as he was learning, once he turned anything into a routine, it became second nature. Even if he didn't consciously remember, his brain would remind him.

"Who knew Boone Murphy was so prepared?" Casey had asked. He knew she hadn't meant it as any more than a throwaway comment, but it still stung. It brought him back to a time when no matter what his intentions, Boone Murphy *wasn't* prepared, nor was he the type of guy you relied on to clean you up after a car accident and send you on your way to a much-anticipated interview.

But that's who you are now, he reminded himself. *Even if she doesn't know.*

She winced as he dabbed at the dried blood on her nose.

"Sorry," he said, his throat tightening at the thought of hurting her—*of hurting anyone,* he rationalized. "But it doesn't look too swollen, which means it's probably just bruised. That's a good sign."

"Still hurts like a mother trucker," she murmured.

Boone chuckled. "And look at Casey Walsh, admitting when something hurts. Guess we've both changed a bit since…" He trailed off, unable to finish the sentence. Then he squeezed his eyes shut, not even wanting to finish the thought.

"Since we were kids," she said, putting as neutral a spin on it as she could. "We all do, don't we?"

He opened his eyes again, her green irises clear and sparkling as she stared back at him, unfazed. Maybe she hadn't changed as much as he'd thought.

"Right," he agreed. "Since we were kids. You still insist that collarbone break didn't hurt?"

Casey rolled her eyes. "I never said it *didn't* hurt. I'm just not a crier. I don't know why that's always been so hard for you—I mean for *people*—to understand."

After that, he finished cleaning her up in silence. She didn't ask about the airbags when he dabbed some ointment on her forehead abrasion—because yes, he had a first aid kit with him as well—so he didn't mention them either.

"Aren't you going to wish me luck?" she finally asked when he'd given her the thumbs-up to head inside.

He shook his head. "I know how good you are at what you do. You don't need luck, Walsh."

If he hadn't known better, he would have sworn her cheeks flushed at the compliment. But then he remembered it was barely forty degrees outside, which—for a Californian—was practically arctic.

Only now when he didn't need to pay attention to the road—or to carefully placing his hands on Casey Walsh's injured face—did he realize that calloused or not, cold was cold.

The revolving doors of Reno's Salon and Cosmetology Institute spun, and Casey emerged. Even though she was a couple hundred feet from where he sat in the parking lot, he could tell she was smiling.

Boone let out a breath, unaware of the tension he'd been holding in his shoulders—probably since he woke up that morning—until his body finally gave him permission to release it.

She strode toward him with her shoulders squared and her head held high—the confident, assured Casey Walsh he'd once known better than he knew himself. He had to steady himself where he leaned on the bike, the memory of who she used to be—who *they'd* once been together—knocking him off-balance.

He righted himself before she was close enough to notice, then reminded his damned unreliable brain that he and Casey Walsh were not a *they* and hadn't been a *they* since they were teens. Sure, there was a time when she'd loved him, but if he wanted to put a clearer spin on the situation, all he had to do was replay the last words she'd spoken to him before they stopped speaking to each other altogether.

"It *hurts*. Loving a boy like you hurts *too* much. I don't think I have enough love left to weather that kind of hurt, Boone. And I—I don't *want* to hurt like this ever again. It's too hard, thinking I can count on you and then being reminded time and again that no matter how long we've been a *we*, I still feel lonely sometimes, and those sometimes matter. Especially *this* time. I don't want to be lonely anymore, Boone. I just want to be...alone." One stupid joyride and a trip to the ER was all it had taken for Casey to finally realize she'd been right, that he'd never be someone she could truly rely on.

Boone might forget his mother's birthday without setting a reminder in his phone. He might get lost in a project, sometimes forgoing food and sleep for days, if he forgot to refill his prescription before the old one ran out. But no matter how hard he tried to forget Casey's final words to him, they were burned into his memory, imprinted for all time as a reminder of the boy he used to be—and the man he hoped he'd become.

"I'm sensing some good news," he said, painting on an easy grin as she approached.

Her confident strides turned into a giddy mix of bouncing on her toes and breaking into some sort of happy dance that involved both flossing *and* dabbing.

Boone snorted. But before she had a chance to give him verbal confirmation of her good news, she stumbled backward, her expression morphing into confusion and then fear as her knees buckled.

Boone watched it happen in slow motion—her bag falling off her shoulder and her eyes rolling to the back of her head—unaware that he was even moving until he somehow caught her just before she hit the ground.

———

"The CT scan looks good, Ms. Walsh. But your description of the accident—the impact of the airbag and the likelihood that you gave your head a good whack on the headrest as a result plus your symptoms all point toward a mild concussion." The young doctor looked down at Casey's chart and then back up at Casey. "You're going to need to rest up for at least the next week and then go see your general practitioner for a follow-up."

"I don't get it," Casey began, pinching the bridge of her nose and then wincing from the pain. "I felt fine after my interview, and then it was all of a sudden, like, lights out. I don't even remember how I got here."

The doctor nodded toward where Boone sat in the chair that was kitty-corner from the emergency room bed. "Your husband rode with you in the ambulance from the cosmetology school parking lot."

"I'm not her husband," Boone said at the same time that Casey blurted, "He's not my husband."

Boone cleared his throat. "You blacked out for, like, thirty seconds and insisted you were fine, which I *knew* you weren't. But you fought me on it every step of the way, even squirming out of my arms and marching over to the bike. But when you tried to perch yourself on the back of my seat, you kept kind of tilting to the side. So I called 911, and here we are."

Casey scoffed. "This conversation you're speaking of never happened. I'd remember it if it did.

And squirmed out of your arms? Like I was ever *in* your arms. That's—that's wishful thinking, my friend." She tried to defiantly cross her arms but then seemed to realize she was connected to an IV and rethought her choices.

"Are you two *sure* you're not married?" the doctor asked. "Or at least dating—for a significant amount of time?"

"*No!*" Boone and Casey yelled, in perfect sync once more.

The doctor raised her brows and shrugged. "Okay then. Well, Ms. Walsh, now that you are a bit more lucid, someone from registration will be in shortly to get your insurance information. It's all via the computer, so you shouldn't have to read any forms with small print or anything like that, which I advise against for someone in your condition. As long as you have your license and insurance card, we should be good to go. Then we'll get your discharge papers together—including your care requirements for the next week or two—and you can be on your way." The doctor pivoted to face Boone. "Did you say bike? I don't think it's in the patient's best interest to ride on the back of a motorcycle in her condition. Is there any other—"

"Her friend Ivy should be here to pick her up within the hour. In a car," Boone interrupted.

"You called Ivy?" Casey asked, her expression softening.

Boone nodded. "I knew you weren't going to make it back on the bike. Plus I figured you needed your friend right about now."

"Perfect," the doctor said. "Then sit tight for a bit until registration makes an appearance. We should have you out of here right about the time your friend arrives."

Casey nodded, and the doctor slipped past a break in the curtain that gave patients the illusion of privacy in an otherwise bustling hospital ER.

Boone pushed himself up from his chair and brushed his hands off on his pants. His damned tuxedo pants. How was he still walking around in this penguin suit and no one was saying a word?

"I should probably get going. Eli's going to pick me up and take me back to my bike. I'll drive a tow truck out for Adeline later this afternoon after I get back and sort some things out." Despite selling his shop, he'd kept the tow truck, parking it at Eli's place, just in case. "I'm glad you're okay, Walsh," he offered, brushing his fingers across the edge of her ER bed.

"Wait…"

Boone froze as Casey wrapped her hand around his wrist.

"Hospitals still freak me out. Do you mind staying, just until Ivy gets here?"

Hospitals freak *her* out? The hospital was where Boone had lost *her*, where he'd almost lost his own father, and where he'd inadvertently found out that he'd been living with a disorder he never knew he had that, if recognized and treated earlier, could have changed the course of his life. Instead, he was here, having messed up yet another important relationship in his life while simultaneously being reminded of the mess he'd made in the past.

"Sure" was all he replied, though. "I'll stay until Ivy comes."

Chapter 6

CASEY FELT THE LIGHT STREAMING IN THROUGH her curtains before she opened her eyes. She counted in her head—Friday, Saturday, Sunday, Monday—four. It had been four days since the accident, and so far, she had not been able to shake the dizziness first thing in the morning. Once she was up and moving, her equilibrium returned. But the first morning after the accident, she'd damn near given herself a second concussion when she sprang out of bed, ready to greet the day, and her bedroom decided to flip itself upside down, causing Casey to pitch forward toward what she swore was the ceiling but was actually the floor. Luckily—or maybe *not* so luckily—Ivy was there to break her fall.

"I tried to catch you," Ivy had said when they both hit the floor. "But you're pretty heavy when you turn into unexpected dead weight."

There were no serious injuries other than Casey's pride—especially after her dizziness sent her crawling to the bathroom to pray to the porcelain god. But Ivy had only slept over that first night to make sure Casey was okay. After that, Casey's parents had tag teamed checking in on her while

they took care of the weekend rush at Midtown
Tavern. This morning, though, she was on her own.
Thankfully, Ivy was taking her to the doctor today
for her follow-up. Now all she had to do was open
her eyes and test her balance.

Please let it be over. Please let it be over. Please *let it
be over*, she repeated to herself as she slowly opened
one eye and then the other.

She squinted at the light, but she felt no sign of
a headache. Next, she pushed herself to sitting, and
the room stayed right side up, which was always a
good sign. Finally, she swung her legs over the edge
of the bed and placed her feet on the floor.

"Here goes nothing," she told herself and then
stood.

The ceiling miraculously stayed above her head,
and the floor remained beneath her feet.

"Yes! Yes! Yes!" she squealed, jumping up and
down like she'd just won the lottery before doing
her floss and dab happy dance.

Her bedroom door swung open while she was
mid floss—in nothing but her sleep cami and
underwear—and Boone Murphy strode in, his ice-
blue eyes lit with worry. Until he noticed she was
dancing. Half naked. At which point he threw his
hand over his eyes and hurriedly backed toward
the door.

"Ivy said to wait outside unless I heard something, that you might fall because of the dizziness. I

heard something. The wood floor creaked, and then there were some stomps or bangs or… I don't *know*," he stammered. "All I *do* know is that Ivy gave me explicit directions, and…and you're dancing. And wearing—er, *not* wearing—" His head slammed into the doorframe. "Ow. *Dammit*." He dropped his hand from his eyes—which he was squeezing shut—to rub the back of his head.

Served him right, barging in on her like that. "At least it got you to shut up about me being half-dressed," Casey mumbled. "And why in the world would Ivy send *you* to check up on me when *she's* the one taking me to the doctor in an hour?"

Casey pulled her cami down over her belly button and grabbed her favorite oversize red wool sweater from where it lay strewn on the floor, throwing it on over her barely there pajamas.

Boone groaned. "You're not even going to ask if I'm okay?"

"You can open your eyes," she insisted, rolling her own. "I'm covered up."

He slowly blinked his eyes open, then let out a relieved breath.

"And *no*," Casey said, referring back to his question. "I am *not* going to ask how you are, because first, you're certainly not bleeding. Second, you're trespassing on personal property. And third…" She paused for several beats, tapping her index finger against her pursed lips. "Fine. I guess I don't have a third right now, but I'm sure I'll come up with one eventually."

He gave his head one final rub, winced, and then dropped his hand at his side. For a second, Casey felt a pang of guilt. Maybe he really *was* hurt. But just when she was about to offer him some sympathy, he crossed his arms, the corner of his mouth turning up in a crooked grin.

"What?" she asked. "Why are you smiling at me like that?"

He pressed his lips together in what looked like an effort to cage his expression, but that half-baked grin was still there.

"Spill it, Murphy. I am *not* a morning person, and in case you've forgotten, you're sort of invading my personal space." It took everything for her not to roll her eyes at herself or wince at the harsh words. No matter what she'd *thought* about Boone Murphy over the years, it never felt right to be outwardly mean to him—or anyone for that matter.

"You still have my sweater," he noted, and she detected a tiny note of surprise.

Casey looked down at the sweater she wore whenever she was knocking about the apartment, then back up at him in his beat-up flannel and jeans—much more the Boone Murphy she remembered than the man in the tux who'd swooped in like some billionaire superhero to save her from a tragic vehicular mishap. She squeezed her eyes shut and shook her head, attempting to shake off the memory. Then she shrugged. "*Your* sweater? You mean *my* sweater? Why wouldn't I still have my sweater?"

Boone cleared his throat, then cocked his head. "You're kidding, right? That's *my* sweater."

Casey's brows furrowed, and now *she* was cocking her head right back at him.

"Why would I have *your* father's sweater?" she asked. "*My* dad brought it for me when I was in the—" She stopped herself before finishing the sentence, before dredging up a memory that didn't need dredging. "Whatever," she continued. "My dad gave it to me over a decade ago. He said it was an old one of his that he didn't wear anymore. That's why it's so big on me." She fidgeted with a loose thread on the cuff of her sleeve, tugging at it like it was a memory she needed to unravel. Only she remembered that morning at the hospital so clearly—her dad explicitly telling her the sweater was his.

Boone's expression faltered, and for a second, he looked wounded. But before Casey could ask him why, he smiled again, letting out a soft chuckle.

"Sorry," he sputtered, shaking his head as he laughed. "I don't know why I thought... I must have hit my head harder than I thought. Maybe I'm the one who's concussed now. I take it from your ridiculous dancing that *you're* feeling much better?"

Casey grinned and started flossing again.

"I. Feel. Amazing. I mean, my face is still bruised, and I haven't shaved my legs in three days because balance and lifting my leg in the shower and... you don't need to know all that. But yeah. I'm a new woman, ready to take on the world *and* a final semester of cosmetology school." She bit her lip and tightened the loose string of her sweater around her index finger until it went numb. "I... um... Did I thank you for Friday?"

Boone waved her off. "Yeah. It's fine. I'm sure you did."

Casey narrowed her eyes and thought back to all the parts of the day that she could clearly remember, and she clearly did *not* remember ever thanking him for what he did.

"Thank you, Boone," she said. "In case I didn't already say it. Because of you, I get a second chance at my future. I should have told you that before now."

He shrugged. "You were concussed. Probably still are."

She laughed. "True. For all I know, I've got short-term memory loss like Drew Barrymore in *50 First Dates*, and you're just humoring me after I thank you over and over again like it's the first time."

A muscle in his jaw ticked before he smiled back at her. "Nope. That was definitely the *only* time you thanked me. I'd have taken out a damned billboard to announce to the world if you'd been repeatedly expressing your gratitude to yours truly."

"Ha. Ha. Ha," she said with the speed of a slow clap. "Now can you *please* tell me what you're doing in my apartment at eight in the morning instead of Ivy?"

He shoved his hands in the front pockets of his jeans, a gesture that made him look so much like the eighteen-year-old boy she knew even though he was taller and more filled and *definitely* a man now. A man she saw every evening through the window of the tavern when he closed up the shop. He only popped into Midtown on the nights she wasn't closing—an unspoken deal the two of them seemed to have made years ago. For all intents and purposes, the man standing just inside her bedroom door was a complete and utter stranger, yet there were things she was sure only *he* knew about her as well as those only *she* knew about him.

"Right," he started. "Ivy didn't exactly ask *me* to come. She asked Sam, but the baby was up all night, which means so was he. And because he's sort of my boss now, he passed the job along to me. So here I am." He shrugged. "You really should lock your door one of these days, you know."

"Oh," Casey said, not sure why she felt a bit deflated that he was only here because he was literally being *paid* to do so. "And why am I going to lock my door when the only other apartment in the hall is the one where my parents live? The day they lock theirs is the day I get a key made for mine." Boone opened his mouth to comment, but she cut him off. "Wait...Sam Callahan is your boss? Sam Callahan the *rancher*. Who owns the *ranch*. I'm so confused. I thought you were a mechanic."

Boone crossed one dusty cowboy boot over the other, clearly reminding Casey that while you may be able to take the boy off the ranch, you never really can take the ranch off the boy.

"I *am* a mechanic. But one without a shop. As soon as I track down the person Elizabeth sold it to, I'm going to buy it back. But since I don't even have my own pot to piss in, I'm going to be staying at the ranch and putting some money in the bank to pay off some...um...recent expenses I incurred."

Casey wanted to ask him what he was talking about, but the second he said *expenses*, something triggered in her brain.

"Oh no!" she cried, padding past him and out into the living room/kitchen where her bag sat on a stool next to the breakfast bar. She pulled out her laptop, which still held enough charge for her to open up the electronic documents the school had emailed her on Friday. "I've been too dizzy to look at a screen, but I need to electronically sign all the paperwork by the end of the day today." She set her laptop on the breakfast bar and tapped furiously at the keyboard. After scrolling through enough of the piles of junk mail she couldn't be bothered to delete, she found it. The subject line read Application Materials for the Spring Semester.

She chewed on her bottom lip as she skimmed through the pages of the application, then sucked in a breath when she got to the part that said Payment Options. She had enough for the initial deposit, but the options suddenly didn't matter, not when the total cost was...

Casey made a choking sound just as Boone appeared next to her.

"Twenty-five *grand*?" he asked, incredulous. "I thought you just had to finish a semester."

She nodded absently, still staring at the number on the screen. "They loved my portfolio, and I have to do a couple of demonstrations to pass out of the classes I already took over a decade ago, but I thought they were going to prorate the tuition. I mean, I know the cost has increased since then, but I thought since we already paid..."

Casey's breathing turned shallow, and her stomach roiled. She worked at her parents' tavern, for crying out loud. They made ends meet, but it wasn't like the Walsh family was ever rolling in Scrooge McDuck piles of gold. Casey had a *few* thousand put away, but certainly *not* twenty-*five* thousand.

"I'm going to be sick," she blurted, slamming the laptop shut.

"Do you need me to—" Boone started.

"No!" Casey called over her shoulder as she made a beeline for the bathroom, kicking the door shut behind her.

She collapsed at the base of the bowl and rested her head on the closed seat, letting the icy porcelain cool her now throbbing head.

Casey didn't *need* Boone Murphy. She didn't need *anyone* to fight her battles for her. She was a grown adult woman who would figure this out just like she figured out everything else in her life. Nothing was going to keep her from reclaiming what she'd lost. Not a stupid car accident and certainly not a surprise tuition payment.

As her breathing slowed, her urge to empty her empty stomach subsided as well. So she stood, dusted herself off, and marched toward the bathroom door— until she remembered Boone was still out there.

Casey cleared her throat. "Murphy?"

"Yeah, Walsh?"

She stumbled back at the sound of his deep voice, closer to the other side of the door than she'd expected.

"False alarm," she called. "I'm…um…I'm okay. Is Ivy still coming to take me to the doctor?"

"Yeah," he said. "She'll be here a few minutes before nine."

Casey nodded, then remembered that he couldn't see her.

"You're satisfied that I'm not going to fall and hurt myself, right?" She didn't wait for him to answer. "So you can get back to the ranch and do whatever it is you're supposed to be doing, okay? I'm going to shower and tackle all that leg hair I've been neglecting."

Leg hair I've been neglecting? Oh. My. Freaking. God.

She buried her face in her hands even though Boone couldn't see her.

"Yeah," Boone said again. "I guess I'm satisfied. Good luck with that leg hair, Walsh. Remember to use a fresh blade."

Casey squeezed her eyes shut and waited for several long beats until she heard the apartment door close. Then she blew out a long breath…and rummaged through the bathroom vanity to find a fresh blade.

Chapter 7

IT DIDN'T MATTER HOW MANY LAPS BOONE took around the arena, how fast he rode, or how many barrels he jumped, he couldn't get the image of Casey Walsh—barely dressed—out of his head. As the ranchland beyond the arena whipped past in a blur, he could still see Casey clear as day.

Silver hair tousled.

Bikini briefs, the band resting just below her hips.

A tank top that rode up the smooth skin of her abdomen, revealing a tattoo of a butterfly he hadn't known was there. He squeezed his eyes shut for a quick moment, hoping to clear the vision from his memory, but it only brought it into sharper focus.

When he opened his eyes, it was too late. The horse he'd been breaking in—a white Arabian rescue named Cirrus—got spooked by an actual *live* butterfly flitting around the barrel they were approaching.

Cirrus jolted to a stop, then bucked his hind legs into the air and, with them, Boone.

Boone landed hard on his back, the wind knocked clear from his lungs. But he still had enough sense to roll out of the way so that Cirrus's hooves didn't land on his chest.

"Shit, Murphy!" a voice called from over his shoulder, but Boone was done caring whether he was trampled into ground beef. He just needed air. "Are you okay?" the same voice asked, the figure approaching and dropping down to a squat beside Boone, who was sprawled on his back gasping for breath. Finally, his shocked lungs obliged and filled with as much oxygen as they could muster.

"The horse," Boone croaked, pushing himself onto his elbows.

Colt Morgan clapped a palm onto Boone's shoulder and gave him a reassuring squeeze. "Jenna's got him," he assured Boone. "But if I can't trust you not to kill yourself on a simple arena ride, I might have to rethink hiring on a mechanic as rancher."

Boone coughed as he tried to suck in some air. "You're only part owner," he got out before needing another breath. "Can't...fire me...without Sam and Ben."

Colt chuckled. "Putting me in my place, eh? Guess I don't need to call 911."

"There you go, boy," Jenna cooed, walking Cirrus past the two men. She paused long enough to wink at Colt. "And *you*," she added, turning her attention to Boone. "You take care of yourself, Boone Murphy. Cirrus needs you."

"Funny," Boone remarked. "I didn't get that impression."

Jenna stroked the horse's flanks, and Cirrus whinnied softly. "He got spooked is all. But I can tell he feels something special for you." She continued walking and calming the horse after that.

"She's been the Cirrus whisperer ever since he came to us a few weeks ago," Colt told him. "If she says he likes you, he likes you, Murphy."

Boone was sitting now, brushing dirt and last night's slight dusting of snow from his jeans.

"Anything broken?" Colt asked, tipping his hat down over his forehead to shield him from the sun.

Boone sent a silent thank-you to the universe for giving him the good sense to wear his down vest over his flannel.

"Just my pride," Boone admitted.

"Good," Colt said. "I know Cirrus is new to the ranch, but I've seen you ride a bucking bronco for fun. What happened out there?"

Boone sighed. "I don't know," he lied. "Lost my focus is all. But for the record, when I *do* ride a bucking bronco on purpose, I already know he's gonna buck."

"Fair enough," Colt agreed, then stood and held out a hand for Boone, which he gladly took.

"Shit," Boone hissed as he stood, feeling an intense pinch in his lower back. "Think I might have tweaked my back while I was at it."

Colt very visibly bit back a smile, and Boone's jaw tightened.

"Just say it, Morgan. You know you want to."

Colt crossed his arms over his chest and chuckled. "Say what? I was just gonna ask if in addition to bruising your pride, that fall might have aged you a decade or two as well."

Boone took what he *wanted* to be an intimidating step toward his friend, but instead he stopped short, the pinch in his lower back sending a shock wave of pain through his ass and straight on down his leg.

"What in the hell?" he growled, not thinking twice as he pressed the heel of his hand against his right butt cheek.

"Sounds like you have a pinched nerve, my friend," Colt said, not even trying to hide his grin. "I've heard that massage works wonders for putting everything back where it was supposed to be. There's a prenatal massage therapist in town. I can get a phone number for you if you want."

Boone gritted his teeth. "Do I look *prenatal* to you?"

Colt pressed a palm to Boone's belly, and if Boone weren't so intent on *not* moving, he'd have swatted the damned hand away.

"I mean, it's hard to tell if it's the vest or if you've gone doughy on us," Colt explained. "Either way, no judgment here, my friend. We should all be grateful for the bodies we have because they let us live another day on this amazing planet. Am I right?"

Boone groaned. "I'll just ice it and I'll be fine."

Colt shrugged. "Suit yourself. Why don't you take the rest of the afternoon off? Things are slow around here anyway. We don't need the extra hands on deck."

Boone nodded once. "Yeah. Okay. Thanks." He needed the money, but what good was he if he could barely stand upright?

"Hey," Colt started, his face growing serious. "You ever gonna give us the whole story about what happened last week with Elizabeth?"

Elizabeth. The woman he *should* have been fantasizing about instead of Casey Walsh. The woman to whom he should have said *I do* but instead said his final goodbye.

Boone sighed. "I'm not even sure I know the whole story myself." That much was the truth. They might have both realized it wasn't right, but Boone couldn't for the life of him figure out why they couldn't just say the stupid words and be happy. Elizabeth was beautiful, smart, and funny. She was his one-way ticket out of the town that had been for all intents and purposes a happiness dead end since he was a teen. Sure, he had friends and family in Meadow Valley—and at one time a thriving business doing what he loved—but for so long, this place he'd always called home had felt like trying to wear another man's boots. Even if they were the right size, they never quite fit the way they were supposed to. That was Meadow Valley for Boone Murphy. Yet somehow all roads led straight back to where he started.

"Well," Colt said, "all kidding aside, I do hope you figure it out. After your prenatal massage, of course."

Boone growled, but Colt only laughed harder.

Speaking of boots, Boone put his right one forward—a baby step on his way to at least solving a type of pain he understood. The physical.

He hissed in a breath but was able to keep moving. "There's an ice machine in the dining hall, right?" he asked.

"And one on each floor of the guesthouse," Colt added. "We upgraded to the good kind too. Those little ice pellets or beads or whatever. Perfect for nursing an old man's back."

Boone waved him off. "We're the same damned age, Morgan." Thirty might have seemed ancient when he was a kid, but now he understood that no matter what age he was, he still felt as clueless as he did when he was a teen. And if he was clueless, then that meant he was still young.

Colt shrugged. "Still look and feel like I'm twenty-five. What's the old cliché? You're only as old as you feel? It's all a state of mind, Murphy. You just gotta find your flow."

"My flow," Boone mumbled as he hobbled out of the arena and toward the guesthouse. He was wishing like hell that he'd driven his bike to the barn this morning after leaving Casey's, but it was sunny and warm enough for November. Plus the walk had given him time to think even if it had *not* provided him with any answers as far as what was next for him. *Just because he's got his shit all figured out, thinks he can give me hell for not figuring out my own.*

And this was how Boone Murphy made his way back to his new—albeit temporary—home at the Meadow Valley Ranch guesthouse: directing unsubstantiated anger at his teasing friend. After all, wasn't displacing anger easier than taking a good look in the mirror and blaming the guy staring right back?

It sure was. For today at least, Boone would welcome the easy way out.

When he got back to his room—bag of ice in hand—he tried every position in the books to make himself comfortable. But the only time his back didn't pinch like hell was when he was lying flat on it, and that was no way to exist. Not even for the day.

Boone sighed and pulled his phone out of his pocket from where he lay on the bed. He googled massage therapist near me and gritted his teeth as he braced himself for his only option, the prenatal masseuse recommended by Sam Callahan's wife,

Delaney. Not that there was anything wrong with pregnant women needing a massage. He just wasn't exactly a pregnant woman and didn't know how he'd feel sitting in a waiting room *with* pregnant women.

It would feel too much like or remind him too much of—

Shit. He didn't have a choice, not when one toss off a horse had all but incapacitated him.

The only problem? Google had given him zero results. *Zero.* At least in a twenty-mile radius from Meadow Valley.

Boone groaned, then pulled up Colt Morgan's number on his phone and tapped the green call button.

"Miss me already?" Colt offered as his greeting.

"Not even a little," Boone replied. "Actually, though, could you send me the information on that massage person you were talking about? The one who helped Delaney with the same issue during pregnancy? Couldn't find anything online myself."

"Hang on a sec. Let me ask Jenna," Colt said.

Boone sighed as he waited. Maybe he should just go to the ER and get a cortisone shot. It helped for his chronic wrist issues, which were just a part of the job when it came to working on cars, trucks, bikes, and tractors for as many years as he'd been doing.

"You need to call Dr. Charlotte," Colt finally told him when he came back to the phone.

Boone's brows furrowed. "Ben Callahan's wife?"

"That's the one," Colt replied.

"The one who's a *pediatrician*."

"Yep," Colt replied. "Dr. Charlotte North-Callahan. Jenna says she has a program for expectant mothers to become acquainted with the practice before their babies are born. Guess the program includes offering prenatal massage. I should probably tell you, though—"

"Thanks," Boone said, cutting Colt off. He wasn't up for any more ribbing from his friend. "Guess I'll give the office a call. Do me a favor, though. Don't tell Eli I got bucked."

"Of course," Colt replied, his voice growing serious.

The last thing Boone's widowed brother needed was more proof that horses were dangerous. Besides, in this scenario, it wasn't the horse's fault. It was entirely Boone's and his damned daydreaming about Casey Walsh in her underwear.

He cleared his throat. "Thanks again. I'm going to fix this thing and be back to work in the morning. Don't want to leave you, Sam, and Ben shorthanded."

"It's winter, Murphy. Slow season for a guest ranch. We'll manage if you need another day or two."

Maybe they would, but Boone needed a paycheck. He reckoned buying back his shop would cost more than what he made selling it—and more than what he'd already laid out for the wedding that wasn't. A down payment was all he would aim for now. The rest would work itself out.

"Thanks again, Morgan," Boone said. "I'll talk to you soon."

It sounded like Colt was starting to say something else as Boone pulled the phone away from his ear, but by the time he realized it, he'd already ended the call.

Colt would call back if it was important enough. But right now, Boone had a pediatrician to see about a masseuse.

An hour later, Boone found himself facedown on an odd padded table that had a doughnut-style pillow for his face, the hole left open so he could breathe and explore the many grooves in the ceramic tile below.

The subdued spa lighting, though, was actually quite calming, as were the trancelike music and the air diffuser that pumped out a soothing eucalyptus scent. And he was surprised to realize that lying facedown actually did not bother his back.

He closed his eyes and felt his whole body relax. Even if the massage didn't heal his injury, he'd at least get a good nap out of the whole situation.

But as soon as he started to drift off, he heard the door to the small room open and then click shut.

"Mr. Roberts?" a female voice asked.

Right. He'd used his middle name as his last

name. Even though Colt had promised not to say anything to Eli, Boone still didn't want word getting back to his brother that he'd been injured, let alone on a horse. Charlotte's practice had been new in town just as Boone was on his way out, so the two hadn't crossed paths much. And the young woman who worked the front desk must have been new as well because she had no idea who Boone was when he walked in, which was why the name Roberts just sort of came out. Better he not be the start of a small-town rumor that would no doubt bring the supposed curse of the Murphy Horse Ranch back to light.

Boone cleared his throat. "Uh, yes. Mr. Roberts. That's me." His voice was muffled in the face cradle. Maybe he was supposed to look up and greet the masseuse, but he was sure the slight movement would send a shock wave of pain straight through his right ass cheek and the rest of the way down his leg.

"My name is Jean, and I'll be taking care of you today. Are you comfortable?"

Jean...Jean... He didn't know anyone in town by that name, which meant he was in the clear from the rumor mill for sure. Maybe Dr. Charlotte had brought her whole staff with her from New York City. Whatever the explanation, Boone was satisfied. He blew out a relieved breath.

"Yes," he finally responded. "As comfortable as a

man can be who messed up his back and now can only be comfortable either in the position you see me now or flipped over onto my back."

"Hmm," Jean hummed, and he heard what sounded like her hands rubbing together. "I'm just going to warm you up, but while I do, can you tell me about the pain? Location, what triggered it, how long you've been feeling this way? That will help me figure out what muscles and fasciae to target."

Her palms met his skin, warm and soothing.

"That already feels amazing," he said.

"My hands aren't cold?" she asked. "You're my first client today, so I was worried."

"Not at all," he assured her. "And the scent—is that the same as the diffuser?"

"Mm-hmm," she hummed. "Eucalyptus spearmint. I hope you like it."

Boone simply hummed his approval.

"So, Mr. Roberts. What seems to be the issue today? I'm guessing it's not disc compression due to prenatal issues." She laughed quietly.

He was about to answer, but as if on cue, the heel of her hand pressed firmly against his right lower back, and Boone hissed in a breath and exhaled with a swear.

"Sorry!" Jean cried. "So sciatica, huh?"

"I guess," Boone grumbled, his voice rough. "Got thrown from a horse about an hour ago, and, well, here I am."

"Yikes," she said. "So you're staying at the ranch, then? The boys over there don't usually let the guests ride horses who get easily spooked. In fact, in the short few years they've been here, I can't remember one horse-riding incident with a guest *or* one of the owners. Not one that caused injury anyway. Hope you'll go easy on the Misters Callahan and Morgan. They're good boys who usually run a tight ship."

"I'm not suing them, if that's what you're getting at," Boone offered, both irritated at the insinuation but also a little touched at this outsider's view of townsfolk looking out for each other.

She let out a nervous laugh. "Good. I mean, accidents happen, right?"

And guests sign waivers before they're even allowed on the back of a horse, let alone given permission to barrel jump first thing in the morning.

But all he said was, "Right."

"Okay then. Let's get to it. This is going to maybe be a little weird and also hurt a bit, but I'm going to dig into your piriformis, which is most likely the trigger point, and see if we can't loosen the muscle and fascia to hopefully get that disc back into place. Just…um…try to remember the other exam rooms are filled with children, and it's probably a good idea not to scare them."

Boone knew he'd heard of the piriformis, but for the life of him he couldn't remember where on his back that was. He was just about to ask when the masseuse buried what he guessed was her elbow in the center of his right ass cheek, and white-hot pain seared the entire back of his leg.

He let loose a muffled string of swears. Hurt a bit? A *bit*? How about *This is maybe going to be a little weird, and also you're going to feel some NEXT-LEVEL SHIT AS FAR AS PAIN*? Except by the time the last swear left his mouth, Boone felt... relief. The pain wasn't *gone*, but it had lessened. He actually felt the muscle or fascia or whatever it was she'd said *loosen*.

"Again, sorry," she whisper shouted. "But you did great. If I told you it was going to hurt a lot, you'd have tensed up, which would have just tightened your muscles even more. Because you stayed relaxed—relatively speaking—I was really able to get in there and work out that knot."

Only now did Boone realize she was still kneading the trigger point.

"What do you do to relax, Mr. Roberts, if you don't mind my asking? I hope it's not riding." She chuckled.

Relax? Boone didn't know how to relax. If he didn't keep moving—keep a regular schedule of working and doing—he might lose focus. He might let all the spinning plates fall, and then what would he have left? His thoughts? No way he wanted to be alone with those.

"I…don't," he finally replied.

"Huh." She started working her way back up his back and to his shoulder. "I hear knitting is good for that. You concentrate so hard on the needles and then basically forget to tense up. At least that's what Pearl says. She runs the Meadow Valley Inn."

Of course he knew who Pearl was, but he wasn't going to chance his anonymity by admitting it.

"Yeah, my hands aren't made for knitting," he said gruffly. Rebuilding an engine or installing aftermarket airbags into a car that shouldn't have been on the streets otherwise? Sure. But knitting?

"Such a man," she muttered under her breath but loud enough for him to hear.

The tone in her voice—the derision—he knew that tone, didn't he?

"I'm just going to move around to the other side," she added, as if she hadn't just written him off as the chauvinist he sounded like. "Gotta even you out. Even though the pain is on your right, any tightness on your left can contribute to the pinched nerve."

He could feel her moving around the face cradle, and on instinct, he opened his eyes in time to catch a glimpse of her feet shuffling along the tile beneath him.

Despite it being the dead of winter, she wore flip-flops, and on the top of her right foot, plain as day, was a tattoo of a vintage pair of scissors.

But not just *any* scissors. Barber shears. He knew because he'd gone with her to get the tattoo—fake IDs in hand—almost fifteen years ago.

Boone braced his hands under his chest and lifted his head just as she passed him.

"*Casey*," he stated. It wasn't a question.

He sat up, making sure the sheet—though paper thin—was covering his underwear and legs.

She stopped short and spun on her heel to face him, eyes wide and somehow at the same time shooting daggers straight at him.

"Boone *Murphy*! What the actual *fu*—"

But he clapped his palm over her mouth before she could finish. "Remember," he told her. "Exam rooms filled with *children*."

Chapter 8

CASEY SPRANG BACK FROM THE TABLE AS IF IT had burst into flames. It might as well have. She'd just driven her elbow deep into Boone Murphy's ass cheek.

He popped up into a sitting position almost as quickly, then winced.

"Okay," he grunted through gritted teeth. "*Not* cured yet." Then he looked at his attire—or lack thereof other than his boxer briefs—and back up at Casey with a crooked grin. "Guess we're even now, huh?" he asked. "It's *your* turn to try banishing *my* almost-naked body from your mind." Then he squeezed his eyes shut and shook his head. "Where is my damned filter?" he griped under his breath.

Casey bit back a smile at the implication of what he'd just admitted, but then she remembered what got them into this filter-free Boone Murphy situation in the first place.

"Mr. Roberts?" she asked, hands on her hips. "You *lied* about your name. Why? Did you know it was me the whole time? Are you—I don't know— spying on me?"

Boone rolled his eyes. "You ever take me for

much of an actor? And even if I was, why in the hell would I drum up an injury that is quite literally a pain in my *ass*? Huh, *Jean*?"

Casey opened her mouth to retort but then closed it, huffing out a breath.

"Took a course at the library a while back on the introduction to massage therapy," she finally answered with a shrug. "Turns out I was good at it, and the instructor liked me. Offered to teach me one-on-one at a reduced rate, so I did it."

Boone scoffed. "And this instructor didn't want *anything* in return from you other than your discounted tuition?"

Casey narrowed her eyes at him. "My instructor was a sixty-five-year-old woman named Mabel, but thanks for the insinuation that someone would only do something nice for me if it meant they were going to get into my pants."

A muscle ticked in Boone's jaw, and he hung his head, shaking it back and forth.

When he met her gaze again, his bright blue eyes seemed to darken.

"I'm sorry, Walsh," he told her, and she could tell he wasn't playing around anymore. "That was uncalled for. I'm just—I mean, you heard what I said to myself before, right? Walking in on you this morning was…unexpected. And it's been preoccupying my thoughts, apparently to the extent where I start saying dumb shit." He chuckled, but the smile didn't quite reach his eyes. "Dumber than usual, I mean."

"*Boone*," she admonished, the feel of his name still foreign on her tongue even if the memory of it was as vivid as the fuchsia that now replaced the silver in her hair. "You know I never thought you were—"

"Stupid enough to lose control on a bucking horse?" he interrupted, throwing up his shield of self-deprecation. She hadn't forgotten his defense mechanism either.

Casey's eyes widened. "You really did get thrown from a horse?"

Boone nodded. "Told ya, Walsh. I'm not putting on a show."

"It was the horse's fault, right?" she asked, wincing as soon as the words left her mouth. "I mean, you weren't—"

"Joyriding on an untamed bronco just to see how far I could push him before he threw me off? I told you, Walsh. I don't do shit like that anymore. Sam and the boys are trying to break in a rescue. Cirrus. He's a good horse. Seems to trust me. But they think he was abused by his former owner. He's skittish and got spooked by a damned butterfly. I was distracted and got thrown. End of story. Used my middle name as my last name just in case the rumor mill got going. I didn't want—"

"Eli to find out," she said, finishing his sentence. Her heart tightened inside her chest.

"It wasn't easy taking over the ranch when our dad got hurt." He sighed. "But we did the best we could, you know? We loved the horses. They were all we knew. Until Eli lost Tess. He barely tolerates me working with horses again. If he knew I got hurt?" He shook his head. "It wasn't the horse's fault. It was mine."

"I get it. You're…" She cleared her throat. "You're a good brother, Boone." The words…the sincerity…felt so foreign on her tongue when they were directed at him, yet at the same time, they felt as familiar as her favorite pair of jeans.

He scrubbed a hand over his jaw. "I don't know about that. I almost left him and our hometown behind for greener pastures. Not sure how good a brother that actually makes me."

Casey sighed, but when her eyes dipped below his, she was reminded of his naked torso—his muscled, naked torso with fine dark hair peppering his chest and narrowing into a small trail that led—

Nope. That hair was leading *no*where. At least Casey wasn't going to let her gaze *follow* where that hair wanted to lead.

"Could you…?" she asked, then picked up a portion of the sheet that had been draped over Boone's body.

"What?" he asked, then added, "*Oh.* Of course." And immediately he pulled the sheet up and over his torso.

"How good a daughter does it make me that I'm using Adeline's middle name as my own so my parents don't worry about how much I've been working—or how much more I'm going to *have* to work—to come up with the rest of my tuition?"

He sighed. "We're quite a pair, aren't we?" Then he coughed and cleared his throat. "I didn't mean… I was just saying that we're similar, you know? Little white lies to protect the ones we love."

Casey nodded, then dropped down onto the rolling stool next to the massage table.

"You know, we've talked more in the past few days than we have in all our adult lives," she said.

His jaw pulsed again. "Wasn't that what you wanted?"

What *she* wanted. Had it really been one-sided? Or hadn't everything between them just simply imploded, and this was the only way they could have survived?

Casey blew out a breath. "We were kids, Boone. We didn't know any better. We didn't know how to…" She didn't want to come right out and say what they'd had—or what they'd lost. There was no point in rehashing the past or reopening old wounds, not when it wouldn't change what happened. But maybe, *finally*, it was time to move on. Hell, hadn't he almost gotten married last week? "Are you ever going to tell anyone what happened with the wedding?" she asked, sending the trajectory of the conversation in a direction she hadn't fully thought out before blurting the words.

Boone narrowed his eyes at her, and the corner of his mouth twitched.

"How do you know I haven't?" he mused. "You been asking around about me?"

Casey's mouth fell open. Her question was pretty much her admission.

This time when Boone let out a soft laugh, his eyes crinkled at the corners.

"Looks like I'm not the only one who's lost their filter this morning," he added. "Small town. Rumor mill." He shrugged. "Just proves why our white lies are necessary, doesn't it? As for the wedding…" His expression softened, and he scratched the back of his neck. Which meant he let go of the sheet, which also meant his lean, muscled, dusted-with-dark-hair torso was on full display once more. The lean, muscled, dusted-with-dark-hair torso that belonged to a *man* Casey barely knew and not the boy she once loved.

Casey coughed, and Boone caught her staring.

"Sorry," he teased, pulling the sheet back up. But the glint in his eyes told Casey he wasn't sorry at all. "But isn't me being back in Meadow Valley—by myself—answer enough?" He shook his head. "Of course it isn't," he added, answering his own question. "But until I can clearly explain things to myself, I don't think I owe anyone else an explanation."

Casey worried her bottom lip between her teeth. "You're right," she said. "It's none of my business or anyone else's. I shouldn't have asked." Even if the question had kept intruding on her thoughts since the moment she saw him hop off his motorcycle in a tux. "As much as I love this town, I've never been a fan of the total lack of privacy that goes along with it."

Boone pressed his lips into a smile. "Walsh? Are we becoming…friends?"

Casey's throat tightened, and her eyes burned, but she swallowed the unexpected rush of emotion.

"Yeah," she replied. "I think we are. If you think that's something you might be interested in trying."

He smiled at her, and his shoulders relaxed. "I think I'd very much be interested in trying that. It'll definitely make moving around town easier."

She huffed out a laugh. "And it'll mean not having to *leave* town for auto repairs or maintenance." She winced. "Sorry. I forgot you sold the shop."

He raised his brows. "Doesn't mean I'm giving up cars. Boys at the ranch have a small empty barn where I can set up temporarily. Didn't sell my equipment. Just have to get it out of storage. And based on what shape those tires of yours were in, I'm willing to bet you haven't actually done much in the way of auto repairs or maintenance in the past decade."

Casey's cheeks burned, and she stood, crossing

her arms. "Are we finishing this massage or what? You paid for the full hour…"

His eyes widened. "It's not weird knowing it's me?"

She shrugged. "A little. But I'm a professional. And you *are* nursing a legitimate injury that you're trying to hide from your brother. Is it weird knowing it's me?"

Boone groaned. "Yeah. It's weird, but you're right. I need to be able to at least pose as a healthy human when I see my brother later. Plus, you were doing a pretty fantastic job."

Casey grinned, her cheeks heating this time for an entirely different reason.

"Then that settles it—friend. Face in the cradle so we can fix you up and send you on your way. Just a fair warning that you'll probably need a few sessions to set everything right. I can recommend another masseuse outside town if you want."

Boone shook his head before pivoting and putting his face back in the cradle.

"I'm not one to take business away from someone who needs it," he said, his voice slightly muffled. "Besides, you're giving me some much-needed business of my own fixing Adeline back up."

Right. Her car. Casey's stomach tightened at the reminder of yet another expense added to her list.

She undraped Boone's back, tucking the sheet around his hips, then pumped some more oil into her palm before rubbing her hands together.

Her stomach dropped when her skin met his, and she chalked it up to muscle memory—her body's physiological response to knowingly touching his again after so many years.

"Thank you," she finally told him as she kneaded his muscles with the heels of her hands. "For coming to my rescue after the accident and—and for the airbags. I can't believe you did that and never told me. You saved my life."

Boone's back tensed and then relaxed.

"You're welcome," he replied. "Also, I…um…I like the new hair."

"Thanks," she said again, an unexpected warmth spreading through her. Silence fell between them, and she felt like there was more she should say— more he wanted to say—but after a while, the moment seemed to pass.

"You're not…um…going to have to do that thing to my ass again, are you?" he finally asked, and Casey laughed, thankful for the break in the tension building between them.

"You mean this?" she asked, then channeled all her weight into her elbow, driving it into his piriformis, a string of curses once again spraying from Boone's lips. "Children," she reminded him in a singsong tone. "Ready for the other side?"

She grinned and rounded the face cradle to even the score.

Casey Walsh and Boone Murphy—*friends*.

Once Meadow Valley got a whiff of the news—because yes *indeed*, this would be news—their little white lies would be safe from the rumor mill.

And they could finally close the door on the past and start again.

Chapter 9

BOONE FINISHED CLEANING UP IN THE TACK room after his trail ride with the smattering of folks who didn't mind vacationing at a guest ranch in the brisk Northern California winter. He was officially off the clock for the night and was looking forward to a long, hot shower and getting to work on tracking down his shop's buyer.

Elizabeth—with her real estate connections—had taken care of the sale and had retained the paperwork. Since she wasn't exactly returning Boone's texts inquiring about the buyer, he had to resort to plan B, which at the moment didn't consist of much more than googling recent real estate transactions in Meadow Valley. He still wasn't sure what he would do once he found whomever it was he was looking for. After all, he'd been so sure that getting *out* of Meadow Valley was what would finally bring him the ever-elusive happiness he'd been unable to find in his hometown. But right now, what other choice did he have other than to go back to his old life and start from square one?

"Looks like you're moving around pretty good,"

a voice crooned from behind as a hand firmly gripped his shoulder.

Boone spun to find Colt Morgan, despite his flannel, fleece, and vest, blowing into his palms and rubbing his hands together.

"Heading to Midtown for a warm-up and a poker game with Sam, Ben, and the firehouse chief. Don't suppose you want to join us?" Colt asked tentatively.

"Who's holding down the fort with the guests tonight?" Boone asked.

"Friday nights are the men's night off. The significant others are on duty." He winked. "And since you don't seem to have a significant other these days, thought you might want to hop on board. But that still begs the question as to whether you might step foot into Midtown tonight."

Boone huffed out a breath. Looked like his avoidance of Meadow Valley's only source of nightlife hadn't gone unnoticed by anyone. It wasn't as if he'd been banned from the joint. He made an appearance every now and then when he was sure anyone other than a Walsh was tending bar. In the beginning, it was just easier *not* to cross Casey's path than to figure out what he was supposed to do if he did. Then the practice simply turned into habit. Kind of like her reasoning for leaving town for car repairs and maintenance, even if she rarely did so.

"You know what, Morgan? I know your gesture is a courtesy gesture and that you're expecting me to say no like I would have any other time you might have asked. But you're right. I *am* moving around pretty good, and I had a hell of a day. I could use a warm-up. As for the game… You boys play for fun or what?"

Colt raised his brows. "There's a twenty-five-dollar buy-in, which you can give me ahead of time. It's low stakes, just a bunch of guys burning off steam. No cash changes hands at the tavern. Just chips. That way, Old Man Walsh turns a blind eye—as do the sheriff and his deputies. Hell, Mayor Cooper even buys in sometimes. But it's all in good fun. Twenty-five bucks, no more or less, and everyone shakes hands at the end of the night no matter who cleans up."

Boone grinned. A little extra cash in his pocket certainly wouldn't hurt. And after his second massage session with *Jean* this week, he *was* feeling pretty damned good and pretty damned confident that he could stroll into Midtown Tavern and not have the night devolve into chaos simply because he and Casey Walsh were in the same room at the same time.

Granted, *Jean* had kept their second session strictly professional—no talk of their elevated status from estranged to possibly becoming friends—but Boone knew their earlier conversation hadn't been a figment of his imagination. He *knew* that he and Casey could do this.

He held a hand out to Colt, and the two men shook.

"All right," Colt began, holding out an empty palm. "Pay up, and then meet us there in an hour."

Boone laughed and then pulled his wallet out of his pocket. "You're lucky I have cash on me." He handed Colt the money, which Colt folded in half and shoved in his own pocket.

"You're the one who's going to need luck tonight, Murphy. It might be a friendly game, but that doesn't mean we're going easy on the new guy."

Boone offered his friend a little salute. "Wouldn't have it any other way. I need to head home and shower. I'll see you all there."

Colt clapped him on the shoulder again. "Glad to have you join the group," he said. "See you soon."

Boone Murphy wasn't a man of many outfits. In fact, the word *outfit* never actually graced his vocabulary. He found a pair of jeans he liked and bought three pairs. He found a thermal or a flannel in his size, and he bought whatever colors were available.

"Wear what you want and whatever makes you feel like *you*," his father had always told him. It was his old man's way of saying that he didn't need to compare himself to Eli or Ash—that just being *him* was enough.

Now, though, as he stood in front of his small

guestroom closet, staring at the sea of denim and plaid—and the tux that hadn't yet made its way back to Carson City—he felt stuck.

He'd *tried* to change, though, hadn't he? Sold his shop, got the hell out of Dodge, and almost very nearly but not quite made it down the aisle and off to a new life. Everything was supposed to be different. Instead, he was right back where he started—right back where he'd always been.

"Screw it," he said, then pivoted toward the dresser opposite the foot of the bed, the one that held the rarely worn navy fisherman's sweater—a sweater he once owned in two different colors—and pulled it from the drawer.

The wool was stiff as he pulled it over his head, and it stretched a bit over his arms. It smelled of cedar, which lined the inside of the drawer, but it also retained the faint earthy scent that reminded him of the last time he wore the garment or its counterpart, all those years ago.

"Keep doing the same old shit and get the same old result," he mumbled to himself, then brushed his palms over the rough wool on his arms. Big changes hadn't worked, so maybe it was time to make small, almost unnoticeable adjustments to see if he could tip the scales to—where? He wasn't sure. Just somewhere *else*.

The tavern was already crowded by the time he pushed through the doors. The second he stepped foot onto the familiar wood floor and smelled the scent of stale beer that never quite washed out of the floors and tables, he was hit with an odd sense of déjà vu. It wasn't as if he'd avoided the tavern altogether over the past decade, but it was as if his whole being knew that tonight was different from all the others.

Every tavern patron must have felt the same way because all eyes seemed to be on him, like he'd triggered some sort of buzzer that told everyone to stop what they were doing and look at the spectacle standing in the entryway.

Goddamn small towns. The man who'd thought he'd never leave had been clawing his way out of Meadow Valley for more years than he cared to count. And he'd made it out—made it almost two whole days. Now here he was, the main subject of town gossip and, apparently, tonight's most anticipated entertainment.

"Evening, folks," he offered, painting on a grin and offering the townsfolk a friendly salute. "Just here for a pint and a friendly game of cards. Appreciate the greeting."

He caught sight of Colt, the Callahan brothers, and Chief Carter Bowen from the fire station at a round table clear on the other side of the tavern and took a deep breath before striding through the sea of onlookers to the relative safety of his companions. Only when he rounded the corner of the long rectangular bar did he see her—Casey Walsh—working the tap and charming every single customer in her periphery. He could tell by the patrons' smiles and the way so many seemed to lean over the edge of the bar to talk to her.

Boone's chest tightened, and for a second, he found it difficult to inhale, like he'd suddenly changed altitude. Instead of continuing on his path to his table, he found himself heading for the bar instead. He needed to rip off the bandage—to let the folks who seemed to be watching his every move see that Boone Murphy was just as welcome in Midtown Tavern as they were.

She didn't see him at first as she finished pouring another draft and slid it across to Old Man Wolcott, proud owner of Meadow Valley's longest-standing retail establishment, Meadow Valley Feed, Seeds, and Fertilizer—better known as the feed store. In fact, Casey Walsh seemed to be the *only* living and breathing human in the entire tavern who hadn't taken notice of Boone's entrance.

Wolcott scratched at the wisp of gray hair that stretched across his otherwise balding crown, gave a less than subtle nod in Boone's direction—which was two occupied stools away—and then loudly cleared his throat.

"Are you okay, Amos?" Casey asked, brows furrowing.

He coughed loudly into his fist, but it sounded

a lot more like *Murphy!* than it did your average, everyday cough.

Finally, Casey sent her gaze in Boone's direction, and her eyes widened as they met his.

Amos Wolcott was still talking as she brushed her hands off on her apron and moved to where Boone stood at the bar.

She smiled nervously as she pulled a clean pint glass from underneath the bar.

"Come here often, cowboy?" she asked, then skimmed her teeth over her bottom lip.

"No," he said matter-of-factly. "I can probably count on two hands how many times I've stepped inside your lovely establishment in the past ten or so years. But I'm trying something new tonight. I was hoping maybe you could tell me whether I made the right choice."

She looked him up and down and nodded slowly.

"You look...nice, Boone. Real nice tonight."

He chuckled. "I didn't mean the clothes, but I guess this is a bit different from the norm."

She tilted the empty glass under the tap and gave the lever a pull.

"Usually, when someone pays you a compliment, you respond with some form of gratitude," she mused, brows raised.

He scratched the back of his neck and shook his head ruefully. "Right. I mean, thank you. You look—I mean you *always* look—"

"Ew, stop!" she interrupted, but she was smiling. "That's not how compliments work. I'm not dishing 'em out just so I can get one back. You look good tonight. End of story. Here." She closed the tap and pushed the glass over to his side of the bar.

"But I didn't tell you what I wanted," he said.

"Your favorite is whatever IPA is on tap as long as it's from a local brewer, which *all* our tap beers are. We just tapped this one tonight."

His brows furrowed. "How did you..." But he didn't need to finish his question. "Word travels fast in a small town, huh? No matter how insignificant the word is." Yet however the word had gotten to her over the years, she'd committed to memory something that *he* liked. Even when she hadn't liked *him*.

"Don't I know it," she agreed. "And word tonight is that Carter is going for a three-week streak as far as mopping up the poker table with everyone else's cash, so good luck."

Boone raised his glass to her, then took a long swig, the familiar bitterness of the hops hitting his tongue.

She was right. It was exactly what he would have ordered if she'd rattled off a menu of what was on tap. But instead she'd simply known.

"Beautiful," he finally said, finishing his earlier and interrupted thought. "You always look *beautiful*. And you shouldn't have to compliment *anyone* to hear that in return. So in case you didn't know it, now you do."

Her mouth fell open, but she didn't make a sound, so he raised his glass once more.

"Put this on my tab? I'll settle up after I put Bowen in his place and mop up the table myself."

Then he spun on his heel and made a beeline for his buddies as he felt all eyes on him once again. This being friends with Casey Walsh thing was going to be fun, especially if all it took to stun her to silence was telling her the truth.

"Evening, boys," Boone said, pulling out the one empty chair at the table. "Let the games begin."

Chapter 10

CASEY HEARD CARTER BOWEN'S FAMILIAR ROAR of conquest, and by the time she made it to the table to clear away their empty pitcher and glasses, he was already in the midst of his victory dance atop his chair.

She pulled her phone out of her pocket and opened the camera app, threatening to take a video.

"If you don't get your drunk ass off that chair, I *will* send this to Ivy, who will send it to Delaney, who will put it on the Meadow Valley Ranch website. I can see the caption now: 'Weekly Attraction of Fire Chief Embarrassing Himself at Local Tavern.'"

Carter laughed, continuing to stir the big pot while winking at Casey's camera. "Love you, Ives!" he called out, and Casey rolled her eyes. Carter Bowen was too beloved by both her best friend *and* the town for him to worry about any sort of embarrassment. Plus, she knew he wasn't drunk—not on beer, anyway. The man just exuded joy, and while Casey loved the guy and how happy he made her friend, that unbounded, unbridled happiness got to her every now and then. Tonight was one of those nows.

Boone Murphy stood and raked a hand through his hair. The navy sweater lay over the back of his chair so that he was only wearing a white under-shirt and his jeans.

Casey swallowed. Despite having seen the man and having touched his nearly naked form on the massage table more than once, she'd been able to remain professional, to turn off any lingering attrac-tion she might still have for the man who used to be the boy she once loved.

But the way the cotton hugged his torso, the way the sleeves tugged against his biceps? There was no rule that a bartender had to turn off what felt like a chemical reaction happening inside her. It was like he was sexier *with* clothes than with-out because the clothes accentuated the form. They reminded her that *this* Boone Murphy was all man—a man who had called her beautiful and then simply walked away.

He started gathering and stacking the empty pint glasses, then grabbed the pitcher with his free hand.

"These still go in the sink in the back?" he asked.

"You don't have to—" she started, but he shook his head.

"I need to escape my own humiliation," he insisted with a crooked grin. "You told me Bowen was good, but you didn't say anything about his ability to gloat."

Casey laughed and nodded toward the kitchen door. "Sink first, then run them through the tunnel washer. I'll be right there."

"Also," Boone added, nudging her shoulder with his own, "your victory dance is way better than his. I'll bet the guy doesn't even know how to floss."

Casey's cheeks burned as Boone strode off toward the kitchen. But she licked her lips and squared her shoulders, collecting herself before turning her attention back to the poker table—the last patrons left in the tavern.

"Time to settle up, boys," she told them, holding her hand out for either cash or debit cards. "You don't have to go home, but you can't stay here."

"Drinks are on the asshole up there," Sam Callahan said, nodding up at the still dancing Carter.

Carter finally hopped off the chair and pulled a wad of cash from his pocket. "Since I still haven't blown through last week's winnings, I might as well," he offered with a self-satisfied grin.

By the time she'd closed out the register, pocketed her tips, and locked the tavern door, Boone still hadn't emerged from the kitchen. She stared for a long moment at the chair where he'd been sitting—at the wool sweater hanging over the back of the chair and how similar it looked to her father's old sweater that Boone had for some reason thought was his. A flash of that night in the hospital

streaked across her memory, her father laying the
sweater over her like a blanket as she shivered from
the cold and the aftereffects of the anesthesia.
The hair on the back of her neck stood up, and an
unexpected chill racked her body. She rummaged
behind the counter of the bar for her hoodie and
threw it on over her Midtown Tavern T-shirt.

Winters must be getting colder in Meadow
Valley.

She rounded the bar, gave Boone's forgotten
sweater one last glance, and then shook her head,
banishing the half memory to the past where it
belonged before pushing through the saloon doors
and into the kitchen.

"You don't have to—" she started, but then she
caught sight of the wireless earbud poking out from
his dark hair. Casey crossed her arms and bit back
a smile as she watched him rinse pint glasses and
beer steins all while subtly shaking his rear end to
whatever was playing in his ears.

Boone Murphy. In *her* kitchen. In her *bar*. The
former hadn't happened since they were teens, and
the latter? She'd hear about it after the fact—every
time he'd shown up on her rare nights off. They'd
tiptoed around each other for twelve years. *Twelve*
years. And now when Casey was finally reclaiming
the life she'd lost, he was back.

The man he'd become was nothing like the boy
she knew. Still, there was a familiarity that drew

her in—and scared the hell out of her. Could they really be friends?

Casey cleared her throat and squared her shoulders. If she was ready to leave the past in the past and finally move forward, then that meant the same for what she and Boone *were*. It was time to see what they could be.

She tapped him on the shoulder, and he startled, spinning toward her with the sink hose in his hand, sprayer aimed at her chest. Casey was soaked before she could scream.

"Shit!" Boone exclaimed, dropping the hose and holding his hands up in the air as if *she* were aiming a fully loaded hose at *him*. "I'm sorry! I didn't mean to—" But before he could finish his apology, he was doubled over. *Laughing.*

Casey dripped from her newly chopped bangs to her red sneakers.

"You think this is funny?" she said, fuming, any trace of cold now replaced with white-hot indignation.

Boone was practically wheezing, his hand on his belly. He finally pulled out the wireless earbuds, and Casey instinctively held out her palm.

His laughing eased as he handed the small yet expensive-looking listening devices over to her.

Without missing a beat, she placed them on a dry counter out of reach, then turned back to where Boone still stood, staring after her. She strode toward him with purpose, stopping in front of the dropped hose, picking it up, and spraying him from his neck to his knees.

He stood there, stunned, for *maybe* a millisecond. And then it was *on*—a one-on-one battle for the hose. When Casey lost it to Boone, she went for the suds in the sink, giving his already wet hair an impromptu shampoo.

She yelped as he retaliated by dropping the hose and scooping her into his arms, threatening to drop her in the oversize sink that, beneath the frothy white suds, was filled with dirty pint water.

Casey locked her arms around his neck and her legs around his waist.

"No, Boone Murphy. Don't you *dare*." Her heart raced, and her breaths came in quick trembles. But it wasn't being dumped in the sink she feared. It was the feeling deep in her core at being this close to *this* man.

Casey felt his chest rise and fall against hers, and she realized he was no longer holding her over the water but had pivoted so his hips rested against the sink's stainless steel edge. His hands—his *big* hands—gripped her thighs, his fingertips kneading the skin beneath the denim of her jeans.

For a moment, neither of them moved.

For a moment, she felt Boone Murphy's breath on her lips.

For a moment, she forgot the two of them had a

past as one single, solitary urge pulsed through her veins.

Kiss. Him.

Kiss Boone Murphy.

Now.

Here.

Tonight.

Except as quickly as the thought entered her mind, Boone gently lowered her to the ground and released his grip on her entirely.

"Sorry," he told her, clearing his throat. "We… uh…made a mess of the place right when I'm sure you want to close up and get the hell out of here." He pressed his hands to her shoulders and gently nudged her back so he could slip out from between her and the sink. "I'll go find a mop and take care of this."

He pivoted away from her, but she grabbed him by the wrist.

"The mop is the other way, in the closet in the back," she said.

"Then tell me something I can do for you up front," he insisted, his voice rough, but he hadn't turned to face her.

"Why?" she asked.

Boone pulled free from her grasp.

"Because, Casey…" He clenched and unclenched his fist. "It's late, I'm not thinking straight, and I'm trying to be a gentleman here. And if I turn back around and lay eyes on you again, I'm going to have to admit to you that I want something I'm not supposed to want. Something I'm mighty sure *you* don't want. I'm not gonna leave you here all by yourself to clean this up, so at least give me something to do up front so I can help get you home at a decent hour."

He ran a hand through his damp hair, tilting his head forward as he scratched the back of his neck.

Casey watched the muscles in his back and shoulders move beneath his now sheer, soaked T-shirt. She sucked in a shaky breath, then blew it out, steeling herself for whatever came next—rejection or…

"How can you be so sure I don't want this thing that *you* want?" she asked. "And how fair is it for you to make a decision *about* my wants without even asking me first? Just another chauvinist parading as a feminist, am I right?"

He groaned, but her goading did the trick. Boone spun on his heel, mouth open and ready, it seemed, to spit fire—until he saw her grinning.

"You're baiting me?" he asked, his expression wounded. *Not* what she expected.

"Sorry," she said. "Wait… *No.* I'm *not* sorry. You did make a decision disregarding *my* input when the decision involves both of us and *not* just you. Maybe the chauvinist thing went a little too far considering I'm nervous as hell right now, so I'm guessing you're *maybe* in the same boat. But still, you shouldn't have—"

"You're nervous?" he interrupted. "Nervous about what? How does my decision affect both of us? How can you possibly know what I want or what is going on in my overloaded-as-hell brain right now?"

She dared to take a step closer. He didn't move but simply stared at her with eyes wide and his jaw tight.

"Dammit, Murph. I want to kiss you. No— *need* to kiss you, like, right now, or I think I might actually explode. Do you want to be responsible for my spontaneous combustion and the end of Meadow Valley's finest nighttime establishment? No. I don't think you do. So let's just do this thing, get it out of our systems, and call it a day. Or night. Or is it tomorrow already?"

The corner of his mouth turned up, and he blinked at her once. Twice.

"Tell me again," he insisted, crossing his arms and giving her the cocky grin that always used to do her in. "What is it you said you wanted?"

Heat crept up her neck and into her cheeks.

"Kiss me," she pleaded, hooking a finger through the belt loop of his jeans. "Please, Boone. Kiss me now."

Twelve Years Ago

Boone let loose a shaky exhale as he nudged the spaghetti strap of Casey's dress off her shoulder.

"Are you nervous?" she asked, smiling as her teeth skimmed over her bottom lip.

"What gave you *that* idea?" he asked with a laugh. "The fact that my hands are trembling? Or can you see my stomach doing all sorts of cartwheels and shit?"

She cupped a palm to his cheek as she slid her arm through the strap. "You. Are. Adorable."

He sighed. "Just what every eighteen-year-old guy about to lose his virginity wants to hear. *Adorable.*"

Casey leaned forward and kissed him.

"I'm scared too, Murph," she whispered, then paused for a long moment. "We don't have to… you know."

He cleared his throat. "Do you not want to?"

"I do," she said without hesitation, and she meant it. "I'm scared because this is big and it means a lot, you know? But I want it to be you. I want it to be tonight. I love you, Murph."

He lowered the other strap and then unzipped the back of her dress.

"I've loved you since I was nine years old," he told her. "I've never been more sure about anyone or anything in my life. And even though I *know* you

mean it, it doesn't stop me from wondering sometimes why you chose *me*."

She sighed. "Right. Because every girl in school
doesn't crush on you."

"Yeah, but you *know* me."

She scoffed. "Love how you didn't even try to
deny it."

He leaned his forehead against hers. "You *know*
me. How I'm shit in school, how I forget birthdays
and anniversaries and sometimes when I'm supposed to meet you after Midtown closes. I'm...
scattered, you know? All over the place."

"You're spontaneous," she said with a smile.
"And always waiting for the other shoe to drop."

He huffed out a laugh, but his smile didn't quite
reach his eyes. "Or maybe I *am* the other shoe."

Casey shook her head. "Not as long as I'm
around. I'm not going to let you be the other shoe."

He kissed her, his lips lingering on hers as he
spoke. "You're *not* always going to be around.
You're going to get some great job in LA, which
you totally deserve, and then who's going to look
after me?"

She laughed, but her heart squeezed in her chest.
What would happen while they were apart?

"What if *you're* not here when I get back from
the great job with enough money to open my own
salon?" The thought had crossed her mind—more
than once.

"Never." He kissed her. "Gonna." He kissed her again. "Happen." He smiled against her. "The only thing that would take me out of Meadow Valley is if *you* weren't here for me anymore. So if you're saying you're *not* planning to come back…"

She nipped at his bottom lip. "I will *always* come back for you, Boone Murphy. As long as you think I'm worth the wait."

"And I will *always* wait," he promised.

But that night, they didn't wait for anything. Because despite not knowing what the future might hold, Boone Murphy was Casey Walsh's first and only love, and she wanted him to be her first—and last—everything. No matter where she went after graduation, Meadow Valley would always be home. *Boone* would be home. Because he was right. Casey *knew* him, all of him, and loved every part, even the parts he didn't love about himself. She had enough love to fill whatever void he couldn't fill on his own. At least she was naïve enough to believe she did.

But they were only eighteen. Kids. And whatever it was they thought they *knew*, they were wrong.

Chapter 11

BOONE TRIED TO REMAIN CALM, BUT CASEY Walsh's index finger tugged at the belt loop of his jeans. Her chest rose and fell with trembling breaths that mirrored his own.

Then she stood on her tiptoes, bracing her free hand on his shoulder for purchase as she whispered, "*Please.*"

Her breath tickled his lips, and that was all it took. He was a goner.

He crushed his lips against hers, and she let his belt loop go, sliding both arms around his waist and grabbing his ass. The ass she'd so professionally pummeled with her elbow on the massage table was now gripped—cheek for cheek—in her palms. And there was *nothing* professional about the way she pressed him closer, her hips rocking against his.

"Wait!" he cried, abruptly stepping back so that Casey's arms fell to her sides. "Get this out of our systems?" he asked, repeating her words and trying to make sense of what seemed to be happening over the past week—and right here in their soaking wet clothes—after twelve years of radio silence.

She nodded, her green eyes wide, her cheeks

flushed, and the skin on her chin already reddened from the stubble on his.

"You said it yourself that you were—you know—affected by seeing me half-naked. And I'm not gonna lie… Finding out it was you on the massage table? Touching you like that after all these years? There's no manual for how to react, and even though I am determined to be the consummate professional, my body's reaction would say otherwise. I just think—I mean, we've just proven that there's an unresolved *physical* attraction between us. Should we acknowledge it so we can move past it and get on with the rest of our lives?"

Physical attraction.

Boone felt himself strain against his jeans at the mention of the words, which meant she wasn't *wrong*. Every nerve in his body stood on end, waiting to see what might happen next. But despite his newfound appreciation of therapy and medication and tools to keep himself grounded and in the moment, right now his brain felt like scrambled eggs. He could throw logic out the window and let his body take over—like he'd already begun to do—but he'd still have to deal with the aftermath.

They'd have to deal with it.

So he closed his eyes and began counting backward from ten.

"What's happening?" Casey asked when he reached the number seven.

He cracked an eye open to find her still staring at him, brows furrowed.

"Do you do this a lot?" she asked.

"Do what?"

"Leave a girl hanging mid kiss so you can launch into a countdown?"

Boone cleared his throat. "I was counting out loud?" Shit. He really wasn't in control.

Casey nodded. "Are you nervous?"

His stomach tightened as he was immediately transported back to that night. The best and worst night because it was the beginning of the end.

He wished he'd known that the first time they'd been together like that was actually the first and *last*. He'd have savored it more, appreciated it more, committed every last piece of it to memory instead of just letting it happen.

Except her words right now had triggered a memory he hadn't realized was there, waiting to be dug up from the rubble of Casey and Boone.

Boone blew out a breath. "Nervous might be the understatement of the year."

Casey let loose a shaky laugh. "Right? I'm kind of terrified myself."

He cocked his head. "You are? I thought nothing could shake the great and confident Supergirl."

Her eyes grew shiny, but then she sniffed and shook her head, squaring her shoulders. "Yeah, well, confident as I am, waiting to find out if I'm being rejected seconds after a guy starts kissing me is a *little* bit terrifying, you know?"

He nodded. He *knew*.

"I'm nervous," he admitted. "Because I want to continue kissing you more than I'd like to admit. I'm nervous to think that after twelve years, we only just found a way to coexist in this town—as friends—and I don't want to mess that up. And I'm nervous for what happens after, because no matter what we say right now about what this does or doesn't mean, there's an *after*, Walsh, because it's you and me."

"Right," she said softly. "It's you and me." She blew out a breath, then stepped into him once more, sliding her arms over his shoulders and clasping her hands behind his neck. "But we're not kids anymore, Boone. We're grown-ass adults who can set boundaries so we don't have to worry about the after. Like just kissing and nothing more."

But he could feel the hard peaks of her breasts through her wet shirt as they pressed against his chest. He glanced down, and she followed his gaze.

Casey groaned. "It's because I'm *cold*."

"Mm-hmm," he hummed. "That's why your cheeks are on fire."

She gasped and then rolled her eyes. "Fine. Kissing and other stuff, but...but no *actual* sex. You know, like fornication or coitus or penetra—"

"I *got* it," he interrupted.

"Are you sure?" she asked with a grin. "Because I was just getting started. There's knockin' boots, taking a trip to pound town, doing the no pants dance…"

He closed his eyes and shook his head.

"I'm just trying to ease your nerves," she said, a sincerity in her voice he wasn't expecting. "Mine too."

When he opened his eyes, she gazed at him earnestly.

"If we don't *do* what got us in trouble before… If we leave *feelings* out of it," she started. "This might actually be—I don't know—fun? What do you say, Murph?"

Murph. Did she know that when she called him that, it was impossible to say no to her?

"No feelings," he noted, trying the words on for size. He'd had purely physical relationships before. How different would this be? "So, like, friends with benefits? For tonight. And then we go back to being just friends?"

She nodded with a grin. "Sounds pretty fun, doesn't it?"

But there would be expectations, wouldn't there? Eventually, even as her friend, he'd fall short like he had in the past—like he did with Elizabeth only a week ago. Boone had thought he'd grown and changed and figured out this adulting thing. But if that was the case, why was he still getting so much of it wrong?

She raised up on her toes and tilted her forehead against his. "You're overthinking it, Murph. Say no if you don't want this, and we can pretend tonight never happened."

He pressed a hand between them, his palm sliding up her torso until his thumb grazed one of those raised peaks.

She sucked in a sharp breath, and Boone bit back a growl.

He wanted this—wanted *her*.

"Just to get it out of our systems," he said, his voice rough. "No other expectations?"

She nodded. "No expectations other than—"

He pinched her between his thumb and forefinger, and she gasped.

"*Fun,*" he finally added, throwing logic out the damned window.

Because fun hadn't felt like this since…well, he couldn't remember when. And with all the upheaval in his life right now, he could use a little bit of what Casey Walsh was offering.

Once again, he pressed his mouth to hers, and she parted her lips and welcomed him inside.

For tonight, he could ignore how her kiss tasted better than he remembered or how simply being this close to her had the hairs on the back of his neck standing on end, his pulse racing, and his breath coming in fits and starts. He could ignore it all if it meant not having to back away and walk out the door.

Tomorrow he'd answer to himself, but tonight he was all hers.

"Call me *Murph* again," he whispered against her, and she nodded.

"Take me upstairs, *Murph*, and get me out of these wet clothes."

His stomach tightened, and for a second, he swore his heart stopped beating.

"Lead the way, Supergirl," he finally said.

And they quickly closed up shop and did exactly as she asked.

Chapter 12

CASEY PACED BACK AND FORTH ACROSS THE floor in Ivy's small office at the back of her boutique.

"Come on. Come on. Come on," she said aloud, as if Ivy could hear her from wherever she was.

Casey checked the time on her phone again: 7:58 a.m.

Ivy always opened at 9:00, which meant she came in to do paperwork at 8:00, but the girl was so punctual, that usually meant 7:30. So where the hell was she?

Finally, at 8:00 on the nose, Casey heard the tell-tale tinkle of the bell above the shop's door, and as Ivy unlocked the door and made her way inside, Casey emerged from the back office.

"Took you long enough!" Casey exclaimed, and Ivy screamed, tossing her travel mug and sketch pad in the air, the former—because the lid was open—spraying a stream of coffee across a beautiful cream-colored hand-knit sweater that was folded on a display table at the front of the store.

"Shit!" Casey hissed, running toward her friend.

"What the *actual*—" Ivy started, but she cut herself off as she placed a palm to her chest and caught her breath. "I think I might faint. Or throw up. Or both." She grabbed Casey's shoulder as she approached, and Casey led her to the stool behind the counter. Not that Ivy *ever* sat down when customers were in the shop, not even when she was artfully wrapping their items in tissue before bagging them. Ivy was always on the other side of the counter, next to her customer, because everyone who walked in the door was family to her. Though Casey was pretty sure *she'd* lost the moniker after scaring her best friend to near fainting.

Ivy took several steady breaths while Casey retrieved her half-spilled coffee and fashion sketchbook along with what she guessed was a ruined sweater that Casey now owned.

"How did you get in here?" Ivy finally asked.

Casey shrugged and offered a sheepish grin as she piled the collected items on the counter. "Your spare key," she said.

Ivy narrowed her eyes. "The one I gave you in case of emergency? Like, say, if the place was burning down and the fire department couldn't get here in time even though they're right down the street?"

Casey nodded slowly and worried her lip between her teeth. "Aren't my woeful financial situation and my impending tuition emergencies?"

Ivy narrowed her eyes. "Is this about your woeful finances and school tuition?"

Casey sighed. "*No.* But it could have been. And I

am *really* freaked out about that whole situation, but for the immediate present, my woeful finances have taken a back seat to the fact that I maybe, sort of, probably just left Boone Murphy sleeping in my bed."

She squeezed her eyes shut, too ashamed—mortified? humiliated?—to see her friend's reaction.

But that wasn't it. Casey didn't feel any of those things. She was scared...scared that Ivy wouldn't approve, because Casey wanted what happened last night to happen again.

She waited several long seconds, eyes still closed, but Ivy said nothing. Not. One. Word.

So Casey opened her eyes.

Ivy was staring at her, mouth hanging open, eyes wide and unblinking.

Casey waved a hand in front of her friend's face. Nothing.

She snapped her fingers at close range, but Ivy didn't even flinch.

So Casey took drastic measures and licked her index finger and then reached for Ivy's ear!

"All right! All right!" Ivy yelled, slapping Casey's hand away. "Save your wet willy for the man in your bed. The *man* in your *bed*! How the hell did you not drag me out of *my* bed to tell me this? How did it happen? *Why* did it happen? Do you still hate each other? Was it hate sex? Are you two dating? Does he know you left? Does—"

Casey pressed her palm to Ivy's mouth, and for a few seconds, muffled questions still escaped the other woman's lips. But Ivy must have realized she needed to breathe, because she finally stopped and inhaled through her nose.

"You go from catatonic to Chatty Cathy in record time!" Casey exclaimed.

"It's a gift," Ivy said as best she could. Then she wrapped her hand around Casey's wrist and lowered her arm. After that, she made a motion of locking her lips and throwing away the key, then motioned for Casey to continue.

Casey blew out a shaky breath.

"Okay. In the order that you asked…the how and the why… We were having a water fight in the tavern kitchen, and one thing led to another. But he stopped it almost as soon as it started, because no, I don't think we hate each other anymore. We decided after he hurt his back and I was his masseuse that maybe it was okay for us to be friends now, like let go of the past and start fresh. I mean, the guy did rescue me on the side of the road *and* inadvertently saved my life by giving Adeline airbags without me ever knowing, so he can't be *that* bad, right?" Her throat tightened, and she swallowed, teenage Casey's broken heart threatening to push through to the surface, but adult Casey wasn't going to let it. "And anyway, friends don't *do* what we were doing. Except I *really* liked it, Ives. Did you know he has, like, all these muscles now? And his hands. God, his big, calloused hands…"

She closed her eyes and let herself relive the fingers of one hand pinching her breast beneath her wet shirt or unbuttoning her jeans after he laid her out on her bed, that same capable hand slipping beneath her panties and sliding effortlessly inside her as if he'd been touching her like that every day for the past twelve years.

"Um…hello? Daydream believer? I don't want to know what's going on behind those eyelids of yours. Okay, *maybe* I do, but you haven't answered the rest of my questions. And I have another to add to the list. What's this whole back injury/massage situation I've not been told of?"

Despite her friend knowing *exactly* what was happening behind her closed eyes, Casey let herself reminisce for a few seconds more before meeting Ivy's wide-eyed stare.

"It wasn't hate sex. It wasn't even *sex*…at least not in the literal sense. I just, I can't, not with him. Not after—"

Ivy nodded. "I know, honey. I know. But the not literal sex…it was good?"

Casey's stomach tightened, and heat crept up her neck to her cheeks.

"Really, really, *really* freaking good. We agreed it would be just for the night. I said we needed to get it out of our systems, and then we could go back to this new friend thing we're trying."

"Friends who massage each other and are really, really, *really* good at kissing each other and stuff?"

Casey groaned. "The massage is legit. I'm moonlighting at Charlotte's office for her pregnant soon-to-be clients."

"Don't you also moonlight as a notary?" Ivy asked.

"Uh, yeah," Casey replied. "Like the one time a month someone needs something notarized." She sighed. "Boone got thrown from the new rescue horse at the ranch and… You don't want to hear about all that. You just want to know if I'm dating my high school sweetheart who *broke* my heart twelve years ago."

She draped her arms over the counter and banged her forehead—*lightly*—on the wooden ledge.

Ivy hooked her finger under Casey's chin and forced her to meet her gaze.

"No, Case," she said. "I want to know if you *want* to date your high school sweetheart who broke your heart twelve years ago. And if you do, I want to support you and Boone and hope for the happiness that I think you both deserve. And before you give me crap for wishing him well after he hurt you, I want to remind you that you were both kids, that there is always another side to the story no matter what we think we know, and that for whatever reason—I'm still trying to figure out all the details—that man was on his way to his own wedding last week, and instead, he was there for *you* in your hour of need. That *has* to mean something."

Casey straightened and made her way around the counter to where Ivy was still perched on her stool. She wrapped her arms around her friend and squeezed.

"Thank you for that—for not judging me. But I think the only way to leave the past in the past is for Boone and me to move forward as friends. We both agreed that last night was a onetime thing, and I think that's the best decision."

She straightened to find Ivy looking at her somberly.

"Whatever you want," Ivy said. "I support you as long as you're happy."

Casey smiled.

What she wanted was more of last night, not just what happened in her bed but the way he helped her clean up after the poker game, even if they made an even bigger mess that she'd have to take care of this morning. It didn't matter. Waking up next to him, Casey felt happy in a way she hadn't in years. And it scared the hell out of her.

Once upon a time, Casey Walsh and Boone Murphy had fallen in love—and then broken each other's heart. And she'd be damned if she'd let either of them risk that again.

But friends she could do.

Friends who kiss? Even better.

Last night didn't have to be a onetime thing if they kept the boundaries clear.

"Right," Casey finally said. "I think I need to go see a naked guy in my bed and make sure we're on the same page."

Ivy huffed out a laugh. "Maybe have him throw on some boxers or something first. Always best to have important conversations when all parties are properly clothed."

"Tighty-whities!" Casey blurted, then threw her hand over her mouth.

Ivy gasped. "Boone *Murphy*! Who *ever* would have guessed?"

"Okay, *not* tighty-whities," Casey amended. "They were colored. Navy, I think. But they were those small, hug-you-everywhere kind of briefs."

Casey squeezed her eyes shut and shook her head free of the image of Boone Murphy *in* hug-you-everywhere kind of briefs...and *out* of them.

"I'm leaving!" she said, then spun on her heel.

"Hey!" Ivy called after her, and Casey pivoted back to face her friend. Ivy held up the coffee-stained sweater. "I know you're in a financial bind right now, so I'm putting this on your tab. You can pay it off with free drinks at Midtown."

Casey rolled her eyes. "You *never* pay for drinks at Midtown."

Ivy laughed. "That's because I'm an excellent tipper. You *do* owe me a coffee. Preferably something with *peppermint* and *mocha* in the name."

"But that was just plain old coffee in your mug, and you still have, like, three quarters of it left."

Ivy shrugged. "Compensation for the emotional distress you caused by almost scaring me to fainting."

Casey lovingly flipped the bird at her friend, and Ivy responded by blowing her a kiss.

"Make it a large!" Ivy called as Casey backed out the door and onto the sidewalk.

Okay. *First*, she'd stop by the inn for one of Pearl's candy cane mochas. *Then* she'd propose her—well—*proposal* to Boone.

Easy peasy lemon squeezy—and maybe, possibly, slightly *queasy*.

Chapter 13

WHAT THE HELL WAS HE DOING HERE?

The question felt like a broken record these days, yet it was also the fitting theme to where he was in his life, which was limbo.

"Can I help you, sir?" a woman asked with a tap on Boone's shoulder.

He spun, his clothes still damp from the night before, making the movement sluggish and uncomfortable.

"Boone!" the older woman exclaimed with a grin. "Well, I didn't realize that was you. Haven't seen you since you came back to town." She raised her brows, making it clear her observation was laced with curiosity.

"Mrs. Davis," Boone said with a nervous laugh. "I wasn't expecting you to be open so early, nor did I realize you had a…um…a knitting section in the bookshop. I was just taking a walk and—"

"When are you boys going to stop addressing me like I'm your middle school teacher? We're both adults here, and if you promise to call me *Trudy* from now on, I'll fix you a cup of coffee on the house. You look like you need it."

The small beagle she held under her arm nipped at her salt-and-pepper braid.

"I see Frederick is still chewing on all the things," Boone said, scratching the dog behind his ear.

Trudy glanced down at her pooch and then kissed him on the snout.

"Poor old guy still doesn't realize he has no teeth." She shrugged. "As long as he's enjoying himself, I pay him no mind. Now what do you say to that coffee?" She nudged Boone with her elbow. "It's the reason I open an hour earlier than I used to. Got me one of those restaurant-grade espresso machines so that the ice cream parlor is also a *coffee* parlor. Pearl wasn't too happy when I started doing it, until I made her a pint of my lemon poppy seed ice cream. That seemed to set things right, especially since it wasn't as if her guests were leaving the inn to get their coffee elsewhere." She sighed. "Did I miss your answer? Was that a yes?"

Boone laughed. Sometimes he forgot the small things he loved about this town—like Trudy Davis and her toothless dog.

"I would *love* a cup of coffee, Mrs.—I mean, *Trudy*." He checked his watch. "Gotta be at the ranch in an hour to start tack room inventory, which is basically desk duty. Think I need to talk to the boys about letting me back on the horse."

Trudy's brows furrowed. "And why do they have you *off* the horse?"

"Shit," he hissed, and Trudy shook her head ruefully.

"Come on upstairs, and you can tell me all about it over a cappuccino," she offered.

"Just a black coffee is good," he said.

Trudy gave him a knowing grin. "Suit yourself, but I think you'll change your mind when you taste my cappuccino."

Boone sighed and followed her out of Storyland's unexpected knitting nook, around several book-shelves, and up the steps painted to look like book spines. When they reached the top, Boone's eyes widened when he found his poker buddies from the night before—Sam, Ben, Colt, *and* Carter all sitting around a table. In front of each man sat a mug covered with foam, and in each of their hands were…knitting needles.

Boone looked behind him, waving his hand through the air.

"Did we just pass through some kind of portal into an alternate dimension?" he asked.

Trudy laughed, and the other men—until now oblivious of their arrival—looked up from their balls of yarn and metal sticks.

"Boone!" Colt called out. "I'd ask how the rest of your night went, but if I'm not mistaken, it looks like you're wearing the same clothes you had on the last time I saw you. What do you think, Carter?"

"Shh!" Carter hissed, then counted to himself

under his breath. "Knit one, purl one. Knit two, purl two. Knit one, purl one."

A long, thin, scarf-looking *thing* draped over Ben's lap onto the floor and had formed a small mountain of yarn. If it *was*, in fact, a scarf, it was a scarf fit for a giant.

"Okay," Boone said. "Seriously. Where the hell am I, and how do I get back to *my* universe?"

Sam laughed and nodded for Boone to come over to the table. "Grab a seat, Murphy. Our club can always use a fifth."

Boone blinked, then looked toward Trudy and Frederick as if they had some sort of explanation for him that would make sense.

"Go on now," Trudy insisted. "I'll get your cappuccino while the boys get you situated. Sam, give him the wooden needles I made you start on. Those are best for beginners."

"You got it, Trudy," Sam called over his shoulder as Trudy set Frederick down in his doggie bed and then slipped behind the ice cream/coffee parlor's counter.

Boone walked in a daze to the round table that barely fit the four men and all their gear as it was, let alone the extra chair Colt slid between him and Ben. Once he sat down, the five of them were practically shoulder to shoulder, yet the other men simply adjusted their positions in their chairs so that no one's elbow bumped another, and they continued as if Boone had never been there.

Boone, however, had no idea where to put his hands. On the table? On his lap? He settled for crossing his arms over his chest, yet tighter than was comfortable so as not to accidentally nudge Colt or Ben. His sweater hugged his damp T-shirt to his torso, and goose bumps rose up and down his arms.

Note to self: Next time you find yourself being undressed by your high school sweetheart, make sure your wet clothes—if your clothes are indeed wet— don't end up in a ball on the floor where they will never get dry.

"What *is* that?" he finally asked Ben, his eyes trailing down the length of the blue-green yarn to where the creation pooled on the floor.

Ben counted a few more stitches before looking up. "It's...*nothing*," he said with a laugh.

"We don't do this to *make* anything," Colt added.

"Just to sort of Zen out," Sam added.

"Zen *out*," Boone repeated. He hadn't *really* taken Casey's suggestion to take up knitting seriously. But when he'd wandered into the bookshop, he'd somehow made a beeline straight for the knitting nook, as if he'd always known it was there. "So," he continued, "you have poker night on Friday and—"

"Knitting club Saturday morning," Carter interrupted, finishing Boone's thought. "Pearl got me started soon after I became chief. Said it's her favorite way to unwind after a busy spell at the inn. Of course I thought she was full of it until she sat me down one night after a stressful shift on call, and…well…here we are." Carter shrugged, then nodded toward the other men at the table. "We're terrible at it."

"The *worst*," Sam added.

"But what a way to start the morning," Ben added, slamming his needles down on the table and then taking a healthy swig of his foamy beverage. When he set his mug down, his nose was covered with a dollop of foam.

"You…um…" Boone started, and Ben's eyes widened.

"What?" Ben asked, with what Boone could tell was mock concern. "Is there something on my face?" He swiped at his clean chin and then at his foam-free cheek.

Boone rolled his eyes. "How long has this—I don't know—club been meeting?"

"Eleven weeks," the four of them said in unison.

"Eleven *weeks*, and I lived and worked down the street and never heard a word of this?" Boone asked.

Trudy slipped out from behind the counter and made her way over to the table. She placed two mugs in front of Boone, one with black coffee and the other a cappuccino.

"You've kept to yourself so much over the years," Trudy noted, ruffling his hair like she did when he was a mischievous preteen. "It's nice to see you out and about now that you're back. Heard you turned quite a few heads at Midtown last night."

Boone let out something akin to a growl and then snatched up the mug with nothing but black coffee. He took a sip and then shuddered, doing everything in his power not to spit what was in his mouth back into the mug.

He finally swallowed. "Hell, Mrs. Da—*Trudy*! What *was* that?"

"Language," Trudy said, as did every other man at the table.

"Trudy doesn't put up with swearing," Sam added.

"It's her place of business," Ben added.

Colt picked up his foam-topped mug and offered Boone a gesture of cheers. "And we have to pay for the coffee if we let any curse words fly." He took a sip. "Much better than the straight espresso, especially with the little bit of magic Trudy sprinkles on top."

Trudy waved Colt off. "Aren't you sweet? It's just cocoa and cinnamon." Then she turned her gaze to Boone. "That was your *second* and final freebie as far as language is concerned. I'm counting the one from downstairs too. Next time, all this"—she motioned to every mug on the table—"is on *you*."

"Yes, ma'am," Boone said like a sulking teen who'd been called out for exactly the same thing.

Trudy laughed. "And to answer your question, the reason it's so bitter is that I don't brew *coffee*. It's an espresso bar, so you can either take it straight or with milk and my little bit of magic. It's up to you."

They all stared at Boone, daring him to either swear or taste the cappuccino or both. He truly didn't know. But somehow he felt like if he *did* choose the cappuccino, it would be the same thing as Neo choosing the red pill in *The Matrix*, that a whole new world was about to open up to him. He just wasn't sure he wanted to be a part of that world if it meant blurring the lines between his work life and personal life. That was what his therapist was for, though he wasn't sure what he was going to tell her at their next appointment.

Hey, Dr. Sharon. So I slept with my high school ex. Well, not slept, but everything but. And when I woke up this morning, she was gone. How fucked up is that?

His eyes widened, ready for Trudy's admonishing, then realized he'd only cursed in his inner monologue. Boone scrubbed a hand over his stubbled jaw as the muscles in his shoulders tightened and he felt the ever-familiar pinch in his lower back.

"Screw it," he finally said. "Wait, that word is okay, right?"

Trudy grinned. "I'll allow it, Mr. Murphy."

He blew out a long breath, then lifted the mug

of cappuccino to his lips and took a sip. He closed his eyes and sighed as the not-quite-sweet yet not-quite-bitter liquid warmed him from the inside out. Then he licked the residual foam from his top lip, tasting what Colt had rightfully called Trudy's little sprinkle of magic.

Well *shit*. The cappuccino was damned good. And he could still swear in his head, which was also pretty damned good.

He opened his eyes to find the whole table staring at him expectantly.

Boone sighed. "Fine," he relented. "Give me the da—darned beginner sticks and show me what the *heck* I'm supposed to do."

"Attaboy!" Ben said, clapping Boone on the shoulder. "Welcome to the club."

And that was how Boone found himself—after waking up alone in Casey Walsh's bed—in a bookshop, drinking cappuccino and knitting absolutely *nothing* with a group of men he'd planned to keep at arm's length until he got his garage back and could do what he did best—fix cars, keep to himself, and make as little mess of his life as possible.

Chapter 14

FIVE DAYS. HOW DID SOMEONE FALL ASLEEP IN your bed and then disappear for *five* days. Okay, fine. Maybe Casey had fled the scene first the morning after the poker game, kitchen water fight, and everything that came after. But that was simply to decompress with Ivy and figure out what the hell she wanted—or at least how *much* she could want—while still keeping her heart safe. But when Casey finally got back to her apartment, Boone was gone.

She'd called the ranch and gotten Barbara Ann, Sam and Ben's mother, who'd said that *all* the men had taken the early morning off for some sort of meeting. She guessed that was where Boone was too. She'd have called or texted Boone directly but didn't actually have the guy's cell phone number.

And now it had been five days of looking up every time the exam room door opened to see if her next massage client was a certain Mr. Roberts. It wasn't. He'd been a no-show at Midtown during the week as well. Not that she'd been paying *too* much attention.

"I'm sure Carter could give you his number,"

Ivy told her the next morning as the two women enjoyed a cup of coffee at the Meadow Valley Inn.

"That feels stalker-ish to me," Casey said, worried. "I mean, we're not dating. We're not *anything*, really, if I can't even talk to the guy and see if he wants what I want or if Friday was just a onetime thing because I *said* it would only be a onetime. Am I overthinking this?"

Ivy laughed. "Do you want me to answer honestly or say what you want to hear?"

Casey narrowed her eyes. "Duh. Tell me what I want to hear. If that's not why best friends exist, then I don't know why the universe brought us together."

"Because I'll always have your back, and you'll always have mine?"

Casey sighed. "Okay, yeah, that too. But..." She trailed off.

"You're *not* overthinking things," Ivy insisted. "It's sort of a big deal that you and Boone hooked up after all these years, so I'm sure he's *not* overthinking things just as much as you are *not*. But you can always just pop by the ranch for a trail ride or something. Or to check up on your car?"

Casey leaned back in her chair and inhaled the comforting aroma of coffee and cinnamon.

"Too soon," she said coolly. "I'm just gonna let the chips fall where they may and go on with my life."

"So breezy of you," Ivy teased with a wink.

"I know, right?" Casey replied.

"Do I hear my daughter's voice?" a man's voice called from the door where the inn's screened-in and heated café connected to the inn proper.

Casey craned her neck to see her father's thick, snow-white hair pop through the door as he peeked out at his daughter and her best friend.

"Hey, Dad," Casey said with a confused smile as she got up to greet him. "I thought you were on kitchen prep this morning."

Every Wednesday, Casey's father met with their local food suppliers to replenish for the weekend.

"I am," he replied, stepping all the way through the door and wrapping his daughter into a hug.

Did he feel thinner than the last time she'd hugged him? When had that even been—a week ago?

"Are you eating enough, Dad?" Casey asked as they both loosened their embrace and she stepped back to get a good look at him. Same flannel button-down and jeans—his *uniform*—that he always wore, but the shirt looked like it hung a little looser over his shoulders, his jeans a bit baggier than she was used to.

Her father waved her off with a smile, the lines at the corners of his eyes setting her at ease.

"Why do you think I'm here? Your mom's talking produce with Anna and sent me here for Pearl's eggs Benedict."

Casey crossed her arms and gave him a long, hard stare.

Her father held up his right hand and said, "Scout's honor," to which Casey rolled her eyes.

"You were never a Boy Scout."

He laughed. "True, but if I *was* one, I'd have been super honorable." He gave his daughter a kiss on the cheek. "I'm all full up with hollandaise and love for my little girl, so I should get back and help your mom. How's things with getting all registered for school? All set to start after the holidays?"

Casey forced a smile and nodded. "All set."

"And they're really prorating the tuition even after all these years?"

Her throat tightened at him repeating her lie, but she nodded again, hoping her smile didn't look as artificial as it felt.

"Mm-hmm. Just a couple thousand, which I already have saved up. Nothing for you and Mom to worry about."

"I'm proud of you, sweetheart," he noted, his expression growing serious. "I know how much this means to you, and your mom and I couldn't be happier."

"Even if it means me spending less time at the bar?" she asked with a wince.

He cupped her cheek in his calloused palm. "*Especially* if it means you spending less time at the bar. Midtown—that was *my* dream. You've waited long enough for yours."

Casey sighed. "How do you always know the right thing to say, Dad?"

He laughed. "Many years and *many* lover's quarrels with your mother. I think I may be finally figuring things out."

Casey's heart squeezed in her chest. "You know you and Mom set the bar too high, don't you?" How she'd ever find what they had was beyond her, so much so that she was willing to settle for friends with benefits, because if there was one thing the other night made her realize, it was that even if she could satisfy her own physical needs, there was something to be said for spending the night with another warm body beside her and waking up in someone else's arms.

He winked at her. "Remember, a lot of years and a *lot* of quarrels. Marriage is work, darling. Your mom and I have our good days and our not-so-good days, but at the end of every one of them, do you want to know what I do?"

Casey's brows furrowed. "You fall asleep in the recliner watching late-night television after closing the bar?"

He laughed. "Yes. But also, when I *do* finally make my way to bed, I pull the book off your mother's chest, close it, and put it on the nightstand. Then I slide her glasses off her nose because she's already snoring. And then I kiss her on the cheek and thank her."

"For what?" she asked.

"For choosing me…and for continuing to choose me every single day."

Casey swallowed the knot in her throat. How had she never known this about her parents?

"Does she even hear you if she's sleeping?"

He shrugged. "Sometimes no. And sometimes she tells me to wait until tomorrow, because she might change her mind."

This time, Casey snorted. "I maintain what I said. Bar. Too. High."

Her father blew a kiss over her shoulder to Ivy. "How's my second daughter?"

Ivy blew a kiss right back. "Just kicking it with my sister from another mister," she called back.

"I'll see you around four," Casey told him. "I have some errands to run today." More like a shift at the pediatrician's office to pay for that nothing-to-worry-about tuition. "But I'll be back for my shift."

Her dad pursed his lips and looked at his watch. "You know, Wednesdays are pretty light, and with tomorrow being Thanksgiving, lots of folks are home preparing meals or out of town to escape the cold. Why don't you take the night off and do something for you."

She opened her mouth to protest but then thought better of it. She *could* use some time to herself—to unwind and maybe unravel the tangled spool of thoughts in her head.

"Are you sure?" she asked, then realized it meant a night without tips. "Maybe I should—"

"Consider it a vacation day," her father replied, interrupting her thought. "Which means vacation *pay* for my girl who always seems to be working. You'll need a little extra in that nest egg once you start classes again."

Casey threw her arms around her dad and squeezed him tight. "Thank you!" she exclaimed and wondered if he suspected how much this small gesture meant to her. She hoped he didn't, at least not to the fullest extent. "Just make sure you take a break and eat a good dinner tonight, okay?"

He held up his right hand again and said, "Scout's honor," and Casey playfully swatted his hand away. "See you at the ranch for Thanksgiving dinner tomorrow?"

Right. Sam, Ben, and Colt had made it a tradition to host a Thanksgiving feast for all who needed or wanted some place to go on Thanksgiving night. Casey assumed that this year, Boone Murphy would be in attendance since he was technically part of the ranch family now. Which meant *she* and *he* would be spending the holiday together, after not talking for five days, after what happened last Friday night.

She forced a smile. "Of course," she replied.

"I'll even help you pack up the keg from the tavern."

He laughed, said goodbye to both of his girls, and pivoted back through the door.

Casey strolled back to the table, pulled out her phone, and brought up the ranch's number.

"Who are you calling?" Ivy asked, but someone on the other line had already picked up.

"Hi," she said. "Sam? It's Casey. Got any last-minute slots for a trail ride early evening? Or maybe a bonfire or something?"

"Ooh, a bonfire sounds fun!" Ivy cried. "Sign me up too!"

Casey shushed her friend. "Uh-huh. He is. Okay. Yeah. Five o'clock. Dress warm. Got it. I'll be there. Thanks!"

Ivy raised her brows. "Did you just leave me out of s'mores and ghost stories?"

Casey huffed out a laugh. "No bonfire tonight. Not enough guests. But there's a couple and their two kids who are doing a trail ride at five, and I'm going to tag along." She paused. "Boone's leading the trail."

Ivy crossed her arms and raised her brows. "Well, color me impressed, Casey Walsh. What happened to letting the chips fall where they may?"

Casey shrugged. "Doesn't mean I can't take the reins and give those chips a little nudge."

Ivy replied with a slow clap. "Assertive *and* punny. I knew I liked you."

Casey blew out a breath. Here was hoping Boone Murphy was in the market for a friend with benefits who was assertive and punny too.

Chapter 15

BOONE GRUMBLED TO HIMSELF AS HE STRODE toward the barn. He could have had the night off, his family of four canceling their trail ride once they saw the temperature was supposed to drop into the thirties. But as soon as he got the cancelation notification from the ranch's online scheduling system, Sam had sent him a text letting him know a solo rider had made a last-minute booking that he hadn't entered into the system, which meant that Boone was still on the clock.

Not that he was complaining about doing his job—or the paycheck that came with it. He'd just set his still jumbled mind to working on the couple of vehicles he had waiting in his makeshift garage—an opportunity to put his brain to work so he could stop thinking about all the things he didn't want to think about.

It was funny. Riding on the back of a horse used to be his own form of meditation. But ever since the morning he accidentally barged in on…

"Casey?" he asked, brows furrowed as he pushed through the barn door and found her standing at Cirrus's stall, patting him on the nose. "What are you—wait, *you're* my solo trail ride?"

Her eyes widened as she turned to face him.

"*Solo* trail ride? But Sam said there was a family of four already booked."

Boone shook his head. "They canceled because of the drop in temperature. Not sure why they waited until the last minute when the forecast has been spot-on all week." He crossed his arms. "Did Sam take your reservation?"

She nodded.

Boone huffed out a laugh, condensation from his breath clouding the air. "Funny, he didn't bother telling me who my solo rider was. Just said he didn't have a chance to put the reservation into the system yet." He scrubbed a hand across his jaw and scratched at the back of his neck.

What was Sam Callahan's angle? Of all the folks in town, he was the last one Boone thought might meddle in anyone else's business. But he could easily have mentioned that Boone's solo rider was Casey Walsh—the woman who disappeared from her bed five days ago and drove him to knitting. He had a long snake of poorly stitched together yarn just like Ben's to prove it.

"I should probably go," Casey admitted, shoving her hands into her red puffer coat pockets. "You don't need to head out just for me."

She gave Cirrus one last pat and then began walking toward Boone, who was still standing just inside the door.

"Hold it," he said, his hand in the air as if stopping traffic. "If you cancel, I'm off the clock. And if I'm off the clock, my hours for the day get cut, which means the same for my paycheck. If I'm going to get my shop back or—I don't know—set up shop somewhere else, I'm going to need a down payment."

Casey halted mid stride. "Somewhere else?" she asked, then shook her head with a laugh. "Sorry. That's none of my business. What you do and where you do it is for you to know and for me... well...not to know, I guess." She winced. "I just mean that we're not... It's not like we..."

Boone cleared his throat. "It's okay, Walsh. I don't need you to spell it all out for me. You were clear where we stood Friday night and even more so Saturday morning. We got it out of our systems, and now we can move forward, right?"

She winced again. "Are you...angry at me, Murph?"

His jaw tightened. He hadn't thought he was angry, but his grinding teeth and the tightness in his chest said otherwise.

"Acknowledge your emotions, Boone," Dr. Sharon had told him at a recent session. "If you don't give voice to how you feel, it will all just simmer below the surface. The only way to keep everything organized in that brain of yours is to give yourself permission to feel how you feel, deal with it, and move forward."

Fine. Baby steps. What did he have to lose when it came to him and Casey Walsh that he hadn't lost already?

"Yes," he finally replied. "I'm a little pissed that you took off the other morning without even having the nerve to look me in the eye and tell me that we made a mistake and it shouldn't happen again."

She swallowed. "Is...is that what you think? That it was a mistake?"

He let out a bitter laugh. "Jesus, Casey. Of all the people who should *not* have wound up in bed together, can you think of any two who are a bigger mistake than us?"

She flinched as if his words had physically hit her, and he wished he could swallow them back up. Just because she'd made *him* feel like a mistake didn't mean he wanted her to feel the same way.

"You're right," she said, squaring her shoulders and looking him straight in the eye. "It never should have happened, and it never will again." Her words bit harder than the frigid air. "If we scrap the trail but I jump some barrels in the arena instead, will you still get your hours for the night?"

He sighed. "Yes, but, Walsh..." His voice was gentler now.

She shook her head. "It's fine. I just wanted to ride and clear my head anyway. This way, we don't have to worry about making conversation or any other mistakes, right? Loki likes the barrels, right?" she asked, referring to Ben Callahan's black stallion.

Boone nodded.

"Great," she said with a cool grin. "I'll just grab his stuff and get him ready to go."

She strode past him and into the tack room, as if this was something she did all the time. For all he knew, maybe it was. He'd only been a part of the ranch for a couple of weeks, but he did know that any guest who signed up for an activity *had* to be accompanied by a ranch employee, and tonight, Casey Walsh was a *guest* at Meadow Valley Ranch.

When Casey walked Loki out into the arena, Boone was already there, sitting in Cirrus's saddle.

Casey groaned. "You seriously don't need to babysit me."

Boone tipped his hat—which he'd have to toss once the sun fully set—and gave her a self-satisfied grin.

"Actually, I do," he said. "Ranch liability and all that. Can't let you out there alone."

She huffed out a cloudy breath. "You could watch from the fence, couldn't you?"

He shrugged. "I probably could, but how can I smoke you in barrel jumping from the sidelines?" He wasn't sure why he was taunting her competitive streak. Even if in reality he was simply moving in circles, at least he'd be *moving*, which was better than standing still.

He gave Cirrus a nudge, which was all it took to launch the still skittish rescue horse into a canter, which quickly escalated to a gallop.

"Cheater!" Casey called after him, and Boone bit back a grin as he and the cloud on which he rode neared the first jump.

"Yah!" he called, tapping his heels on Cirrus's flanks as they cleared the first hurdle. They picked up speed and raced toward the first turn of their lap. But despite the wind rushing in his ears, he could hear the rhythm of Loki's hooves against the dirt, the stallion's speed increasing.

He held his breath, focusing on the silent interruption to the gallop followed by the front and then back hooves hitting the ground as Casey and Loki cleared the first hurdle as well.

Boone bent low, angling his torso along Cirrus's neck to cut down on wind resistance. But he could hear his opponent gaining speed, closing the distance between them.

He and Cirrus jumped the next hurdle and approached the second turn. He glanced over his shoulder and found Casey and Loki only a few yards away. Cirrus shocked him by barely slowing on the turn, which bought them a few more yards as they bolted toward the next jump.

"Yah!" he called again, not even bothering to suppress his victorious grin. Once over barrel number three, he'd be in the home stretch. He gave

Casey one last glance before readying for the jump, but when he turned back to face what was ahead, he saw it too late—the goddamned trash panda that sat atop the center barrel taunting Cirrus just as Boone had taunted Casey.

If a butterfly was enough to spook his horse in daylight, what were the odds a raccoon at dusk would make Cirrus gentle as a lamb?

Cirrus skidded to a halt before hitting the barrel, which—at the speed they were going—was enough to lift Boone out of his saddle. But he held tight to the reins and had the wherewithal to keep his legs long and hips relaxed, sitting deep into his pockets and attempting to ride out the horse's panic.

He tried pulling on one of the reins to flex Cirrus's head and get him to change direction, but the raccoon, rather than run from danger, snarled and snorted and then let loose a screech that broke through any sort of control Cirrus might have still had.

"Shit," he swore softly to himself when he realized karma was about to bite him in the ass yet again. Cirrus gave his hindquarters another violent kick, and Boone finally lost his grip.

He willed himself not to tense up, to protect his head, and to try to roll in the direction of the fall. He heard Casey scream his name before his shoulder hit the dirt. A sharp pain rocketed up his arm and neck, and he swore. But he let his body keep moving in the direction the momentum sent him, which was thankfully toward the fence and out of Casey and Loki's way.

Boone could breathe this time, and his lower back seemed to be intact. But he knew two very important facts. One, his shoulder was messed up. And two, nobody was here to horse whisper Cirrus out of being spooked. He'd have to do it himself before Loki reacted and did the same thing to Casey.

He pushed himself up with his good arm, teeth gritted against the pain in his other. The raccoon was still there—little shit—hissing at Cirrus and at Loki and Casey, who were only a couple yards back. Loki wasn't bucking, but he was starting to dance backward in a way that told Boone he had a finite amount of time to set things right before someone else got hurt. As much as he wanted to curse the hell out of the rodent to get it to move, he knew the animal was also reacting out of fear and that scaring it even more wasn't going to help anyone.

He moved along the fence until he hoped he was in Cirrus's peripheral vision and calmly called the horse's name.

"Hey, Cirrus," he said, just loud enough to hear himself over the commotion of hooves slamming against the dirt. "Hey, boy. I'm right here."

Cirrus turned toward the sound of Boone's voice, but then the raccoon chittered, and the horse shook his head and backed away. But he wasn't bucking, so Boone took a chance and gingerly stepped toward the stallion.

"It's me, Cirrus," he said, taking another step. "It's Boone. We're both new here, remember? I'm the first rider you tolerated, even though you tossed me once before." He knew Cirrus didn't understand a word he was saying but hoped the soothing tone of his voice would hold the Arabian's attention long enough for him to get close enough to grab the reins, to pat Cirrus's nose and let him know that he was safe. "I'm sorry if they didn't treat you right where you were before," he told him, closing the distance between them. "But you're safe here, Cirrus. You're safe with me. No matter how many times you test me, you're safe. You hear?"

The horse backed up another step, but then he stopped. Boone could feel Casey staring at him from his left, and to his right, he detected a flash of movement that he hoped was the raccoon finally running away, but he didn't dare break eye contact with Cirrus.

"You're safe," he said again, taking the final steps needed to finally get a hold of the reins. "You can trust me, Cirrus. I won't hurt you."

With the reins in his right hand, he tried to lift his left to give Cirrus a gentle pet between his eyes, but the pain damn near made him pass out. He clamped his jaw shut, unable to quiet the growl that escaped his lips. He was ready for Cirrus to jerk the reins right out of his good hand when he saw Casey's palm land gently on Cirrus's nose.

"It's okay, boy," she cooed, petting him gently.

"In my right pocket," Boone noted through gritted teeth. "Sugar cubes."

Casey nodded, keeping one hand on the horse's nose while sliding the other into Boone's pocket to retrieve the treat. On any other night, Casey Walsh's touch might have set his nerve endings on fire. But right now, he could barely see through the pain.

He closed his eyes and exhaled as he heard Cirrus whinny and lap up the sugar from Casey's palm. Soon, she had Cirrus's reins in one hand and Loki's—from where she'd tied him to the fence—in the other.

"I'll get these boys settled," she told him. "Can you make it to your garage or barn or whatever you call it?"

Boone held his injured arm against his chest and nodded. As long as he made it there before the rest of his adrenaline waned, he'd be good.

"Okay," she said. "Go there, sit down, and do *not* move. Do you understand? I'll be right there."

"Yes, ma'am," he agreed, forcing a smile, then did as he was told. He wasn't sure what Casey could do to fix the situation he was in, but he didn't have it in him to argue.

He'd cleared off his desk—which was really just

a folding table from the hardware store—with a sweep of his good arm after carefully setting his laptop on the floor. Funny how when he saw the gesture in countless movies, it preceded some pretty passionate sex scenes. But when *he* did it, it was so he could use the table like a gurney, laying himself flat on his back to keep his shoulder immobilized.

Note to self: Next time I violently clear off my desk, make sure it's for something involving a shitload more pleasure than pain.

A gust of cold air woke him from his stupor as Casey slid the barn door open and found him on his poor excuse for a bed.

"Hey," she said, flipping on one of the hanging lights he'd rigged from the rafters before approaching where he lay. "I called Charlotte, but she has the day off tomorrow for Thanksgiving because—duh—we all do. And, well, she's in the middle of drunk karaoke at Midtown right now. I wanted to try to avoid the ER on a holiday weekend because they're usually slammed, and I didn't want you to have to wait if you were in a lot of pain, so…"

Another figure strode through the doorway, and Boone had to squint against the light to make out who it was.

He bolted upright when he figured it out, pain be damned.

"Shit, Casey," he growled. "You had *no* right."

Chapter 16

"WATCH YOUR MOUTH, LITTLE BROTHER," ELI scolded. "From the looks of that dislocated shoulder, she did you one hell of a favor getting a hold of me rather than making you wait in the emergency room in what I bet is a *hell* of a lot of pain."

Casey's chest tightened. Her endgame tonight had been her and Boone finding some common ground on this friends-with-benefits situation. They should have been on top of his office desk *together* doing things to each other that were a lot more fun than Casey ratting Boone out to his brother after a second fall from a horse. So Eli could hopefully fix Boone up without him having to go to the hospital.

"So you called a *vet*?" Boone asked, eyes narrowed at Casey.

She crossed her arms, her anger surpassing any guilt she felt at having done what she needed to do.

"Eli's a doctor," Casey reminded him. "And he fixed up Chewbarka's shoulder—RIP to the best mutt in the world—several years back when he was still in vet school. Figured he could do the same for you, especially after all his years of experience since then."

Boone squeezed his eyes shut, and for a second Casey wondered if he missed the dog they'd named together as much as she did.

"So what you're saying is that I'm a *dog* in this scenario?" he inquired, meeting her gaze again.

Eli sighed. "What she's saying is that you got knocked off a horse *twice* since you've been back in town and haven't said a damned word to me because you think I can't handle it. News flash, Little Brother. I'm not so damned fragile, and even if I was, it's not your job to keep me safe, especially when you can't seem to get the job done for yourself. Now you're in a heap of trouble and pain, and Casey cared enough to ask for my help so you're not spending Thanksgiving in the hospital. If you ask me, I'd say a thank-you is in order for your friendly neighborhood bartender here."

Casey raised her brows and waited.

Boone growled, but amid the noise, Casey detected a couple of words that sounded like *thank* and *you*.

"You're welcome," she crooned with a self-satisfied grin.

"Okay," Eli started, clapping his hands together. "Lie back down. I can sedate you if you want, but you'll be groggy for a while after that. Or we can just do this, which will hurt like hell, but then it'll feel a lot better."

Boone blew out a breath. "I don't want to be all loopy. Let's just get it over with."

Eli nodded. "Then you're coming back with me to the clinic so I can do an X-ray to figure out how long you need to keep it immobilized. I'll fix you up with a sling as well, and then I'm putting Casey in charge of making sure you go straight home to rest and ice it."

"What?" Casey asked. "That wasn't... You didn't tell me—"

"I'll be fine on my own," Boone insisted, interrupting her stammering.

Eli shrugged. "Forgive me if I don't trust you to do as you're told. You can stay at my place. Though a pissed-off brother might not have the best bedside manner."

Boone groaned. "Can we call it even if I let her take me back to my place, get me situated, and then we go our separate ways?"

Casey's cheeks burned. "If you *let* me take you home. Seriously, I don't know who you think you are that it would be my *privilege* to take care of you, but—"

"Okay," Eli said. "It's settled. We put your shoulder back where it's supposed to be, X-ray it and make sure all that's needed is the closed reduction, and then Casey takes you home, sets you up with a bag of ice and maybe locks your door from the outside so you stay put, and then you two can go your separate ways. Deal?"

Casey opened her mouth to protest, a little voice in her head telling her it would serve Boone right to have Eli babysit him for the night. But this time, her anger gave way to sympathy. Boone wouldn't have been out on Cirrus, racing her, if she hadn't taunted him in the first place. In fact, if she hadn't decided to take charge of her fate or destiny or where the chips fell, Boone would have had the night off and would have been injury free.

She sighed. "Yeah. Okay. Deal," she finally replied.

"Deal," Boone grumbled as well. Then he laid himself back down and let Eli get to work.

A little over an hour later, the two stood outside Boone's door at the Meadow Valley Ranch guesthouse. His arm was in a sling, which—according to Eli—he'd only have to wear through the weekend since there was luckily no other damage from the fall other than the dislocation, which was now *re*located.

Casey could still hear the growl of pain that tore from Boone's throat when Eli set his shoulder. God, the man was stubborn, refusing sedation. But then again, she still remembered her own confusion coming out of general anesthesia all those years ago. She'd been sick to her stomach and so turned around, at first not even remembering why she was at the hospital and then feeling the loss all over again when everything clicked back into place. So maybe she could understand wanting to stay lucid, but she couldn't wrap her head around him *choosing* pain when he had an alternative.

"You look kind of pale," she told him.

He huffed out a laugh. "Yeah, well, it's been a night. And I haven't eaten since breakfast."

"Shit," Casey said. "And you took those pain meds at Eli's on an empty stomach." Eli had mentioned the medication would probably make him groggy, but Boone hadn't mentioned his empty belly to his brother. She grabbed the keys from his hand and hastily opened his door. "We need to get some food in you, or you are going to lose whatever is left of that breakfast really quickly."

She burst through the door, tore off her coat and tossed it over a chair, and then slipped between the two counters that made up the room's kitchenette and started rifling through Boone's small refrigerator. When she finally came up for air, she was hugging half a loaf of bread, a jar of peanut butter, and another jar of raspberry jam. Boone was still standing just inside the doorway, staring at her with his brows furrowed.

"What are you doing?" he asked.

She sighed. "What are *you* doing? I told your brother I'd make sure you got right in bed and iced that shoulder. So get your butt into that bed, and let me do my job." Boone raised a brow, and Casey's cheeks flushed. "You know what I mean, Murphy."

She glanced down at the items in her arms. "And I'm going to make you something to eat so your stomach settles. I wish I could say I'm surprised that this is all you have in your fridge, but I can make do if you have a pan or a skillet of some sort."

Boone shrugged off his vest, which was only half on to begin with, and let it fall onto the same chair that held Casey's coat. But when he sat on the foot of the bed and tried to pull off his boots one-handed, he wasn't as successful.

Casey dropped her fridge bounty onto the counter and rounded the corner to meet him at the bed. She lowered herself to her knees and pulled off his first boot, then the other.

"This is ridiculous," he grumbled. "Why the hell did I get on that damned horse again?"

She sat back on her heels. "Maybe because you see something in him? Like a need in him that you're trying to fulfill. Animals who are mistreated have a hard time trusting, so they act out or get spooked easily. I'm guessing that can start a cycle of neglect if they're not rescued by the right person." She shrugged. "You gave him a second chance. And maybe he made the same mistake again, but you didn't punish him for it. I saw you out there. You showed him love and kindness, and that brought him out of whatever that damned rodent triggered in his head and back to the present, to the sound of *your* voice. He needed someone to trust, Murph.

And he found that tonight in you. *That's* why you got on that damned horse again and why I'm pretty sure you will once more, when you get the good doctor's permission, of course." She cleared her throat. "Also, I'm—I'm sorry."

Boone's brows rose. "For what?"

Casey swallowed, pushed herself to her feet, and then sat down next to him on the edge of the bed.

"For taking off Saturday morning before you woke up. In my defense, I *did* come back to talk to you after I cleared my head as best I could, but you were already gone."

He sighed. "I could have called or texted, but—"

"We don't have each other's numbers," she interrupted, finishing his sentence.

Boone laughed. "I could have asked Ivy."

"And I could have asked Carter," she admitted. "But instead I just showed up uninvited and took what could have been a quiet evening in a whole other direction." She nudged his shoulder with her own, and he turned his gaze to hers. "Do you think it's some sort of sign from the universe that after all these years, our paths start crossing again, but only due to emergency room–caliber injuries?"

He narrowed his gaze at her. "I guess it *was* your fault I spaced out the first time Cirrus tossed me. And tonight you *did* sort of push my buttons in an attempt to goad me, which has left me unable to even take off my own boots. So if you're asking whether the universe thinks all we're good for is hurting one another, the answer might be yes."

He pressed his lips into a smile, but Casey saw another kind of hurt in his stormy blue eyes.

She blew out a shaky breath. She could play into his humorous deflection. After all, she was the one who'd suggested the correlation between their injuries and the two of them reconnecting after more than a decade. Or she could let one tiny ounce of realness seep through. Not enough to put herself in danger but enough to let him know he wasn't only deserving of pain, if that was what he truly believed.

"If you hadn't given Adeline those airbags, I'd have been a lot worse off than just a mild concussion and a few bumps and bruises. So *no*, Boone Murphy. I don't think we're only good at hurting each other. I think maybe we might be able to heal some of those wounds too." She swallowed the lump forming in her throat, then stood and squared her shoulders. "Speaking of healing, time to get some food in that belly of yours so you can rest and recuperate."

She spun back toward the kitchen, grateful for a reason to change the subject.

"Pan's under the sink," he called over her shoulder, and she nodded as she retrieved it and then found a half stick of butter in the refrigerator door.

As she busied herself upgrading the everyday PB and J to a buttery, *grilled* PB and J, Boone slid back on the bed, awkwardly yet successfully propping himself up against the headboard on his two pillows.

She flipped the sandwich in the pan as she watched Boone lean back and close his eyes.

"I hoped to hell you'd never need those air-bags," he noted. "But I'm so damned grateful they worked. I can't imagine if I'd—" He opened his eyes and cleared his throat. "If something worse had happened and your parents and Ivy had—" He shook his head but didn't finish either sentence. "Holy hell, that smells good," he said, glancing up at her as she plated the one-course meal and cut the sandwich into two gooey triangles.

She dragged a chair from the small round table on the kitchen's outer wall to the side of Boone's bed, setting the plate on the nightstand.

"You mean to tell me you've only ever eaten a peanut butter and jelly sandwich cold?" she asked.

He nodded. "No offense, but the last time you tried cooking for me, it didn't go well."

She furrowed her brows, then threw her hand over her mouth as she gasped. "Your birthday brownies!" she exclaimed with a laugh. "When I confused the sugar with the salt! In my defense, I was *sixteen*, and I'll have you know that we label *all* canisters in the tavern kitchen now." She glanced down at the still untouched sandwich and then picked up one of the halves as she perched herself precariously on the edge of the bed, waving her creation under Boone's nose. "What's the matter? Are you afraid I somehow confused the ketchup for jam? I thought you said it smelled *good*."

He leaned forward and tore off a hunk with his teeth, molten peanut butter and jam dripping onto his chin.

"Hot!" he cried, his mouth hanging open. "Shit! Burning my tongue. *And* my face."

Casey burst into a fit of laughter, then realized there was no napkin nearby. So she swiped at the sticky glob on his chin with her thumb and hastily ate the cooling mess herself.

Boone was laughing too as he was finally able to chew and swallow. "Are you *sure* the universe doesn't have it in for us? Because I don't think I have any taste buds left."

Casey snorted, then lost her balance, bracing her free hand against the headboard—right next to Boone's head—to keep from falling onto his injured shoulder.

Their laughing ceased.

She licked her lips as she stared at his. "If the universe is plotting against us, why does it also keep putting us close enough to do things to each other that are very much the opposite of inflicting pain?"

He let loose a shaky exhale. "Walsh," he whispered.

"Murph," she whispered back. Then she dropped

the sandwich back on the plate, pressing her other hand to the other side of his head.

"I don't think Dr. Eli would approve of whatever it is that's going on in your head," he admitted, his voice rough as gravel. "And I sure as hell *know* he wouldn't approve of what's going on in mine."

"Should I call him and ask?" Casey teased, and for a second, she didn't even recognize the sound of her own voice.

His chest rose and fell against hers, and she thought she might actually explode—disintegrate into millions of tiny particles—if she didn't kiss him soon.

"It's *not* out of my system," she said softly, just putting it all out there. "I came back on Saturday morning to tell you that I didn't want it to be just that one night. Not after we—I mean, we were really good at it, weren't we? Like you just knew where to… I knew exactly how to… I'm just saying that I don't think we should put our excellent skills to waste, you know?"

He closed his eyes and sighed, any trace of a smile leaving his face.

Oh god. Maybe it *wasn't* as good for him as it was for her. What if she *thought* her skills were excellent when in reality they were barely mediocre? It wasn't like she was new at this, but she also hadn't been doling out exit interviews in previous relationships, however fleeting they were.

She pushed herself off the headboard and let her hands fall to her lap. Only then, when he likely felt her absence, did Boone finally open his eyes.

"Fine," Casey grumbled with a shrug that she hoped looked a hundred times more breezy than it felt. "I get that my physical enjoyment of the other evening was completely one-sided. Just... um...forget I said anything, okay? I'll clean up the kitchen while you finish your sandwich and then get you a bag of ice for that shoulder. I'll head out after that. I didn't mean to make things weird."

Except she was feeling fifty freaking shades of weird and other locked-away emotions she couldn't name. But her stomach churned, and her head swam. If she didn't get out of his small room, which felt like it was shrinking by the second, she feared she would either vomit or faint, neither of which sounded appealing at the moment—or ever.

She moved to stand, but Boone's good hand wrapped around her wrist, squeezing her tight enough to say *don't go* but loose enough that if she wanted to wriggle free and get the hell out of Dodge, she could.

"It wasn't one-sided, Walsh," he admitted, his voice low and even yet somehow on the verge of something that made her want to run before another word escaped his lips. Except he was still holding on to her, and she wasn't trying to wriggle free. "And I don't think…" He groaned and banged his head softly against the headboard.

Run, Casey. Shake him loose, and run straight out the damned door.

The voice in her head grew louder, repeating its request. But she didn't move. *Couldn't* move until she heard the rest of his thought.

"You don't think *what*?" she asked.

He straightened and set his blue eyes on hers.

"I don't think it was only physical for me. I think that maybe I know why I couldn't go through with the wedding. Casey, I think it was because of you."

Chapter 17

BOONE WOKE TO THE SUN STREAMING THROUGH the curtains, a ray of warm light smacking him straight across the eyes.

He startled, bolting upright and then swearing loud enough to wake anyone within a five-mile radius if they hadn't also been accosted by the too-bright California sun despite it being almost winter.

Where was he? *When* was he? Also why the—*Oh*. Right. Cirrus had tossed him on his ass again, this time making sure Boone couldn't sit in his saddle anytime soon.

He blinked away the last relics of sleep and then inhaled through his nose, swearing he could smell something buttery sweet, which made zero sense in a one-room living space where only a single, thirty-year-old man lived. Boone wasn't above keeping himself clean and groomed, but he was certain he never gave off the aroma of something fresh out of the oven at the corner bakery.

He wasn't even sure he could smell whatever it was he was smelling anymore once he was fully awake. Maybe it was simply some remnant of a dream he couldn't remember.

The initial pain of moving too quickly subsided into a dull ache, and Boone was able to clumsily maneuver himself out of the bed with his good arm, the injured one still strapped to his torso in the sling.

He scratched at his bare abdomen, yawned, and then massaged his closed eyelids with his thumb and forefinger.

Wait. His *bare* abdomen?

The last thing he remembered was collapsing into bed, fully clothed except for his boots, which Casey had to help him remove.

He looked down at his briefs, chuckling softly at his morning wood salute until he remembered *why* he was curious about his attire in the first place.

He spun to find his phone charging on the nightstand, grabbed it, and fired off a call to his brother.

"Mornin', sunshine," Eli said after the first ring. "I thought I was the only one who woke with roosters."

Boone scratched at his stubbled jaw. "I thought you only had hens over there."

Eli had converted their family's property from a horse farm to a veterinary clinic and, now that Jenna Owens had moved from the San Luis Obispo region on up to Meadow Valley, a slowly growing egg farm.

"It's a figure of speech," Eli explained. "*Up with the hens* doesn't quite have the same ring to it since they don't sing like roosters do."

"What roosters do is *not* singing," Boone insisted.

"All sounds animals make are music," Eli countered with a chuckle. "But I'm guessing you aren't calling me at the ass crack of dawn to talk roosters versus hens."

"No," Boone said. "I want to know what the hell was in those pills you gave me last night and why I can't remember taking off my own clothes before going to sleep."

Eli's chuckle turned into a genuine laugh. "Did a little bit of hydrocodone knock big, bad Boone Murphy on his ass?"

Boone's jaw tightened. "I didn't say it knocked me... *Wait*. People don't actually call me that—big, bad Boone Murphy—do they?"

Eli didn't answer right away, which to Boone was answer enough. But right now, he didn't have time to deal with whatever reputation he'd built up over the years. Right now, he needed to know what had happened between him and Casey last night and if he'd been stupid enough to have forgotten the whole thing.

"Don't answer that," Boone added. "Just, what was in that stuff? I thought I told you I wanted to be lucid."

Eli sighed. "You went through a traumatic fall and then—for whatever stubborn reason when you could have just slept in my guesthouse— wouldn't let me anesthetize you for a few *minutes* while I patched you up. The pain you must have been in…" He trailed off.

Boone's stomach twisted. "Eli, are you… I mean, are you pissed at me for getting a second chance when Tess didn't?"

"Jesus, Boone. How could you even ask that? I loved Tess, and I lost her." The last part came out through gritted teeth. Then Eli blew out a long, shaky breath. "You're my *brother*. I'm *pissed* at you for not coming to me sooner, but my anger ends there. And as for the meds… You would have been in too much pain to sleep if I hadn't given you something to take the edge off. The German shepherd with the broken leg that Delaney rescued?" he asked. "Slept like a baby when I set his leg and gave him a couple of those."

Boone groaned. "You gave me *dog* meds? Jesus, Eli. I know I piss you off sometimes, but I didn't think I'd reached the same level as a mangy rescue dog."

"Careful," Eli chided, "or I'll tell Delaney you're bad-mouthing her guests."

Boone lowered himself to the foot of his bed, realizing he was rushing out of it to—where? It was Thanksgiving, and other than dinner tonight at the ranch, he was laid up for pretty much the rest of the weekend.

"Humans and dogs can take many of the same medications. I gave you one that was the perfect dosage for your height, give or take a paw." Eli laughed at his own joke, but Boone remained silent. "You have not reached dog level...*yet*," Eli added. "But the day is still pretty young."

"Fine," Boone said. "But we're circling back to *dog level* soon. Right now, I just want to know *how* unconscious those two dog pills could have made me and if there is any chance that I was undressed and tucked into bed last night by someone *other* than myself."

Someone like—say—Casey Walsh, who was getting really damned good at her morning-after disappearing act. The question was, though, morning-after *what*?

"Hydrocodone doesn't usually mess with lucidity. If you don't have enough food in you, it might make you nauseous or a little groggy, but that's the extent of it. But the adrenaline rush you must have had dealing with Cirrus and calming him down— Casey told me how good you were with him—and the subsequent letdown? That could have contributed to your reaction as well."

Boone had a sudden recollection of a warm peanut butter and jelly sandwich—of Casey on top of him. But after that, everything went fuzzy at the edges.

"I don't think I had much food in me," he told Eli. And he was sure Casey would not have let anything happen between them while he was under the influence of narcotics. Hell, she probably didn't *want* anything else to happen between them after getting whatever was in her system out of it last week. Still, the not knowing was killing him. Had he said or done something to upset her? Or had she simply helped him to bed and then gone home herself since there was nothing left for her to do for him?

"Boone?" his brother asked after a few moments of silence.

"Yeah?"

Eli cleared his throat. "You still taking your other medication?"

Boone's throat tightened. "Of course I am," he insisted, fighting not to grit his teeth. "But I appreciate the trust," he added bitterly.

"I had to ask," Eli said without an ounce of regret in his voice. "You've been making some pretty impulsive decisions lately—the wedding that wasn't, hopping in the saddle of a volatile horse not once but *twice*. When you take risks like that…I don't know. Just reminds me of how you used to be, and I worry. If I don't look after you, who's going to?"

"I don't need looking after," Boone told his brother, even if he did feel more lost than he'd ever been. "If you want a project, why don't you try tracking Ash down. All you need to do is follow the trail of trashed hotel rooms. Shouldn't be that difficult."

Eli let out a soft laugh, but Boone knew his older brother wasn't *really* smiling. "Because you're the brother who *wants* to figure his shit out. At least I hope to hell you are. You don't think I'm scared every day that we'll get the kind of phone call about him we've been dreading for years? At least with you I have a chance to..." Eli sighed. "I don't know."

"Save me?" Boone asked but didn't wait for Eli to answer. "Don't you get it, Big Bro? I'm in therapy. I'm taking my meds. Hell, I think I might even be in a knitting club now. I'm saving my damned self bit by freaking bit. Even walking out on Elizabeth—or us walking out on each other? I might not totally understand *why* I couldn't make things work with someone who on paper seemed like the real deal, but it wasn't right, so I got out before it was too late. But it can't be on your timeline, Eli. I have to figure my shit out for myself. And the same goes for Ash. I hope to hell he doesn't hit rock bottom before he decides to get his shit together, but again, *his* timeline, and we'll be here for him if and when he's ready."

"Good," Eli said coolly. "Save yourself. But Jesus, Boone. You don't *have* to do it alone. You can save yourself *and* let me help. It doesn't make you any less capable to admit you don't want to do it alone."

Boone blew out a long breath. "Like you've been doing it alone? I know you kind of took on Dad's role after he got hurt and that after losing Tess—"

"Don't," Eli interrupted. "Don't bring Tess into this."

"You don't even know what I was going to say."

"It doesn't matter," Eli explained. "Until you know what it's like to lose the best part of yourself, you don't get to say a fucking word about *my* life and the way I live it."

"But you're *not*, Eli," Boone told him, even though he knew he should probably bite his tongue. "You're going through the motions, but you're not *truly* living it, are you? But if you have a menagerie of animals to look after or a brother or two to worry about, you don't have to look in the goddamned mirror, do you?"

The words came out more resentful than he'd meant them to. He only wanted to show his brother that maybe after letting himself grieve for years, it was time to do some saving of his own.

A long silence rang out between them until finally Eli spoke.

"Ice your shoulder, and take your damned meds."

And then Boone's brother—the one who'd always been there for his parents, him, and Ash and for his wife before he lost her far too soon—ended the call.

"Dammit," Boone said, then pushed himself back to his feet. He strode into the bathroom, his steps heavy and a weight pressing down on his chest. He turned on the sink and splashed water on his face, awkwardly and messily with one hand, before taking a good long look at his own reflection.

Until you know what it's like to lose the best part of yourself...

I might not totally understand why I couldn't make things work with someone who on paper seemed like the real deal...

"Oh my god," he said out loud to the clueless jerk staring back at him from the glass.

I think that maybe I know why I couldn't go through with the wedding. Casey, I think it was because of you.

Boone still loved Casey Walsh. Always had. And his loopy, groggy, always-playing-tricks-on-him brain had already figured it out and didn't even try to make him censor himself when the light bulb finally clicked on.

He *told* Casey it had always been her...and she ran straight out the door.

Speaking of doors, he heard the one to his guest room click open and then slam shut once more.

She came back.

Boone scrambled out of the bathroom, forgetting his center of gravity had shifted now that he was in a sling, and he pitched forward, tripping over the threshold between the door and the main room, only to be caught with a palm to the chest by one Ivy Serrano.

"Slow your roll, bucko," Ivy told him, her eyes narrowed at the nearly naked Boone. "And tell me what the hell you did to my friend."

Chapter 18

"Ivy." Boone steadied himself with a hand on her shoulder. "What did Casey tell you?"

Ivy sighed and wrapped her hand around Boone's wrist—well, as best she could.

"Wow," Ivy said, brows raised. "You've *really* filled out since high school." She gently removed his hand so she could take a step back, cross her arms, and look him up and down. "Like *really*. But if we're going to have a conversation, you need to put some clothes on. I'll…uh…just make us some coffee while you"—she waved a finger in the air—"while you do whatever it is you need to do to cover yourself up. Unless you need help?"

"No," Boone countered, more quickly than he should have. Because the truth was, he had no idea how he'd gotten *un*dressed, which meant he wasn't entirely sure how to reverse the process. But the thought of Casey's best friend helping him figure it out just felt weird and wrong, especially when she was most likely here to accuse him of doing something wrong. Story of his life. "I'll just…um…go in here," he sputtered, grabbing his jeans from where they lay over a chair and a clean T-shirt from his dresser drawer. Then he slipped back into the bathroom, kicking the door shut behind him.

He wasn't much better off when he reemerged. His jeans were on but unbuttoned. And he'd gotten his head and his good arm through the T-shirt, but the one in the sling was still strapped to his body beneath the shirt.

Ivy stifled a chuckle when she saw him, and Boone shook his head and huffed out a breath. "It's fine," he said. "You can laugh."

Ivy blew out a breath and regained her composure. "No. No. I'm not going to laugh at an injured man, not before I know what made my best friend skip town for the day and if *he* had anything to do with it." She took a tentative step toward him, then nodded toward his groin. "Um…may I?"

Boone glanced down at his open fly and unbuttoned jeans. Unless he wanted to spend Thanksgiving in his guest room, by himself, he was going to need someone to dress him the rest of the way.

"Yes," he groaned. "Man, I do *not* like feeling helpless."

Ivy did let herself laugh this time. "Sounds a *lot* like someone else I know." Then she set her gaze on his. "Look away," she said firmly. "Don't make this weird."

Boone laughed and did as he was told. "So are you going to tell me where Casey is and why you think it's *my* fault?" He tried to sound clueless, but Ivy gave him a knowing glance.

"She told me to come over here and make sure you were okay and that you weren't going to be stuck in your tiny little briefs all day. I gotta say, Boone Murphy, I did *not* peg you for such an old-fashioned guy."

He rolled his eyes. "They're…um…supportive. Especially on my bike."

Ivy snorted. "I'm sorry." She snorted again. "Okay, no, I'm not."

He waited for her to finish enjoying her amusement at his expense, which lasted several seconds longer than he'd expected, but Boone Murphy wasn't about to apologize or feel self-conscious about his choice of undergarments, especially when he remembered how much Casey had enjoyed re*moving* said undergarment last week.

Casey. Right. He needed to find Casey.

"I think I know why Casey took off," he started. "Did she say where she went?"

Ivy shook her head. "She didn't tell me, not exactly. She just said she needed to remind herself what she really wanted, but I'm her *best* friend. Aren't I supposed to know what she really wants?"

Boone sighed. "I think I might know. Do you have to cook anything for tonight?"

Ivy shook her head and pulled out her phone,

brandishing it at Boone. It was part of a text from Casey.

> Couldn't sleep last night. Check Boone's fridge when you get there. You don't have to worry about dessert anymore. I made enough for both of us.

Despite the ranch hosting Thanksgiving, the dinner was a potluck. Everyone who came had to bring a dish. Boone guessed that Casey and Ivy had both signed up to bring something sweet. What he couldn't guess was what the hell was in his fridge.

Boone and Ivy glanced at each other and then at the fridge. Together they moved around the wall and toward the tiny galley kitchen until Boone's good hand was on the refrigerator door. He pulled it open, his breath catching in his throat as he and Ivy stared down at not one, not two, but *three* home-baked pies.

"I slept through that?" he asked softly, more to himself than to Ivy.

"Oh, Case," Ivy said with a melancholy sigh, and Boone felt like he'd been punched in the gut.

"I didn't know she still did this," he added, his voice rough.

Ivy pressed her lips into a sad smile. "Stress baked? She hasn't in a long time. Not since—" She stopped short of finishing the thought, but it didn't matter. Boone could finish it for her.

————————

Twelve Years Ago

Boone gave Casey her space for as long as he could handle it, which was barely a day after she got home from the hospital. It started at the bookstore, where he'd gone to grab a book on motorcycle repair for his spring semester autos class. He found Mrs. Davis, the owner, nibbling on a brownie at the register.

"You selling bakery stuff now?" he asked, sliding a book on Yamaha bikes across the counter.

Mrs. Davis's cheeks reddened. "No," she said, clearing her throat. "Boone, honey, you know I'm not one to take sides with you kids, but that girl sure was in a state when she dropped these off." She took another bite of the brownie and moaned with a pleasure that made Boone blush as well.

"What girl?" he asked, clueless.

Mrs. Davis rang up his book and took his money. She raised her brows. "*What* girl? Oh dear. I'm guessing you haven't been to the inn? Possibly the firehouse? Honey, the whole town is knee-deep in some of the best pastries I've ever eaten. I mean you *must* taste these lemon bars." She dipped below the counter and came up with a plate full of

Boone's favorite dessert. "Here. Try one. Even if it was baked with a little bit of Casey's sadness."

Boone's throat tightened, and his lungs suddenly forgot how to take in air.

He swallowed hard. "She's..." His voice cracked. "She's home?"

Mrs. Davis nodded. "And baking up a storm, it seems. She only just left here about ten minutes before you arrived."

His body was moving before his brain could catch up, pivoting away from the counter and bolting for the door.

"Your book!" he heard Mrs. Davis call over his shoulder, but he didn't care about books or bikes or the fact that Casey had baked lemon bars for someone other than him. She was out there, hurting just as much as he was, and he needed to fix it. Fix *them*. However he could.

Once he was out the door, Boone ran to every storefront on the street, throwing open door after door, asking if Casey was there.

"You *just* missed her!" he heard at the feed store.

"I think she slipped out the back door," they told him at the market.

"Heard you caused some trouble at the hospital the other night, son," one of the sheriff's deputies said with eyes narrowed as Boone burst into the sheriff's department and quickly back out of it when he still couldn't find Casey.

Finally he found himself in front of the only door he hadn't yet opened, the one to Midtown Tavern.

Boone hesitated only long enough to blow out a shaky breath. Then he squared his shoulders and strode through the door expecting... He had no idea what to expect. All he knew was that Casey's parents probably hated him by now.

He wasn't prepared for laughter. Or for it to cease the second the door closed behind him.

Mr. and Mrs. Walsh stood behind the bar prepping for the tavern's lunchtime opening, but whatever had them in stitches before he walked in was ancient history now.

"She's *not* here, and she doesn't want to see you again, Murphy," Mr. Walsh said through gritted teeth. But Mrs. Walsh's expression softened as she laid a hand on her husband's arm.

"You need to give her time, Boone," she said. "I think we *all* need time to process what happened and how to move forward from here. I'm sure your parents—"

"My parents have enough on their plate dealing with my father's injury and the ranch and..." He thought he knew what he was going to say when he got here, but all he could hear was *She doesn't want to see you again* spinning in his head like a cyclone.

He couldn't focus, not on anything but those words and making them disappear.

Boone was sure he heard shouting as he dove halfway over the bar, grabbed the first bottle he could get his hands on, and ran.

But he didn't turn back. He just ran and ran and ran until his feet couldn't carry him anymore. And then he drank until he silenced the flurry in his head.

He woke up and vomited into the garbage can he somehow knew was next to the bed.

"Good, you're awake," someone said. A girl's voice.

"Walsh?" he croaked, his head throbbing as he opened his eyes.

"No, silly," she cooed. "It's Layla, remember? Found you in my bushes, got you in bed." She smiled down at him from where she sat on the side of the bed.

Boone's blurry vision came into focus enough to see her face.

"Layla?" he said, his voice hoarse. "We didn't…?"

She laughed, then stroked the hair on his forehead. "Please, Murphy. When you and I finally… you *know*…" She paused. "You'll *know*. Now go back to sleep. It's barely eight o'clock, and you so aren't ready to get out of bed yet."

Even though he felt like death or something possibly worse, Boone sighed with relief.

A doorbell rang.

"Hmm," Layla hummed. "I wonder who that

could be so early in the morning. I'll be right back."

Boone might not have clearly remembered *how* he'd ended up in Layla Whittier's bed with a poached hospital IV in his arm, but he *did* remember why he'd drunk himself dangerously into oblivion.

Casey.

He felt the pockets of his jeans—grateful they were still on—but couldn't find his phone. He saw it on Layla's nightstand just as he heard the front door opening not too far from the open bedroom door, and his heart soared when he saw the most recent text was from Casey.

We should talk. Where are you?

But it had already been answered.

"Hey, Walsh," he heard Layla practically sing. "Now's *really* not a good time."

"No!" Boone tried to yell, but he could barely make a sound. He scrambled out of the bed and just as quickly collapsed to his knees, the pain in his skull causing him to retch again.

He was curled up on the floor when he heard the front door close and Layla's footsteps approach the room.

And he knew from the look on her face that it was over, that he and Casey were truly and completely over.

Present Day

"I didn't sleep with Layla Whittier," Boone said. "Not then. Not ever."

Ivy stood there in stunned silence for several long beats, her mouth hanging open.

"I don't get it," she finally said. "Layla told Casey—I mean, she *implied*..."

"Right," Boone agreed. "She *implied*. And I'm not defending her wanting to get a rise out of Casey or putting me in the position she did. We do some dumb shit when we're kids, myself included. But Casey *knew* me. She loved me. But she obviously didn't trust me, and in hindsight, I can't blame her for that." He closed his eyes and pinched the bridge of his nose. "Look, I don't even know why I'm defending myself. What's done is done. I can't change it. I can't get back the last twelve years. Or *un*lose the love of my life."

Ivy blinked. The refrigerator door still sat open between them, the cold air escaping into the small room. "You can't unlose the girl who *was* the love of your life. Past tense. That's what you meant."

It was a statement, not a question, like she was trying to convince herself that he hadn't said what he'd said.

Boone shook his head slowly.

"Everyone's been asking for the story about why I didn't go through with the wedding. But there was no story, because I didn't have the answers. At least not on a conscious level. But I do now. And I'm pretty sure I admitted as much to Casey last night, which is why I think she baked three pies and disappeared."

Ivy backhanded him on his good shoulder with more force than he would have expected, had he been expecting it at all. Which he hadn't.

"Um, ow?" he said. "What the hell was that for?"

Her expression softened, and she brushed off the spot where she'd just made contact as if to wipe her reaction away. "Sorry. I just… Dammit, Boone. Why didn't you fight harder for her? Why didn't you *make* her see the truth if she had it all wrong?"

He let out a weary sigh. "I didn't think I deserved her forgiveness for the things I *did* do regardless of the things I didn't. I'm still not sure I do, especially since it took me this long to admit to myself that I still love her. I've done a *lot* of work, Ives—learned things about myself that had I known earlier might have changed how everything panned out." He gave her a one-shoulder shrug. "But I still have a shit ton more to figure out. What if it's not the right time for us yet?"

Or ever? Just because he'd never fallen out of love with Casey didn't mean everything that happened between them was magically fixed.

"You're never going to know if you don't tell her," Ivy insisted. "It's as simple as that. You've both spent the past decade of your lives *not* talking to each other, and where has it gotten both of you other than right back where you started?" She gently patted his stubbled cheek with her palm. "Do you really think you might know where she is?"

He nodded.

"Okay," Ivy said with renewed vigor in her voice. Then she clapped her hands together. "Let's get you a *little* better dressed, and then we'll go find her so you can tell her everything you just told me."

He looked down at his arm buried underneath his T-shirt, his bare feet poking out from the bottom of his jeans, and then ran a hand through his rumpled hair, a product of his coma-level sleep the night before.

"Deal," he said. Whether Casey shot him down or gave him another chance didn't matter. Okay, it *did* matter. A whole hell of a lot. But he couldn't control how she reacted. All he could do was put himself out there and make sure that at the very least, *she* knew how *he* felt, even if she couldn't offer him the same in return.

Chapter 19

Twelve Years Ago

EVEN THOUGH BOONE'S MOTORCYCLE HAD COME to a stop, Casey still squeezed his torso tight, pressing her cheek to the denim jacket covering his back. After riding for two hours like this from Meadow Valley to Chico, it felt odd and even a little disconcerting to let go. Or maybe it was just that she liked being with him like this—the two of them against the world if only for a finite amount of time.

"We're here," he called over his shoulder, and she could barely hear him through her helmet but nodded against him so he knew she had. "Are you holding on because you're scared or because you just can't stand to be away from me for even a second?" he teased, and she finally let go, leaning away from him so she could take the helmet off.

He hopped off the bike and did the same.

She narrowed her eyes at him. "I am *not* afraid of a vehicle with two wheels, an animal with four hooves, or anything in between unless it involves *you* pushing the limits of either safety, legal speed, or *both*."

She'd always known Boone Murphy was a risk taker, whether it was in the horse arena or on the open road, but he was also a skilled rider in both respects. It had been sexy at first, when he'd shown off riding bareback on a horse they'd barely broken in. Or that time he took his bike out on a quiet country road and showed her a few tricks he'd taught himself. But wheelies and doughnuts only impressed the first couple of times. After that, she started to wonder why he kept pushing the limits of what any human—let alone a teenage boy—should do.

She handed him her helmet and swung her right leg over the seat. Boone wrapped his free arm around her waist and helped lower her to the ground. It didn't matter that they'd been together for nearly four years. Her pulse still quickened when she was this close to him—chest to chest with his head tilted down at her, that look of adoration and also mischief in his ice-blue eyes.

"Hey," he said softly, his chest vibrating against hers. "I may not be book smart like the rest of 'em, but I know horses and bikes." He kissed the top of her head. "And you, Walsh. I know *you*. Which is why we're spending our last day of summer here."

He opened his arm wide and gestured to the small building they were parked in front of.

She spun so her back was to him and read the sign painted on the front window beneath the green awning:

KC Hair Lounge and Day Spa

Casey blinked twice but wasn't sure what to say.

Boone wrapped his arms around her waist and rested his head on her shoulder.

"At first, I just wanted to show you one of those fancy places that were going to hire you the second you got your license because of how damned talented you are. But then I found this place, and it felt kind of like a sign, you know? Like a guarantee that someday you *will* be back in Meadow Valley with your own place. Figured since I found this KC's that it might mean I'll be a part of *your* Casey's someday."

His breath tickled her ear, and when he pressed his lips to her neck, she swore some tiny woodland creature did flip-flops in her belly.

She rested her hands over his, and he squeezed her tight.

"You drove for two hours on our last day of summer before senior year to—to show me my dream?" She spun to face him, pressing her palms to his cheeks. "I don't even know what to say."

He pressed his forehead to hers. "Say you love me and that you always will."

Her throat tightened, and her eyes burned. "I *love* you, Murph. And I *always* will."

He kissed her, then smiled against her.

"We better get inside," he said. "Your appointment starts in five minutes."

Present Day

Casey stared at the neon sign in the window and thought she might be sick.

BURGER SHACK

She double-checked the address, but it didn't matter. The green awning was still there, and when she got close enough to peer inside—the place luckily empty since it was Thanksgiving—she could see the faint outline of two letters that used to be painted on the glass.

K and *C*.

This was it, the landmark reminder of her dream, of how much Boone Murphy had believed in her—had believed in *them*—and it was gone. If, twelve years ago, this place had been a sign of what her future could be, what did it mean now that it was gone? That she might be falling again for the man who had broken her heart all those years ago?

I think that maybe I know why I couldn't go through with the wedding. Casey, I think it was because of you.

He was loopy from pain meds. He didn't know what he was saying. They'd only just decided to be friends *after* he came back from Nevada. If he didn't get married because of her, then that meant that he… It meant that they…

She didn't want to think of the implications of

what it meant, of the time they might have lost had she let go of the past earlier.

She shook her head, still peering in the window of the burger joint that used to be some other KC's dream gone wrong.

Casey shoved her hands in her pockets and buried her face in the collar of her coat. She needed to walk. Needed to think. Needed to figure out how she was going to spend the time in Chico—on *zero* budget with likely the whole town shut down for the holiday—until the one and only bus back to Meadow Valley arrived.

"Shouldn't have even dropped the ten bucks on the ticket in the first place," she mumbled to herself as she picked up the pace, trying to get as far from Burger Shack as possible.

She wandered for nearly an hour before she found herself in front of a store called Bird in Hand that not only sold everything from kitschy knick-knacks to fashionable apparel but also housed the country's National Yo-Yo Museum. How had she lived two hours from such a wonder her entire life and never known it was here? The place was actually open, opting for a Thanksgiving morning sale in lieu of Black Friday, so Casey hurried inside, grateful for a respite from the cold until she figured out what to do next.

After pretending for almost as long as she'd been wandering downtown Chico that she was actually going to buy something at Bird in Hand, Casey finally made her way into the museum. She found herself staring at a giant, circular piece of wood—which she quickly realized was one side of a yo-yo—that had the words *No Jive* carved into it, with a placard below that read WORLD'S LARGEST WOOD YOYO. She wondered how heavy it was, if it actually worked, and how one would yo-yo with this wooden object if one was not a giant.

"Two hundred and fifty-six pounds," a deep voice rumbled behind her. "I googled it on the way here once we figured out exactly where you were." Casey's heart both rose into her throat and sank through her feet and into the floor.

Casey slowly spun away from Paul Bunyan's toy and came face-to-face with Boone Murphy. His dark hair was an adorable mess, and there was a spot of dried blood on his neck where it looked like he'd tried to shave what was the makings of a new beard but then thought better of it.

Ivy peeked out from behind Boone's shoulder, her hair tucked into a cream floral embroidered beanie—an Ivy Serrano original. She offered Casey something between a wince and a smile.

"What are you guys doing here? How did you find me?"

Boone cleared his throat. "I…um…I had a hunch. And then when we got here and saw that…"

"I remembered we had that app where you could

find a friend's location," Ivy added. "Which was how we ended up here. You're not pissed, are you? Boone wanted to find you, and he couldn't drive, so..." She trailed off. "How did you even get here?"

"Bus," Casey answered with a sigh. "Since Adeline is still out of commission."

Boone shook his head. "Shit, Casey. I didn't know KC's place was gone. I'm not sure what you were looking for coming here or why what I said last night might have driven you to do it—after baking three pies—but you know that doesn't mean anything, right?"

She swallowed and forced herself to smile. "I know," she lied. "And what do you mean about what you mentioned last night? You were hopped up on pain meds with an empty stomach. It's not like I took anything you might have said to heart."

Ivy stepped around Boone and came face-to-face with Casey. She placed her mittened hands on Casey's cheeks and sighed. "I'm going to check out the adorable store part of all this." She waved her hands around the museum space. "Just maybe listen to him, okay?" Casey opened her mouth to protest, but Ivy didn't give her a chance. "I'm *not* saying I'm taking sides or anything." She pursed her lips. "No. You know what? I *am* taking sides. I'm on *your* side, Casey Walsh. Always have been. And because of that—and because I just drove two hours to find you and do *not* want to regret it—listen to what the man has to say." Then she kissed Casey on the nose and spun in the direction of Bird in Hand and all its merchandise, leaving Casey and Boone alone with an over-two-hundred-pound yo-yo.

They stared at each other for several long beats until Boone let out a nervous laugh.

"Never thought I'd be having this conversation with you in a yo-yo museum, which I never even knew existed, by the way, but here we are."

What conversation? she wanted to ask, but Casey wasn't sure she was ready for the answer.

"How's your shoulder?" she asked instead.

Boone sighed. "Stiff and sore, leaving me unable to shave, fix my bedhead, or dress myself, but other than that, not too bad. I'm not taking Eli's dog meds again, that's for sure."

"Dog meds?" she asked.

He huffed out a laugh. "Long story. Look, Casey, there's a lot that's happened with me over the past twelve years that you don't know, a lot I think I'd really like to tell you. And maybe I was hopped up on the dog meds last night, but I remember what I said—about why I didn't marry Elizabeth—and I stand by my reasoning. I guess I was just wondering if maybe, possibly, you stress baking and coming back to the scene of what I think is one of your happiest memories means that maybe, possibly, you'd want to try doing this thing with me for real."

Her mouth fell open and her eyes burned, but

this proposal from Boone wasn't what she'd had in mind when she woke up in his arms last week. What had been happening between them was physical, wasn't it? That was why it had felt so good when he'd touched her and kissed her and…

"I'm not saying I deserve another chance with you," he continued when she'd yet to find any words of her own. "Or that I have any idea why it took me so long to figure out how I really felt about you—how I think I've always felt—but maybe if we take it slow and start over as adults…" He let out a shaky breath. "I just think there's something here that's worth exploring if you're willing to give us that chance."

Casey twirled and untwirled a lock of her own hair—now a vivid shade of violet—around her index finger.

"I'm just so focused on getting enough tuition together for school," she finally said. "At least for the next payment I have to make. I don't know how much time I'll have to do much else." Ugh. The fountain of lies just kept spewing forth. Of course she was focused on the tuition, but she had been all set to suggest a friends with benefits scenario to him before his accident, which meant she was willing to find the time for such extracurricular activities. But this? What he was suggesting was *real*. How did she do real with Boone Murphy after all this time?

"I'm scared too," Boone admitted, pulling her out of her tornado of thoughts. "Scared I'll screw up and hurt you again. Scared that even after all the work I've done on myself—and am still doing—that it won't be enough. That *I* won't be enough. But do you want to know what's worse than being scared?"

Casey swallowed. "What?"

"Regret. I've already got buckets full of the stuff, Walsh. I don't want any more."

Casey sniffed back the threat of tears and squared her shoulders. Because hell if she couldn't do with emptying a little of her own bucket of regret.

"Fine," she said, holding out her hand like they were making a business deal. "But I have one condition."

"Name it," Boone told her. "Whatever it is, I'm on board. Even if the no-sex thing is still on the table for now, since I think we already found some pretty successful workarounds." He raised his brows mischievously, but she could see the tension in his set jaw. He *was* scared. And so was she.

"We leave the past in the past," she finally said. "No mention of what happened when we were kids that night in the hospital or…or after, okay? We just move forward from here."

Boone stared at her, his expression unreadable, but then he nodded his head once.

"Deal," he agreed, wrapping his hand around hers. "And since we're in agreement, Casey Walsh, I'd like permission to kiss you right here in front of that giant yo-yo."

Casey bit back a grin, but her stomach was a mess of cartwheels and flip-flops and basically all the acrobatics.

"Permission granted," she said and then stepped into him, wrapping her arms around his neck as he dipped his head and pressed his lips to hers.

Boone's touch was soft and gentle, a simple brush of his mouth over hers, nothing akin to the frantic hunger of what happened in the tavern kitchen. Still, Casey's stomach coiled, and warmth spread from her belly to her cheeks, to the tips of her fingers and toes.

This was...new. Unexpected. Terrifying. Yet whatever was happening, Casey wanted more.

"Hey, lovers!" Casey heard over Boone's shoulder. "What do you think? Will Carter love it or hate it?"

They both laughed and broke away to see what Ivy had found.

Against her torso she held a hanger on which hung a Hawaiian-style shirt that, instead of palm trees, was covered in brown hexagonal frames with colorful turkeys or cornucopias inside each.

"Love it!" Casey called at the same time that Boone yelled, "Hate it!"

All three of them laughed.

"That settles it. I'm buying it." Ivy waved them off. "As you were, for a few more minutes, and then it's time to head home."

Meadow Valley had always been home, but when they arrived back in town today, everything would be different.

"It's going to be different this time," Boone said, reading Casey's mind and slipping his hand into hers and giving her a gentle squeeze. "*I'm* different this time around. You'll see."

They both were, though, weren't they? Different meant good. Different meant safer. Different meant not repeating the mistakes of the past.

Different *had* to mean not getting hurt again.

Chapter 20

BOONE LAY PROPPED UP AGAINST HIS HEAD-board, a half-eaten blueberry pie resting on his belly while a half-naked Casey Walsh fed him another bite.

He closed his eyes and let loose a soft moan as he chewed and swallowed.

"If I had written the script for the perfect Sunday evening, it would have been this," he told her, licking his lips and setting his gaze on the beautiful woman in his bed.

Casey narrowed her eyes at him, then licked the rogue pieces of crust still stuck to the fork clean. "The pie or *me*? And be careful, mister, because there is a right answer *and* a wrong answer here."

He laughed. "Can't it be both?"

She pursed her lips and thought for a moment. "It can," she replied. "But that answer is going to require a ranking system. I need to know where I stand against the pie."

He dipped a finger into the pie tin, scooping up a small dollop of blueberries and swiping it messily across Casey's lips.

She scoffed in mock horror.

"*You* made the pie, so without you, there is no pie, let alone feeding me pie in bed. So you, Supergirl, are most definitely number one in the rankings."

Her expression softened at his utterance of *Supergirl*, and he let out a relieved breath.

"I can still call you that?" he asked, still unsure if leaving the past in the past meant that *all* aspects of the Boone and Casey from *then* were not allowed to be part of the Boone and Casey from *now*.

He was still having trouble wrapping his head around the fact that Casey Walsh was here in his bed—had been since Thanksgiving night—and that it wasn't a dream.

"You obviously cannot fend for yourself until you're out of that sling," she'd said after dinner. "So I'm just going to have to stay at your place until Monday when Eli hopefully sets you free."

And that was that. She'd fallen asleep by his side for the past three nights and woken up curled into his chest the past three mornings. She hadn't even questioned helping him get dressed so he could head to the bookstore early Saturday morning.

"I have a meeting with Colt and the Callahans," he'd noted. "Ranch stuff. And they…uh…they like Trudy's coffee."

Maybe he couldn't join in with the meditative nature of the knitting, but he could be present with his friends—with this new life he'd come home to that somehow included Casey Walsh.

"Yeah," Casey said, pulling him out of his head and back into the moment. "You can still call me that." She licked the blueberries on her lip, and Boone shook his head.

"Oh no you don't, Walsh. I clean up my own messes." He set the pie tin on the nightstand and grabbed the fork out of her hand, doing the same. Then he slid his fingers into her hair, cradling her head in his palm as he pulled her to him, his tongue sweeping across her bottom lip.

Casey hummed a soft sigh, then slid her knee over his hips so she was now straddling him, wearing only a thin white tank top and matching cotton panties.

"Somebody's happy to see me under those snug little briefs," she teased, sliding against him.

"Always," he growled, then slipped his tongue past her lips and rocked his pelvis toward her.

Casey moaned. "Murph..." she whispered.

God, he loved the sound of his nickname on her lips.

He slid his hand down her torso, pausing to cup her breast in his palm. She whimpered as his thumb brushed over her hardened peak, and her knees hugged his hips.

"The things I'm going to do to you when I have two hands," he teased, then let his hand travel farther south, his fingers slipping between them and inside the hem of her bikini briefs.

She braced herself against the headboard, giving him room to slide farther still until one finger, then two, dipped into her warmth.

Casey cried out, her breath coming in short pants as he let his fingers explore.

She lowered her head to his, kissing him hard, her tongue tangling with his.

"You taste so good," he insisted. "Like blueberries and—and—"

And my future, he wanted to add. But it was too soon. Too much. He didn't want to scare her away before he had a chance to show her how he'd changed, before he could somehow rewrite their history so that she remembered more than how he'd let her down.

He might have agreed to her deal to leave the past in the past, and he would—for now. But it was Boone's past too, and he was slowly starting to believe that he deserved the chance to set the record straight. For now, he simply wanted to enjoy the woman who lit up his world with blueberry pie and the permission to kiss her and so very much more.

"Your arms are shaking," he said as he slid his fingers out from between them, and Casey sat back on her knees.

"Yeah, well," she started, breathless. "I like to think I'm in shape, but this never-ending Thanksgiving dessert fest is probably making it a little harder to support my body weight while you perform feats of magic in my panties."

She laughed, but Boone groaned.

"Boone Murphy, do you not *enjoy* performing feats of magic in my panties?"

"What?" he asked. "God, *no*. I mean *yes*, I enjoy the hell out of anything that involves me inside your panties, though I cannot believe how many times we've said the word *panties* in the last thirty seconds."

"Three," she surmised. "Which means one feat of panty magic every ten seconds. A girl could get used to that. And now it's four."

Boone huffed out a laugh. "I just can't stand this thing," he said, nodding toward the sling that not only immobilized his shoulder but kept his arm strapped to his torso. "It's driving me crazy not being able to hold you or to properly pleasure you like I damn well should be able to do."

Casey's cheeks turned pink, and she smiled down at him. "Murph, I promise you that you are pleasuring me just fine. I just needed to give my arms a little break. That's all."

"Fine?" he asked. "*Fine?* There's no way in hell I'm letting my girl settle for fine." He unstrapped the Velcro that kept his hand in place and then loosened the strap slung over his shoulder.

"What are you doing?" Casey asked. "Boone, I don't need you to injure yourself even worse just so we can—"

"Walsh," he said, interrupting her admonishment. "I appreciate your concern, but I am *hours* away from Eli telling me I can lose this contraption for good. I promise I'll be careful and put it back on as soon as we're finished, but if you don't let me *finish* you how I want to—and I mean the kind of finishing that makes you forget your own damned name—then I think I'm going to lose my damned mind. You can help me out or watch me struggle, but either way, this thing is coming off, and so are your panties."

"And now that's five," Casey said. She sighed, then helped him remove the sling and toss it to the floor.

He'd taken it off to shower and had fared well enough. His shoulder was sore, but the pain was nothing like it had been when he'd dislocated it.

"Does it hurt?" she asked, and he could hear the worry in her voice.

He shook his head. "I'm fine," he replied, then caught himself. "*Better* than fine. I promise. Just lie down and rest your arms, okay?"

She crossed her arms and narrowed her eyes. "Are you bossing me around now, Murph?"

The corner of his mouth turned up. "*Please*," he added, and she climbed off him, doing as he said.

Once she was sprawled on her back, he climbed over her. She stared up at him, her green eyes sparkling with need, and for a moment, he was brought back to that night in the barn—a night he'd never erase no matter what Casey said about leaving the past in the past and no matter how badly things had fallen apart soon after. It was the night he'd known he would love this girl for the rest of his life. Maybe he'd forgotten along the way, letting himself get sidetracked by life. By fear. By not believing he deserved another chance with her.

But here they were, grown adults, Casey giving him that chance and Boone grasping for the reins like he was on a bucking horse.

"I'm going to win you back," he told her.

She smiled at him, then stuck her fingers inside the waistband of his briefs.

"Don't you get it? You already have, Murph." She tugged at the white cotton, lowering it enough to expose his unbridled need for the woman he still couldn't believe was lying in his bed. "You already have."

Then she shimmied out of her own panties and grabbed hold of his thighs.

Boone's heart rose into his throat.

"Casey," he said tenderly. "Are you sure?"

She skimmed her teeth over her bottom lip and nodded. "I'm on the pill. Never miss a dose. I don't even mess up the time," she added with a nervous laugh. "Have a reminder in my phone's calendar and everything."

Jesus, how alike they were, and she didn't even realize it.

"So," she continued. "It's safe. *We're* safe, Murph. If you're ready."

If you're ready…

He wasn't sure he'd ever be ready to go down this road again. There was no manual, no preparation, no guarantee that they wouldn't crash and burn again. But he'd already lived the alternative, had *been* living it for twelve years, and he'd had enough.

Boone answered her by sliding his briefs the rest of the way down until he kicked them to the floor. Then he hesitated.

"I can't," he started. "I mean, usually I *can*, but…"

Casey laughed sweetly.

"Let's switch," she told him, then helped him down to his back as she crawled over him.

"This is a damned good view." He stared up at her, still not sure that this was really happening. That *they* were happening.

Then she leaned down and kissed him, soft yet earnest, as she wrapped her hand around his length, positioned him just right, and sank down over him until he was buried to the hilt.

Casey cried out and wrapped her arms around him, hugging him tightly with her knees.

"Welcome home, Murph," she whispered in his ear.

Boone's heart squeezed in his chest, and his throat burned.

"It's good to be back, Supergirl."

Now that he'd figured his shit out, it was damned good to be back.

Chapter 21

THIS TIME, CASEY GAVE IVY A HEADS-UP.

> I'm in the shop already. Came prepared with a latte on the off chance I scare your coffee out of your hands again. Now kick that fire chief of yours out of bed and get your ass to work so I can stop freaking out.

She hoped her best friend didn't have her phone on Do Not Disturb and would actually see the text before arriving at the shop.

Casey paced, stopped, then paced some more. This time, she at least hadn't run out on Boone while he was still sleeping. She had waited until he was in his brother's capable hands, being admonished for not entirely adhering to doctor's orders.

"You took it off early, didn't you?" Eli had accused after he carefully and methodically unstrapped Boone's arm and slid the sling off Boone's shoulder.

"I—what? How would you even know that?" Boone asked, not even trying to lie.

Eli narrowed his eyes at his younger brother. "Your mobility right now," he said, nodding at

Boone, who'd already started rolling his shoulder back and forth. "It's like you've done this before. Do I even want to ask why you risked surgery—or maybe even permanent damage—when all you had to do was get through *one* weekend taking it easy?"

Boone had glanced at Casey, who'd been pretending to admire Eli's framed certificates and awards displayed on the exam room wall. When she didn't return his gaze, Boone turned his attention back to his brother while Casey watched the two men out of the corner of her eye.

"I wasn't riding—the horse or my bike—if that's what you're getting at," Boone said. "I was careful, and it was necessary, and it was only for a little while before I strapped myself back in again. I told you I don't need saving, Eli. I can take care of myself now."

That had been Casey's cue to leave or, to put a finer point on it, run away before things got too real.

"You're in good hands," she'd told Boone with a little too much vigor as she patted him firmly on the back. "So I'm gonna go...do a thing." She nodded at Dr. Murphy. "Eli," she added before hightailing it out the door and into her father's borrowed truck, leaving Boone stranded with his brother as she sped into town to take refuge first in her makeshift salon—better known as her apartment bathroom—and soon after with her best friend.

It felt like hours before Ivy finally walked through the shop's front door, but really, it had only been six minutes since Casey had let herself in. She'd been counting.

Ivy's dark eyes were still sleep glazed when she shuffled through the door.

"I close the shop at noon on Mondays following holidays. Boss's rule, and since I'm the boss, I gotta follow the rules I make," she said with a yawn. "So this better be good."

"Oh shit." Casey winced. "I forgot about the Monday thing. But...I slept with Boone? That should account for my brain fog," Casey said with a shrug and a nervous laugh.

Ivy's eyes widened. "Yeah. Okay. This is good. Tell me *everything*." Then she snorted. "Okay, maybe not *every*thing. But I do already know about the briefs. I've even seen 'em."

Casey's mouth fell open. "You what? When? *How?*" But her brain started connecting the dots, and soon she was cracking up too. "Did he even realize I swiped his room key and gave it to you that morning? Or was he too concerned with being caught in his briefs by his girlfriend's best friend?" She threw her hand over her mouth, but Ivy slapped it away.

"What...did you...just call yourself?" Ivy asked, her voice tentative but not without accusation.

"I don't know," Casey said. And she really didn't

have any clue where the—the—the *G* word came from. This was all still so new, but at the same time, it wasn't.

Ivy narrowed her eyes, but all Casey could do was laugh nervously.

"Seriously, Ives. I'm freaking out. Again. What am I even doing? I barely have a month to secure my first payment to finish school, let alone figure out how I'm going to manage any sort of payment plan after that initial deposit. And then what? If I figure it all out, I get my certificate and do what I was supposed to do twelve years ago and *leave* Meadow Valley for somewhere that will give me the professional experience I need in order to open my own place? It's déjà vu or history repeating itself or—" She gasped for air. "I. Don't. *Know.*" She ripped her beanie off her head. "And *look…*"

Ivy blinked a few times before her lips broke into a smile, albeit a hesitant one. "It's lavender!" she cried, her grin widening into near maniacal proportions. "And *shorter*," she added, acknowledging Casey's now chin-length bob.

Casey rolled her eyes. "I look like an Easter egg. In November. And my ends were not having it with the lightening, so I had to hack them off, and I hacked more than I intended. Let's face it. I'm a thirty-year-old beauty school dropout who stress bakes and stress colors rather than process what's actually going on in my head." She pouted and dropped down to a squat, then collapsed onto her ass immediately after, huffing out a long breath as she dropped her head to her knees. "Not only am I Frenchy from *Grease*, but I've *stayed* Frenchy for the past twelve years."

Ivy chuckled, and even though Casey wasn't looking at her, she could tell the sound was genuine and not forced like her expression after seeing Casey's hair. She could feel Ivy kiss the top of her head, then heard her plop down opposite her.

"You didn't drop out of cosmetology school because you couldn't hack it," Ivy said softly.

Casey sighed and tilted her head up to meet her friend's gaze. Both women rested their heads on their knees, their arms wrapped around their shins.

"I could totally hack it," Casey admitted with a weak smile. Then she shook out her new do. "And *hack* it I did."

They both burst into a fit of laughter, which helped ease the tension in Casey's shoulders and lighten the invisible weight pressing down on her chest.

"How is it that you have all your shit together, and I feel like I'm spinning plates while riding a unicycle and playing an accordion?"

Ivy gasped. "Do you know how to play an accordion? Have you been holding out on me? When's your next concert?"

Casey huffed out a laugh. "But nothing of my prowess as a unicycling plate spinner?"

"Please," Ivy scoffed and waved her off. "Everyone knows you're an expert at *that*."

"True," Casey sighed. "You can't argue with talent."

Ivy's expression softened into a tender smile. "You're allowed to get caught up in your own life every now and then. That's the beauty of our friendship. Even when you might be a *little* scattered, I always know you love me."

Casey's throat tightened. "I *do* love you, Ives."

"And I love you, my little Easter egg." Ivy glanced around the shop, to the checkout desk several feet away from where they'd taken up residence on the floor. "Am I mistaken, or did you say something about coffee, because I think we're going to be here for a while?"

Casey blew out a shaky breath. "Has anyone ever told you that you're the best?"

"Only every single day." Ivy shrugged. "Carter's sort of head over heels for me like that."

Casey laughed. "As he should be. You can add me to that list as well." She pushed herself up, strode to the desk, and then returned with two insulated coffee tumblers, one with a latte and the other with black coffee and cinnamon. She handed the latte to Ivy.

"Now," Ivy started, "since I'm here and you're here in a darling clothing boutique that is closed for the day and we're doing this whole figure-you-out kind of thing, what would you say to a good old-fashioned *fashion* show?"

Casey gasped. "Like we did in high school? Should I see if my dad still has a bottle of peach brandy hiding behind the bar?"

Ivy wrinkled up her nose. "God *no*. But are you working today…or tonight?"

"Mom and Dad take Monday nights," Casey said with a shake of her head. "And apparently Dr. Charlotte follows the same rule as you. Pediatrician's office is technically closed, but the good doctor is, of course, on call for the emergency ear infection or strep test. But that means no extra income for Casey today." She sighed.

Ivy pursed her lips. "You know you could always work here. I could afford to pay you for some part-time help. And if you need a loan—"

"You just shut your pretty little mouth, Ivy Serrano," Casey demanded. "You and Carter are getting married in the spring, and I will *not* let you dip into the wedding fund, not even a little bit. And as for the part-time help, the most fashionable attire I own is the denim jumpsuit I wore for my interview. The rest is Midtown tees and a whole lot of denim that is not nearly as cute as that jumpsuit."

Ivy cleared her throat. "Yeah, I'm going to need that jumpsuit back, Walsh. You left the tags on, right?"

"See?" Casey raised her brows. "It's not even *my* jumpsuit. I'd definitely hinder rather than garner you any extra sales. Besides, things are just slow because of the holiday weekend. It'll pick back up soon, and I'll be moonlighting my way to beauty school graduate." She paused. "Right?"

"*Right!*" Ivy insisted with enough confidence that Casey practically believed her. Ivy held up her travel mug, and Casey clinked it with the bottom of hers. "To the *year* of Casey. Because you deserve so much more than a day."

The two women took long swigs of their morning beverages like Casey was standing behind the bar and had just poured them each a pint.

"And because it's *almost* lunchtime," Ivy said, "and we both technically have the day off, I have some single serving cans of Crossroads Sparkling Rosé in the mini fridge. I hear it's much better than peach brandy."

Ivy stood and then held a hand out for her friend.

Casey grabbed on and let Ivy pull her up. "This is *perfect*," she agreed. "Exactly what I need to clear my head. A throwback fashion show with a little present-day bubbly. Let's do it!"

———

Twelve Years Ago

Boone and his buddy Peyton sat atop the fence to the Murphy Horse Ranch's arena, their boots tucked behind a slat for purchase.

"You boys ready?" Ivy asked, peeking out from the barn door. "Because this is Casey Walsh like you've never seen her before."

Casey's palms were sweaty, and her cheeks and throat and belly felt hot. She wasn't sure if it was the awful peach-flavored liquor she and Ivy had just downed or the aftereffects, like everything in her stomach threatening to come back up.

She squared her shoulders and smoothed the fitted—and now cropped after Ivy's scissors had their way—white ribbed tank over her torso. Then she tugged at the black striped tie she'd stolen from her dad's closet, onto which she'd let Ivy embroider bright pink and yellow flowers, loosening it even more. Even the cargo jeans were stolen—er, repurposed—from Ivy's brother Charlie's collection. They were huge on Casey and had to be held up with a belt. She'd watched Ivy take a cheese grater to the thighs of Charlie's jeans to make them look perfectly ripped. "Without having to pay perfectly ripped prices!" Ivy had exclaimed. "Which is exactly how they *should* be," she had added, "if we're going to pull off this retro Avril Lavigne skater girl vibe—with an Ivy Serrano twist, of course."

Ivy twirled the lone blue lock of Casey's otherwise blond hair around her finger.

"You're *perfect* for this look. Just promise me you'll always stay blond like the Disney princess you were born to be with that tall, dark, and handsome prince waiting for you outside."

Casey snorted. "I am *so* not a Disney princess, which means I don't have to adhere to any rules that might pigeonhole me as such. I am my own person, blond hair or not."

"Fine," Ivy said. "Badass princess who chooses her *own* path and her *own* happily ever after, whether it's with a prince, a rancher who likes to work on cars and ride motorcycles, or whoever." She winked at Casey and then pushed her through the barn door.

Chapter 22

AFTER ELI'S ADMONISHMENT—BUT ALSO A clean bill of shoulder health so long as he stayed away from bucking broncos for another few weeks—Boone was back in the barn, mucking out stalls.

"Isn't that the exact opposite of something that's safe for a shoulder injury?" he'd asked his friends and current employers.

Colt had shrugged. "We checked with Eli. He said as long as you're using your dominant shoulder for any heavy lifting, you'd be okay. And since you're a righty and the shoulder in question is your left…"

Not exactly the grand return to meaningful work he'd hoped for, but it did give him and Cirrus some good one-on-one time to have a little chat since Colt and the Callahans had taken care of *his* stall already.

"Looks like it's just you and me, buddy," Boone commented as Cirrus poked his head out of the stall to watch Boone clean out the one that belonged to his next-door neighbor. "How you been?"

Cirrus snorted and whinnied, which Boone took as a good sign, so he paused what he was doing, grabbed a stool, and sat down in front of Cirrus's stall so they could have a real sort of man-to-man heart-to-heart.

"So," Boone continued, taking off his gloves and giving Cirrus's nose a pat. "How did they hurt you, boy? What's got you so afraid to trust me?"

At his words, Cirrus shook his head and took a couple of steps back into his stall, as if understanding what Boone had just asked him.

"The authorities are still investigating," Sam had told everyone upon Cirrus joining the ranch. "So they can't give us too many details. All we know is that Cirrus was removed from his owner's care in Bakersfield and sent to the rescue portion of our ranch. We hope to integrate him into the general population, make him officially part of the Meadow Valley Ranch experience, but we can't do that until we know he's safe to ride. Until he can trust us and vice versa."

Boone sighed. "It's okay, boy. I think I get it. If no one showed you proper affection before, it must be hard to believe I'm being genuine." He wondered if Casey felt the same way, if even after saying yes to giving it another shot, she was afraid to trust him after all the history between them—history he still thought they should revisit someday.

Cirrus slowly approached the stall entrance again. Boone reached a hand into his pocket and retrieved a few carrot slices he'd brought with him just in case. He stood and reached his arm over the stall gate, then stood perfectly still while Cirrus contemplated another step forward. For a long moment, the stallion didn't move, and Boone waited patiently.

Cirrus sniffed and then took a small step toward Boone's outstretched hand. He sniffed again, then took the final step, finally dipping his head to gobble up the carrot pieces, then immediately taking a step back as soon as he was done.

"Wow," Boone whispered softly. "Our little incident the other night really had an impact on our relationship, huh?"

Boone dropped his hand and crossed his arms over the top of the gate, resting his chin on his forearms.

"I'm just gonna stand here and talk if that's okay. No expectations. Just two guys shooting the shit." Boone chuckled as he realized that was exactly what he was doing this afternoon. Literally. Cirrus didn't respond, so he took that as an invitation to keep going. "So this is the story. I am a thirty-year-old man who lost his business, left a woman at the altar—although technically, we left each other—admitted to his high school sweetheart that even after being estranged for more than a decade, *she* was the reason I couldn't go through with the wedding, and now we're back together, which is great, but I still feel like there's something hanging between us that needs to be acknowledged or dealt with or *something* if this is really going to work."

He sucked in a breath, then blew it out slowly.

"Sorry, buddy. My therapist is on vacation for the holiday, so I guess I'm letting it all out on you."

Cirrus gave a soft whinny and took a step in Boone's direction.

Boone laughed. "So you like chatting, huh? Didn't used to be my thing, but I guess I'm not the same guy I used to be. Also it's easy to talk to you." He reached out a hand, and Cirrus surprised him by nuzzling Boone's palm with his nose. Boone raised a brow. "I'm guessing that means you're not hating this either?" He laughed softly. "Well then, you should try your hand—or I guess hoof—at knitting. It's almost as soothing as lying on a creeper, rolling beneath a car's undercarriage, and being able to fix what's broken."

Cirrus nudged Boone's palm again, and he laughed, reaching into his pocket to produce what was left of his just-in-case treats. The horse not only gobbled up the carrots but this time *didn't* back away when he was finished. Instead, he let Boone pat his nose and pet him between the eyes.

"I've always loved horses. Don't get me wrong," Boone said. "But when I started learning cars—the intricacies of how all the parts worked together to serve the whole—it just kind of clicked, you know?

Problems had definitive solutions, ones that despite any of my academic shortcomings at the time, *I* could solve." He shrugged. "I don't know why, but even before my diagnosis, I was able to stay focused and in the moment every single time I set foot in my school's garage and soon my own."

Cirrus moved all the way to the stall door, softly nudging Boone's chin with his nose.

"Whoa," he said with a laugh. "I think we're making progress."

"Look at *you* two," a voice called over his shoulder—a voice he'd know anywhere. He gave Cirrus one more good pat and then spun to face Casey Walsh.

Even beneath her puffy red coat, he could tell she wasn't dressed in her typical Casey Walsh attire—the requisite jeans and Midtown Tavern sweatshirt or tee. Maybe it was the bare knees that gave her away or the mid-length cowboy boots that were adorned with the trademark Ivy Serrano flair—brightly colored floral embroidery.

"Let me guess," he mused. "Another one of Ivy's special makeovers? *Not* that you need one." He added the last part with a nervous laugh.

Casey tugged at the beanie on top of her head, and her cheeks flushed.

"We were just having some fun. Sort of a girls' day."

She took a step toward him and then a small stumble straight into Boone's chest.

"Hey there," he began, wrapping his arms around her as she righted herself and stood up straight. "You okay?"

Casey huffed out a laugh. "These boots are pinching my toes, and I maybe possibly had a few cans of sparkling rosé on an empty stomach over the past couple of hours. Stopped by to see if you'd eaten yet?"

Boone grinned. "Depends on which meal you're talking about, seeing as it's barely three o'clock. Had a quick lunch in the dining hall, and it's too early for dinner, even by senior citizen standards. This is all just to say that I'm not quite sure how to answer your question. But I am confident enough to say that no matter what is happening under that coat of yours, you, my tipsy Supergirl, look good enough to eat."

Her eyes widened, and Boone shook his head ruefully.

"What? You don't think I remember what I said when you had that sexy skater-girl thing going on in high school?" He scratched the back of his neck. "I don't suppose there's a cutoff tank top hiding underneath all that goose down, is there?"

Casey laughed but dipped her head as if embarrassed.

"I'm too old to pull that off anymore. This was stupid. I'm just going to head home and get out of these damned boots that—while cute as hell—are most definitely a half size too small."

She made a move to turn away from him, but his arms were still wrapped around her waist.

"Uh-uh," he told her. "I'm not letting you go that easily. Not when you only just got here." He hooked a finger under her chin and tilted her head up so her eyes met his again. "Show me," he said softly.

She wrinkled her nose.

"I mean this in the nicest possibly way," she started, "but you sort of—"

"Stink?" he asked with a laugh. "I'm surprised it took you this long to notice." Only then did he drop his arms, and Casey took a small step back.

"Colt told me you were working in the stables. I guess I was just too excited to see you to take into account the implications of what that work would entail."

Too excited to see you...

Boone had to refrain from lifting her into his arms and kissing the hell out of her right then and there.

"Can you say that one more time? I'm not sure I heard you right."

She sighed. "You know, you'd think a girl who practically grew up in a tavern would have a better filter even when she's a little tipsy."

Boone cupped a hand to his ear like he was still unable to decipher her words.

"I'm sorry," he teased. "I didn't quite get that. Can you slow down, enunciate, and maybe talk a little louder?"

Casey rolled her eyes. "I...was...excited...to... see...you. There. Slow and with full enunciation. Was it loud enough for you?"

He crossed his arms and beamed. "Perfect," he said. "Loud, clear, and permanently recorded in my brain." He scratched the back of his neck. "You know, you took off from Eli's so quickly this morning that I didn't have a chance to ask you... And now that you're here and obviously not working tonight...um... What would you think about me taking you out on a proper date? Tonight. Here in Meadow Valley." He swallowed, only now realizing as the words stammered their way out of his mouth that he was nervous.

Casey tugged at her beanie again and cleared her throat. "You mean like a public debut of us as a couple? Where everyone would see us?"

Boone's heart sank as Casey confirmed his worry.

"Wait!" she exclaimed. "No! That's not what I meant. I'm not afraid of people seeing us together. Like *together* together. I swear."

"Are you some kind of mind reader?" he asked.

She laughed, and simply seeing her smile at him put his mind at ease. "No, but that wounded puppy look of yours is hard to mistake."

"Wounded *puppy*?" he asked, incredulous. "I do *not* look, nor have I ever looked, like a wounded puppy."

Casey placed a palm on his cheek, and it was

all he could do to hold his resolve and not lean into that touch. "It's sweet," she admitted softly. "I think I'm the only one who's ever been privy to it. And seeing it just now—it took me back to us *then*. To all the things that made me fall for you. Not that I'm falling for you. We just started dating. This is brand new, and we're different than we used to be, and—"

"Walsh," he said, interrupting her verbal out-pouring. "It's okay to remember the good stuff about us, even if it seems like it happened to two people we no longer know. I like hearing that it wasn't all bad for you, that you can still smile about some of the memories of us."

Her eyes widened, and she looked stricken.

"Is that what you think?" she asked. "That I don't remember the *years* of good before it fell apart? Just because I don't want to rehash the part where it did go wrong doesn't mean I've wiped my memory of the rest of it."

Boone nodded slowly. "I didn't mean it like that." He cleared his throat. "Wait. Maybe I did. We've been playing by your rules here, Supergirl, so I'm still not yet on solid ground about what does and what doesn't constitute rehashing the past."

Casey sighed. "You're right. I'm sorry. You *have* been letting me take the lead, and I appreciate that. Can we just—" She groaned and pulled off her beanie, revealing a very lavender and much shorter new do hiding beneath.

"Oh," he noted, still taking it in.

"Oh," Casey echoed. "*This* is why I'm nervous to make our public debut. Not because it's us but because the whole town knows I'm headed back—or at least I *hope* I'm headed back—to cosmetology school next semester, and I look like the frosting on an Easter cupcake or one of those weird fruit-flavored marshmallows... Or a fairy from Pixie Hollow."

Boone's brows wrinkled, and Casey scoffed.

"Pixie Hollow? Where Tinker Bell and her fairy friends live?" she asked and then groaned.

"Okay," he said. "I know who Tinker Bell is. I just didn't realize she had her own little town or whatever." He reached for her hair but then dropped his hand. "I really want to run my fingers through that hair of yours, but we'd both need a shower after that. And as much as I'd love to invite you to join me, it's gonna be a minute before Cirrus and I finish our chat and put a pin in this afternoon's job. So how about you grab yourself a snack. Change those shoes if you want, but don't lose the outfit. I'm a big fan of those legs of yours, and I sure as hell won't mind showing them off on our date."

She rolled her eyes, but she didn't argue.

"So that means it's a yes?" he asked, just to be sure.

Casey nodded and bit her bottom lip in that way that made him feel just a little bit drunk and drove him just a little bit mad.

"Pick you up at six? Just…um…tell me where?"

She pursed her lips. "Depends. Will this date be happening at the tavern or at the fine dining establishment that is the Meadow Valley Inn?"

Boone laughed. "Those are our only options, aren't they? I'll call Pearl and get us a table at the inn. Nothing but the best for my girl."

Casey's eyes widened, but then she smiled. "I guess that's me now, huh? Boone Murphy's girl?"

He nodded but then shook his head. "No," he insisted, and she narrowed her eyes at him. "I take it back. You're *you*, Walsh. You belong to no one but yourself. I'm just the lucky guy who gets to sit across the table from you tonight…and maybe wake up with you tomorrow morning despite not needing someone to help me put my pants on anymore."

She shrugged. "I guess that'll depend on how well you wine and dine me, Mr. Murphy. And since this is our first official date, like *ever*, because I can't recall being wined and dined as a teen, I think you should pick me up at my apartment door."

She wasn't wrong. They'd started out as childhood friends, and then things just sort of evolved in high school when Casey finally caught up to Boone's feelings for her. There was no wooing. No fancy dates. One day they were friends, and the next they were more. Simple as that.

"Should I bring something?" he asked. "Flowers? Balloon animal? Maybe a small wood carving?"

"Balloon animal?" she asked with a laugh. "What I wouldn't give to see you try to make one of those."

"Oh no," he said. "I wouldn't trust such a creation to an amateur like myself. It'd take some googling, but I'm sure I could find a balloon master not too far away if that's what the lady wishes."

She was still laughing as she shook her head. "God, no. I hate balloons, especially the squeaky sound they make when someone is twisting them." She pulled her beanie back onto her head, tugging it down over her ears. "And any plant that enters my apartment dies almost on arrival. So that's a no on the flowers too. Just bring yourself, Boone Murphy. That's all I need." She shoved her hands in her coat pockets. "Which means I guess you'll have to wait for the big reveal until then. I am *so* losing the shoes, though." She rocked back and forth on her heels and winced before taking a couple steps forward, rising up on her toes, and kissing him softly on his newly bearded cheek. "That's all you get until you shower, cowboy."

He scratched at his cheek. "I should probably shave too now that I have two hands, huh?"

"Or I could help with that. Wielding a straight

razor was part of my cosmetology training—albeit over a decade ago. But I've done it a few times since then."

He swallowed, the thought of Casey Walsh taking a razor to his neck both thrilling and terrifying. But mostly thrilling, in a ridiculously sexy kind of way.

"You need to go before I forget all about finishing work and taking that shower and just let you have your way with me in the tack room."

Casey laughed and started backing away. "Six o'clock, cowboy. Don't be late."

Her smile faltered so quickly that if he blinked, he'd have missed it. But he didn't miss it.

Don't forget was what he knew she was thinking in that moment. *Prove you have your life under control.*

Boone's watch beeped, and his eyes dipped from Casey to his wrist—to his reminder to take his afternoon dose of his daily medication.

"I'll be there at five fifty-five," he assured her, clearing his throat and painting on his best devil-may-care grin. "But I should get back to what I was doing."

She nodded, her gaze wary, but then she gave him the same artificial smile, the two of them easily falling into the roles of the dual performance they were in.

"See you soon, Murph." And then she spun on her heel and was gone.

Boone strode to the utility sink that sat outside the tack room, gave his hands a good scrub, and then reached inside his vest pocket for the prescription bottle he'd tossed in that morning when Casey wasn't looking.

He wasn't ashamed of needing medication to balance the chemicals in his brain. He'd had years to get used to it, years to put his life together in a sort of routine that worked for him. But he wasn't perfect. He slipped up sometimes, still sometimes made rash decisions that weren't always for the best—like selling his shop and running off to marry a very good woman for very wrong reasons or getting back on a horse who'd already thrown him once and then hiding the incident from his brother.

How could he prove to Casey that he'd changed, that all the steps he'd taken over the years had been to better himself even if better didn't mean perfect?

"One night," he mused, turning back to Cirrus's stall. "All I need is for us to have one good night where I can show her that I'm not impulsive or rash, that I won't forget what's important, and then I'll tell her everything—from the therapy to the knitting to the medication, *all* of it. And we'll just see, right?"

Cirrus whinnied and nudged Boone's outstretched hand with his nose.

"See?" he asked. "All it takes is a little trust that there are people out there who see the good in you even if whoever you were with before made you feel different."

Easy words to say to a horse, but to believe about himself? Boone was still working on that.

Chapter 23

CASEY GOT UP CLOSE AND PERSONAL WITH HER bathroom mirror as she fought with a stubborn poppy seed that had likely been stuck between her two front teeth for *hours*, considering she'd snagged a lemon poppy seed muffin from Storyland's ice cream parlor/coffee shop. The muffin was fantastic, and Trudy Davis was kind enough to give Casey her recipe as long as she promised not to put them on the Midtown Tavern menu. The staying power of poppy seeds in Casey's teeth? Not so fantastic. At least not for a woman preparing for her first date with her first love.

It was time to get serious. She pulled out the drawer under her sink and retrieved the waxed floss. *Nothing*—not even Casey's too-close-together teeth—could withstand the waxed floss. At least that was what she hoped.

She checked the time on her phone: 5:40 p.m. Based on Boone's promise not only to be on time but to be at her door five minutes early, she had plenty of time to take care of dental business, throw on some lip gloss, and figure out what she was going to swap for the too-small boots that would be sensible yet still fashionable enough to pair with the above-the-knee flouncy floral dress thingy Ivy had dolled her up in this afternoon.

Casey sighed. She really was too old to pull off the retro Avril Lavigne skater-girl look these days. Then again, so was Avril Lavigne. Not that Casey was knocking women in their thirties. She *was* a woman in her thirties. She just didn't remember when she grew up.

"I'm a grown-up," she told herself as she slid the floss between her teeth to evict her unwanted guest. It took a slide here and a twist there—maybe a tiny shimmy—but the poppy seed was soon gone. When she went to remove the floss, however, the long strands of thin string held together by wax and maybe a bit of sheer will shredded between her two front teeth so that now she had floss hanging in front of her teeth and behind her teeth, *and* there was a tangled, shredded nest of the string that separated from the group balled up right in front of her chompers.

"This is *not* happening," she said.

Casey dug at the floss with her fingernail, but she always clipped them as close to the quick as she could without making herself bleed that she was no help to herself.

She brought up Ivy's number on her phone and hit the green button to call her.

"Who's ready for a hot date?" Ivy answered after one ring.

"Ives?"

"Uh-oh," Ivy said. "That's your uh-oh tone. Why are we uh-ohing when you're about to embark on romance-a-rama? Or should it be date-a-rama? Do you think he's going to pull out all the stops? Maybe some over-the-top first-date grand gesture? Ooh! Maybe he'll whisk you off in a helicopter to another city—or in a private jet to another *country*!"

"*Ivy!*" Casey finally yelled.

"Right!" Ivy cried. "Sorry. You have an uh-oh tone, and I am clearly watching too many romcoms. I just can't help it. I love love, especially when we get closer to the holidays. Ooh! I should watch *The Holiday*!"

"*Ivy.*"

"Zipping my lips until you tell me what you need."

"Floss," Casey confessed with a small whimper. "I have *floss* stuck between my two front teeth, and Boone is going to be here in"—she pulled the phone away from her ear to get a quick look—"*six* minutes!" she concluded. "Ives, I cannot leave my apartment with floss hanging between my teeth!"

Ivy made a stifled sound, one Casey swore sounded a hell of a lot like a laugh.

"Is this funny?" Casey asked, irritated. "Is my pre-date plight here for your entertainment?"

Ivy snorted. "I'm sorry! For real, Case. I am. But is it doing that little shreddy ball thing it did that time we let Jenna drag us out line dancing?"

"It's *hardly* dragging when you go with her at least once a week," Casey said. "And *yes*. It's doing the little ball thing."

She heard Ivy sigh. "Honey, I thought after that night that we decided no more waxed floss."

Casey's eyes widened as recognition bloomed. "No more waxed floss!" she exclaimed, so proud as if she'd just solved the climate crisis or just remembered the quadratic formula. "I wasn't supposed to use the waxed floss," she added, tapping her index finger to her forehead. "So what do I do?"

"Um," Ivy began. "Let me google… Okay! Here's something. You could try cutting it so it's shorter, and then it will blend in better with your teeth."

Casey rolled her eyes but then realized her friend couldn't see her. "I'm rolling my eyes at you, you know.

"Can you floss it out with more floss?" Ivy asked.

Casey blew out a breath. "And risk getting multiple strands caught between my stupid teeth? Should I get braces? People do that as adults, right?"

She pulled another piece of floss from the dispenser and readied herself to try Ivy's suggestions, because it wasn't like she had another choice.

"You have beautiful teeth and a gorgeous smile," Ivy insisted. "Your teeth are just snuggled a bit too close for comfort. That's all."

"Okay," Casey said, looking down at the phone on the counter. "I'm going in with strand number two."

"Best of luck," Ivy cheered. "Wait! Switch to video chat so I can see what's going on."

Casey sighed but then picked up the phone, pressing the camera icon on the call. Ivy's face soon appeared with Casey's in the smaller thumbnail in the corner.

Ivy snorted. "Oh my god. You look like you tried to swallow the Lorax's mustache or something."

Casey glared at her friend, even though the description was pretty on point.

"Seriously, Ives. What the heck do I do?"

"Has this ever happened before?"

Casey shook her head. "I usually use a different kind of floss, but this damned poppy seed was just hanging on for dear life. So I busted out the thicker, waxed stuff the dentist gave me last time I had a cleaning and, well, here I am."

Ivy tried to suppress her grin. Casey could *see* the effort. But it was no use.

"Fine," Casey groaned. "Just get your giggles out of the way already. We both know if the tables were turned, I'd be laughing too."

"Ohmygod, thank you!" Ivy squeaked before bursting into a fit of giggles until she finally calmed down and caught her breath.

"Are you done?" Casey asked, brows raised.

Ivy nodded. "Now officially reporting for best friend duty. But, honey, you know this is just Boone, right? Why are you so nervous?"

Casey's palms were damp, and her cheeks flushed at the question.

"Be*cause* it's Boone," she admitted after a long pause. "This is—I mean us as a couple again… I don't even know." She blew out a shaky breath. "I'm scared, Ives. Scared that I want this to work when for *so* many years, I convinced myself that I was over him and that the only thing he was capable of was hurting me."

Ivy smiled sweetly at her friend now, no trace of laughter or amusement left on her face. "But you know that assessment of him is wrong? Does this mean you two have talked about the past?"

Casey's stomach sank at the thought. "No," she told her. "That's the one thing we *don't* need to do. If we could just erase all that and move forward… That's why tonight needs to be perfect. Our official fresh start, you know?"

Ivy raised a brow, and Casey let out a nervous laugh.

"Okay, our official *public* fresh start after a very sexy private reunion."

"Attagirl," Ivy said.

A knock sounded on Casey's apartment door.

"Oh shit!" she and Ivy cried in unison.

"It's only five fifty," Ivy noted. "It can't be Boone yet, can it?"

"I might have accidentally made a comment about him showing up on time, so he said he'd be here at five fifty-five. I'm guessing he tacked on another five minutes to prove himself, and I'm basically the worst for making him feel like I'm still judging him based on the past that we are *not* discussing, and this is karma's way of saying I should have just trusted him."

Boone knocked again, because of course it was going to be Boone and no one else, and Casey shrugged.

"I guess this is it, right?" she asked.

Ivy bit her bottom lip, which meant she was back to being amused.

"If it's any consolation," Ivy started, "I don't think there's anything you could do that would be a turnoff for Boone Murphy. So go get him, kiddo. You *and* the Lorax you're trying to eat."

She snorted again, and Casey glared again.

"Byeeee!" Ivy added and then blew her friend a kiss before ending the call.

Casey looked at herself in the mirror, from her Easter egg hair to the frayed string hanging between her teeth to the beautiful and sexy dress she wasn't sure she could even pull off to her bare feet, her toes bruised from trying to cram them into the boots she never should have worn.

"Thanks a ton, karma. You couldn't have just tossed *one* obstacle at me tonight?" She pointed at the woman in the mirror as if she were the embodiment of karma herself. "I'm keeping tabs, okay?

This is more than enough. I've learned my lesson."
Though Casey was still trying to figure out what
that lesson was exactly.

A third knock came from the front of her apartment, and Casey finally called out, "Coming!"

She padded toward the sound, squared her
shoulders, and smoothed out her dress before
finally turning the handle and throwing open
the door. She was ready to spread her arms and
announce *Ta-da!* But instead her mouth simply fell
open in a silent *Oh* as she drank in the tall, dark,
and *suited* man before her. Not the tuxedo he was
wearing the day he found her on the side of the
road but a midnight-blue suit with a *lavender* shirt
and tie beneath his jacket.

"Oh," she said out loud this time, then grinned
when she saw his dusty riding boots poking out
from the bottom of his pants. "You look—wow."
He even kept the beard.

"Wow yourself," he echoed with a warm smile.
"Except it looks like I caught you mid floss?
Dammit. I'm *too* early. I should have waited. I was
just—" He cleared his throat. "I was *really* excited
to see you," he revealed, echoing her own admission when she'd turned up tipsy at the barn.

She sighed. "You're not too early. I mean, you are
but it's okay. And I'm not mid floss. I mean, I am
but... You told me to get some food in me since I
was tipsy, and I did. Trudy has these amazing lemon

poppy seed muffins that you would *love* if you haven't tried them yet, since I know how you feel about lemon pastry." She smiled, then covered her mouth with her palm. "Anyway, I should have known better than to eat anything with seeds because my giant, overcrowded teeth like to hold on to seeds for dear life, and I used the extra thick waxed floss to get the seed out, which I did, but now the floss is stuck and frayed, and Ivy said it looks like I tried to swallow the Lorax's mustache, and she's right, and now I think that maybe the universe really is conspiring against us."

"With floss?" Boone asked. "Also, are you going to invite me in to help, or would you like me to wait out here until you sort this Lorax thing out?"

He bit back a grin, and Casey pouted. "Do you really think you can help?"

"I don't know. I mean, I can rebuild a car engine, install aftermarket airbags to a car that has no business being on the road otherwise, *and* I can tie my shoes. Which, you know, means I have experience with strings." Boone chuckled.

Casey, hand still over her mouth, stepped back and held out her free arm, welcoming him in.

"I can't believe this is how our date is starting," she grumbled, her voice muffled behind her palm.

"Do you have tweezers?" he asked, clapping his hands together like he was ready to get to work.

Casey nodded, headed back to the bathroom,

and returned with a small pouch containing at least ten different kinds of tweezers and a small wastebasket, which she set on the floor next to her stool.

She shrugged as his eyes widened. "Different types of brows need different types of plucking. Depends on how fine or coarse the hair is."

"And how many sets of eyebrows do you have?" he asked, nodding for her to take a seat on one of the stools opposite her small breakfast bar.

Casey rolled her eyes. "Just because I'm not licensed—*yet*—doesn't mean friends don't come to me for certain beauty-related services. After a while, you develop a collection of tools depending on your clientele."

He set the pouch on the bar and wrapped a gentle hand around her wrist, urging her to uncover her mouth.

Her shoulders sagged as she dropped her hand.

"Hey, Supergirl," he said softly. "Sometimes a heroine needs an assist, okay?"

Her heart squeezed like it did every time he called her by the nickname, and she nodded.

And just like that, he went to work, sifting through her bag of "tools" until he found what he was looking for. And like a surgeon, with one set of tweezers in each hand and Casey tilting her head up and toward the ceiling light, he had the Lorax's mustache removed and disposed of in less than fifteen seconds.

"How did you...? I mean, I should have thought of..." Casey groaned.

"You panicked," he answered matter-of-factly. "Sometimes when we panic, it's hard to think of the right thing to do or say. That's why all superheroes need a trusty sidekick."

She huffed out a laugh. Most days, Casey Walsh felt nothing like a superhero. And Boone Murphy... did he think himself only worthy of sidekick status?

"You *are* pretty trusty," she said instead of asking him flat out. The night was already off to a strange start, and she wanted to steer it back to something resembling normal—whatever that meant.

"I'm glad you think so." He grinned, then dipped his head to kiss her, but before his lips met hers, she threw her hand up between them as a barrier.

"Wait!" she cried, pressing her palm against his mouth. "I need to brush again after that ordeal. What if I taste like—I don't know—string or something?"

Boone laughed and lowered her hand. "It was mint-flavored floss, and you'll taste like *you*."

He didn't wait for her to argue again but instead brushed his lips against hers and, taking her sigh of delight as permission to proceed, kissed her for *real*. He nipped at her with his teeth, slipped his tongue past her parted lips, and turned her bones to pure liquid as she clasped her fingers behind his neck and held on for dear life, thanking the conspiring universe for letting her still be seated on the stool for this particular kiss.

Her feet hooked around his calves and then rose to his knees, and she yanked him forward.

Boone laughed as he braced his hands on the breakfast bar behind her.

"Careful there, Walsh," he said softly, his beard tickling her chin. "While I don't think the universe is out to get us, we *have* both suffered our share of bodily harm in the past few weeks. We may want to proceed with caution so that we make it to the end of the night."

She leaned up and kissed him again, humming against his lips. "And what happens at the end of the night?" she teased.

"Board games," he whispered, his breath warm against her ear. "Lots and *lots* of board games."

They both started laughing, and any tension Casey felt about how this night would go—and whether the universe had nefarious plans for the two of them—disintegrated into pure nothingness.

"Now," he began when they'd both finally regained their composure. "Are we ready to put the gossip to rest?"

"Or give everyone even *more* to talk about? I'm in," Casey said. "Let's do this."

Five minutes later, Casey had gloss on her lips, Converse sneakers on her feet, and her elbow linked with Boone's.

"I almost forgot," he mentioned just before she opened her apartment door. "Instead of balloon animals…" He reached into the pocket of his suit jacket and retrieved a yo-yo.

Casey's throat tightened as he handed her the small toy, still in its package.

"It's just a kid's one," he admitted, a nervous smile playing at his lips. "That was all I could find in Trudy's small toy section."

"I love it," she said, staring at it for several long moments before slipping it into the pocket of her coat. When Casey met his eyes again, something shifted in the air around them. She couldn't put her finger on it other than the assuredness that whatever life threw at them tonight, they'd come out on top.

With a renewed sense of confidence, Casey threw open the door, ready to take on the town—and nearly bulldozed her own father in the process.

"Dad! Why aren't you downstairs at work?"

He winced. "Your…um…your mom and I sort of had a little argument. Minor, really. Nothing to worry about."

"Then why were you about to knock on my door?" Casey asked.

"Because she walked out on me—for the night, not for good—which means I have no one to tend bar while I run the kitchen, since we gave everyone else the night off for the holiday."

Casey groaned. "When is this town going to learn that holidays don't extend into the week *following*."

It was only then that her dad glanced past Casey and acknowledged her date.

"Oh," Bill Walsh said to the other man. "I didn't realize you had—" He cleared his throat, and Casey expected her father to give Boone the cold shoulder or something worse, but instead the older man looked chagrined. "I guess the rumors are true and you two *are* an item again, which means I'm interrupting a date." He waved the two of them off. "Forget you saw me and enjoy your night." He pivoted away from the door, but Boone clapped a hand over her father's shoulder.

"You worry about the kitchen, Mr. Walsh. Casey and I will tend the bar."

Chapter 24

BOONE'S SHIRT WAS BEER SOAKED. HIS TIE? WELL, the blender won that one. But also, who orders a piña colada in November? At a tavern? In a small ranching town?

A large group of empty-nester couples on a cross-country road trip who probably took the wrong exit, that's who.

"Boone, honey?" one of them called from the other side of the bar, tapping her empty glass. "Another one of your yummy treats?"

Casey appeared from the other side of the bar with a stack of empty pint glasses and dropped them in the bus bin just as Boone's flirty customer waggled her brows at him.

Casey bumped her hip against his and winked at him. "I got this one, Boone, *honey*."

She bellied up to the bar across from the older woman and reached for her empty glass as Boone watched with anticipation.

"Another colada, or can I interest you in a local brew?"

The woman nodded over Casey's shoulder. "Is that one of your local brews?"

Casey leaned closer and whispered something in the woman's ear, something Boone couldn't hear but desperately wanted to.

When Casey pulled away, both women were laughing, and Boone sure hoped he wasn't the butt of the joke.

A moment later, Casey pivoted back to face him with the woman's empty glass in her hand and a triumphant grin on her face.

"Do I even want to know?" Boone asked.

Casey set the glass in the bus bin and got to work making a fresh frozen beverage for the woman.

"That's Eileen," she told him. "She and her husband, Paul, started doing this small-town road-trip thing a few years back once their kids were grown and had kids of their own. They've got six of 'em," Casey said, staring at the blender rather than making eye contact with Boone. "Kids, I mean. Scattered all over the country. So they make a trip of it each year—visiting each and every one—but always with a stop in Meadow Valley. Looks like this year, they joined a road-trip meetup group, and the meeting spot is here."

She shrugged, her back still to him.

"And you ladies were laughing because...?" he asked coolly, even though he was dying to know. He wanted to trust that she saw him differently now—that she trusted him, regardless of the situation. But damn, how easy it was to fall into the old self-talk that convinced him, once upon a time, that he wasn't worthy of her forgiveness.

"Because," Casey replied, spinning to face him as the blender did its thing, "I told her that if she kept making eyes at my man while hers was in the bathroom, I was going to run off with Paul and tell all her grandbabies to start calling *me* Nana." She blew her overgrown lavender bangs out of her eyes, and Boone forgot they were tending bar in Meadow Valley's most popular—and *only*—spot for any sort of nightlife. He wrapped his arms around Casey's waist, lifted her off the ground, and planted one on her right there for all to see.

And based on the whistles and hollers from the surrounding patrons, all *did* see. And all seemed to approve as well, including Casey, who hooked her legs over his hips and kissed him right back, right there for all to see.

"I guess we made our public debut after all," Boone said when he finally set her back on her feet.

Her cheeks and neck were flushed, and her chin was bright red from the rough bristle of his beard.

"That's it," he insisted. "I'm shaving tonight."

"What? Why? I mean, I know I said I'd help, but I think I kind of like it." Her hand instinctively went to the raw skin beneath her bottom lip. "Despite what you think," she added, since she was a mind reader now. "Also, what was that delicious public display of affection even for?" she asked.

He raised his brows, forgetting for a second about the beard and basking in the glow of Casey's words.

"You said *my man*." He crossed his arms. "You, Casey Walsh, *claimed* me. In public. So I thought it was best that I do the same."

"I suppose I did claim you, Mr. Murphy. Didn't I?" She tapped her index finger against her kiss-swollen lips. "Now that I think of it, I might actually need some clarification on that. Could you…um… claim me again?"

The blender's timer stopped, which meant Eileen's drink was done mixing, but Casey spun toward her customer and held up a finger. "Just a second, Eileen!" she called. "I'm getting *claimed*!"

"No rush, sweetheart!" Eileen called back. "I'm just going to continue enjoying the show with the rest of the crowd."

Casey pivoted back to Boone and grinned. "You heard the lady. Midtown Tavern is looking for a show, so we better give 'em something to feed the gossip mill until the next scandal rolls through town."

Boone was—thankfully—fresh out of scandal now that everyone likely knew why he couldn't go through with the wedding. But he sure was happy to put on a repeat performance, especially if Casey Walsh requested it.

"Aren't we supposed to get a fifteen-minute

break?" he asked, and Casey nodded. "In that case..." He picked her up again and walked her straight out from behind the bar just as Casey's father poked his head out from the kitchen.

"Watch the bar for a few, Dad!" she called, then yelped with laughter as Boone bounced her higher onto his hips, through the larger-than-normal Monday-night crowd, and out into the cold.

Once outside, though, he set Casey down, then rubbed his hands together and blew on them to warm them up.

"I didn't quite think this through," he admitted with a shiver and a laugh.

Casey, in her definitely-not-made-for-winter dress and bare legs, danced back and forth on her toes.

"N-n-no," she sputtered, teeth chattering. "We didn't."

"What on earth are you two doing?" a woman asked from over Casey's shoulder.

They spun to face the hooded figure as she came into the pool of light from the streetlamp up above.

"Mom?" Casey asked as the woman removed her hood. "Where have you been? I texted you. The bar is crazy busy, and Boone and I were supposed to be on a date, and Dad said you got in a fight." Casey blew out a breath. "And I was worried."

Casey's mom wrapped her gloved hand around her daughter's bare and goose-bumped wrist.

"Come upstairs. I'll make you something warm to drink and tell you what happened." The older woman lifted her gaze to Boone. "Can I—is it all right if I have a few minutes alone with my daughter?"

Boone heard Mrs. Walsh speaking to him, but a light above a shop window across the street distracted him, as did the sign in the window that definitely wasn't there the day before.

FOR SALE.

And below the words was a phone number—a phone number for anyone who wanted to buy Boone Murphy's auto shop.

"Yeah," he noted absently. "You two go talk. I'll meet you back at the bar in fifteen minutes."

"Are—are you okay?" Casey asked, teeth chattering.

Boone turned to face her and nodded. "Yeah. I'm good. I just need to take care of something really quickly. Go warm up, and I'll be right back."

Casey's brows furrowed, but her confusion or concern or whatever it was lost out to the promise of warmth.

"Okay!" She stood on her toes and planted a kiss on his lips, then pivoted back toward her mom, who rushed her inside and out of the cold.

Boone forgot all about the winter temps and strode across the street until he was standing in front of the window that still had MURPHY'S AUTO painted on the glass.

He pulled out his phone and hurriedly tapped in the numbers on the sign, then blew out a long breath as he listened.

After four rings, there was a slight pause and then the practiced *Hello* of a voicemail greeting followed by a message that tied his stomach in knots.

"Hello. You've reached Elizabeth Westfield of Westfield Realty. If you're calling about a property of interest, please leave a detailed message, and I'll get back to you during regular business hours. If you are inquiring about our newly listed property—the *former* Murphy's Auto Shop—that building comes with a few caveats, mainly that it *not* fall back into the hands of Boone Murphy or anyone in the Murphy family. Thank you for choosing Westfield Realty for all your real estate needs. I cannot wait to do business with you."

Despite the cold, Boone could feel the beads of sweat form on his neck.

Elizabeth had come to *him* before the ceremony. They'd made the decision together not to go through with it, hadn't they?

He squeezed his eyes shut, forcing his racing thoughts to calm and rearrange themselves into a coherent memory he could trust.

"Our hearts aren't in this, Boone," she'd said.

Wait. No.

He concentrated on his breathing—an exercise

he'd learned in therapy—and waited until his pulse wasn't beating through his temples anymore.

Remember, he told himself. Everyone's mind played tricks on them when it came to memories, filling in the gaps to make the past make sense. But Boone had the added bonus of a brain that—when overloaded—sometimes erased certain things to make room for others. And the day of the wedding and then seeing Casey and everything else that followed? Yeah, that was overload even for a man who finally felt like he had his life under some semblance of control.

He closed his eyes again, slowed his breathing, and then let the scene replay itself to the best of his ability.

"Hey," Elizabeth had said as she tapped Boone on the shoulder as he stared out over the bluff.

He'd spun, then covered his eyes with his hand. "Whoa! Isn't it bad luck to see the bride before the ceremony?" He remembered laughing but also his throat tightening as he thought of Elizabeth as his bride.

She wrapped a hand around his wrist and urged him to drop his arm, so he did.

She was beautiful in the simple, long-sleeved, silk white gown that hugged her body and then pooled into a small train around her feet. Her dark, wavy hair hung over her shoulders in sharp contrast to the pale fabric of her dress. She was everything a man should want—confident, successful, loving, and *his*. Yet he knew in that very moment that he couldn't do it.

"You're not in love with me, Boone, are you?" she asked like she was asking him if he did or didn't want another cup of coffee.

"I love you, Liz," he told her, but she shook her head.

"That's not what I asked, Boone. And we can't get married on a technicality. Are you *in* love with me? Just answer with one simple word—yes or no."

He blew out a shaky breath. "No."

She gave him a sad smile. "I know. I mean, I knew. I feel like I've always known, but come on. Look at me. I'm pretty damned fabulous, aren't I? I deserve the real deal."

He laughed softly. "You *are*, and you *do*."

"And you are *not* the real deal, Boone Murphy. Not when you don't truly know what you want."

His brows furrowed. "How are you so sure I don't know what I want?" He *thought* he wanted marriage, someone he cared about lying next to him in bed, a future. Wasn't that what he was chasing with Liz?

She sighed. "Because you wouldn't be here with me—the *wrong* person for you—if you knew who the right one was."

The right one? How about there was *no* one. It was just Boone and his shop, and he didn't even have that now.

"Can I ask you one more thing?"

Boone nodded. "Anything."

"Would you have gone through with this if I hadn't said something?"

He thought for a long beat, tried to imagine himself saying *I do*, and realized he couldn't. Not even his imagination would go through with it.

"I think my timing would have been a lot shittier than yours," he admitted. "But no. I wouldn't have gone through with it. I wouldn't have done that to you." Maybe it was Eli's words in the hotel room, or maybe Boone had always known that while he might have been physically able to escape what had been holding him back from happiness, his head and his heart still knew that *this* wasn't the answer.

"I'm sorry, Elizabeth. I'm so sorry."

She huffed out a mirthless laugh. "Already it's back to Elizabeth and not *Liz*, huh?"

He scrubbed a hand across his jaw. "I don't have the right to call you by a nickname. You deserve so much better than a guy who thought he had it all figured out but apparently is still just as clueless as he was when he was a kid."

She sniffed and squared her shoulders, holding her head high.

"I'm gonna be fine, you know. In case you were worried. And it's not like you're alone in this as far as the blame game goes. I stayed in this thing knowing it wasn't right. You should go," she warned him.

"You definitely don't want to be here when my parents find out we're not going through with it. I'll tell everyone."

But Boone shook his head. "One thing I'm not doing anymore is taking the easy way out." He threaded his fingers through hers, and for a second, she just stared at him with wide, incredulous eyes. "It's not like you're in this alone," he added, echoing her words. Then she squeezed his hand as they both spun to face the small congregation of guests—as Boone Murphy made the first big step toward facing his truth.

A sharp gust of frigid wind brought him back to the present, to the phone in his hand and the outgoing message that had just played.

"Elizabeth," he said after what may or may not have been a pause too long for her to keep listening. "I'm so sorry for hurting you. Truly, I am. But you—you were the one who bought my shop? I don't understand. Can we please talk? Call me. Text me. Anything. Please. I just want to sort this all out so we can both move on. That's what you want too, right? It's Boone, by the way. But you already knew that."

He ended the call.

He'd hurt Elizabeth. Boone owned that. But wouldn't it have been worse if he'd gone through with the wedding and locked her into a loveless marriage when she deserved so much more? Now that he was so close to maybe, possibly, winning the love of his life back for good, he realized that all he was doing was repeating the same cycle over and over again—skipping out on his mistakes only for them to follow him wherever he decided to go.

A text popped up on his screen. Elizabeth.

> I'm at the Meadow Valley Inn. I'll be here through the end of the week meeting with potential buyers. If you want to set up a meeting, let me know what day works best. But I'm not giving you your shop back, Boone. I have to somehow come out on top here, don't I? This is the only way I know how.

Boone looked at the time on his phone. He still had ten minutes before he needed to be back at the tavern. So he set a timer and made a beeline for the Meadow Valley Inn. Ten minutes was hardly enough time to plead his case, but he couldn't sit by and wait, not when his future—when Casey—was counting on him to be the man he promised her he could be.

Boone needed to fix this. Tonight.

Chapter 25

"Mom, Dad is not having an affair. You two have been happily married for almost forty years. How could you even think that?"

Casey's mom rose from the small kitchen table to unplug the whistling teakettle. Her silver-streaked blond hair was cut shorter these days. "I like to just wash and go, you know? Not have to worry about whether I can still pull off a certain style," she'd told her daughter when she'd convinced Casey to lop off her shoulder-length locks.

"What about color?" Casey had asked. "You could pull off something really bold with your coloring if you wanted to. Or maybe just some honey highlights?"

But her mother had shaken her head. "What you see is what you get with me, sweetheart. Don't get me wrong. I love the way you change your look as quickly as you change your mind, but I'm simply not wired that way. I want to look in the mirror and see just…me."

Casey had done what her mother had asked, and of course the woman looked just as beautiful with her new do. But that last sentence—*I want to look in the mirror and see just me*—had hidden itself in the recesses of Casey's mind, popping out every now and then to what—needle her? Challenge her? Plenty of women colored their hair and still maintained their own identity. Why now, whenever she admired her mother's newer look, was Casey starting to question her own?

As if her mom could feel Casey staring at her from behind, the older woman rubbed a hand at the nape of her neck and shook her head as she poured hot water into one mug and then another.

She spun back to face her daughter. "Maybe I *should* have let you color my hair. Or teach me how to do makeup like you do. Maybe a smoky eye? Or what do you call it when you do that little wing thingy at the end of your eyelid?"

"Um…*wings*?" Casey replied, brows furrowed. "Or cat eyes?"

"That's it!" her mother said, setting the mugs down on the table before taking her seat again. "Cat eyes! Do you think your father wants me to have cat eyes?"

"*Mom*…." Casey placed her hand over her mother's. "Tell me where all this is coming from."

The other woman sighed. "He's been getting up early—before dawn—even on the days we don't have inventory delivery. He's gone for hours sometimes, and when he comes home, he gets right in the shower and then crawls back into bed like he's been there the whole time."

Casey narrowed her eyes at her mom, then lifted her mug to her lips, inhaling the comforting aroma of vanilla and almond.

"What?" her mom asked, understanding Casey's accusation just from a look.

Casey took a long, slow sip of her tea and then set her mug down. "Mom? How do you know that Dad is disappearing early in the morning, sneaking back in the door, showering, and then sneaking back into bed?"

The other woman sighed. "I am the lightest sleeper in the world. I didn't used to be, by the way. When I was a teen, in my twenties even? I could stay up all night and sleep until the next afternoon. It's how I knew I was cut out for being a tavern wench."

Casey gasped, and her mom winked.

"Aw, come on. You've never heard me swear? Not that *wench* is a swear word. But, sweetheart, I'm human, just like anyone else. I used to be thirty years old with everything ahead of me and nothing to wake me in the morning. Then I turned thirty-one and had a baby girl, and I've never slept through the night since. It just happens. Someday, when you're a mom—if you decide to go that route—you'll see."

Casey opened her moth to respond but then closed it.

"Oh, honey," her mom said. "I'm sorry I mentioned the baby thing. I wasn't thinking."

Casey shook her head. "No, Mom. It's okay. It's been twelve years."

"But you've barely ever talked about it," her mother reminded her. "I guess that's why sometimes I forget it even happened."

Casey shrugged. "And right now we're talking about *you*. So you're awake when Dad leaves early in the morning and again when he sneaks back into bed, but you're pretending to be asleep?"

"Well, when you say it like that," her mom started, "you make it sound a little foolish."

"That's because it *is* foolish. Why don't you just *ask* Dad what's going on?"

Her mother stared down at her mug of tea and sighed. "I did, finally. Tonight. It's why I walked out of the tavern…and apparently ruined a date with Boone Murphy? Or does he work for us now—in a tailored suit?" Her mom gave her a knowing grin, but then she sniffled and swiped at a tear under her eye. "You've seen him, right? Your father? How he's changed?"

Casey nodded, her eyes wide. "I was afraid he was sick or something. Is he? Have you checked with his doctor? Did you fight because he's keeping some sort of illness from you? Oh my god, Mom. Tell me!"

Her mother huffed out a laugh. "I'm sorry, sweetheart. Your fears aren't funny. We're just very much alike is all. I took him to the doctor myself when he started losing weight, and he's fine. Better than fine. His cholesterol is down, and his thyroid is doing all the things a thyroid is supposed to do—whatever that is. But he's...I don't know how to say this... He has *definition*."

Casey flinched and squeezed her eyes shut. She had *no* idea what her mom meant, but she knew without a doubt that she did *not* want to hear the word *definition* used in relation to her father—in *any* way.

"Oh, Casey," her mom said with a laugh, waving her off. "I mean *muscle* definition. Do you know that where he used to have a little beer paunch he now has...well, I guess it's a four-pack right now? Not quite a six-pack."

"What?" Casey snorted. "So Dad is, like, working out? But where? Why?" She started connecting the dots, and her smile fell. "You think he's doing this for another woman? Come on, Mom. That's impossible."

Her mother looked up from her mug and met Casey's gaze. "Is it? You said it yourself. We've been married for almost forty years. I've never once shamed your father about his appearance. Nor he me, by the way. But for him to all of a sudden make this kind of change without telling me, it has to be for someone else, right?"

Casey opened her mouth to argue with her mom but couldn't come up with the right words.

The woman *did* kind of have a point. This change in her father was a bit odd and out of the blue. Even when Casey questioned him about his health, he brushed her off. Was her father—a man she trusted more than any other—having an affair?

Casey wrapped both hands around her mug and comforted herself with another sip of tea.

"Well, what did Dad say when you confronted him about—about the affair?" she finally asked, not able to believe those words had just come out of her mouth.

Her mom rose from the table and busied herself with dishes at the sink, her back now to her daughter.

"I didn't exactly *confront* him," her mom admitted. "I just decided the next time he slipped away before dawn and then dared to slip back into our bed without so much as a word that I was going to do…*something*. So tonight, when he handed me my apron and said he heard it was going to be a tourist-heavy night, I just snapped. I tossed my apron back at him, told him he could ask his lover for help, and then I left."

Casey sprang up from her chair, nearly knocking the table over with her knees.

"*Mom!*"

Her mother spun to face her.

"Okay, first, bravo for standing up for yourself. Truly. I'm all for you being a strong, powerful, take-charge kind of woman. But do you mean to tell me that without any sort of confirmation other than a hunch, you accused the man who thanks you nightly for choosing him of having another lover?"

"How did you...?" her mother started. "He told you about that?"

Casey nodded. "You and Dad have something most people spend a lifetime searching for. Trust me. I speak from experience." She blew out a breath. "Has Dad ever given you a reason not to trust him before now?"

Her mom shook her head. "But—"

"But *nothing*," Casey said. "Unless he *stops* thanking you, every single night before he goes to sleep, for choosing him, then you need to give the man you've trusted for nearly forty years the benefit of the doubt and *talk to him*." Casey glanced at the clock above the sink and gasped. "I have to get back. Boone and I promised Dad we'd only be gone for fifteen minutes. He doesn't have anyone else behind the bar since *someone* had a little crisis of trust." She raised her brows but offered her mother a conciliatory grin to let her know that she was on her side. Casey was on *both* of their sides.

"I'm coming too," her mom told her. "You and Boone should get back to your date." Then she returned Casey's grin with one of her own, but hers was full of worry and concern. "You and *Boone*, huh? How did that happen?"

Casey shrugged. "I'm not entirely sure myself. But ever since that day he found me on the road after the accident, it's been like—I don't know. All these feelings I thought I didn't have anymore… Or maybe they're new feelings? But it's *something*." Something bigger than she was ready to admit.

Her mother placed a palm on her cheek and kissed the top of her head. "I want you to find whatever it is you've been searching for, and if Boone Murphy is it, then I'm happy for you. I just want you to be careful. It took so long for you to make it through everything that happened last time. Now you're going back to school. You're finally picking up from where you left off all those years ago. I don't want anything to get in the way of that again."

Like thousands of dollars she hadn't anticipated? There was more on the line than just Casey's heart. But this time around, she and Boone were different, weren't they? History only repeated itself if you didn't learn from it. She and Boone had learned… *something*. They wouldn't be where they were now if they hadn't. "I know, Mom. I know," she insisted. "You have nothing to worry about. Not when it comes to me and Boone." Although Casey wasn't sure who she was trying to convince more: her mother or herself.

"I'm going to clean up here and collect my thoughts, figure out the right words to say to your dad after behaving so rashly. Do you and Boone mind giving me a few more minutes? Then the rest of the night is yours."

"Of course, Mom," Casey said. "Whatever you need."

Her mother smiled. "Why don't you get back downstairs to your father…before Eileen ditches Paul and I really do have another woman to worry about."

"Were they at the bar last night too?" Casey asked.

Her mother nodded. "They got in just before closing, and she flirted her way to a piña colada even though it was past last call."

The two of them laughed, and all the tension left Casey's shoulders. "Don't worry. She's already got her eye on Boone."

But Boone wasn't going anywhere. Not this time. He might have vanished from her life once before, even if he'd been in plain sight the whole time. But he was hers now.

She smiled at the thought.

Hers. Boone Murphy. *Hers.*

———

Pearl Sweeney eyed Boone warily as he drummed his fingers on the check-in desk.

"What game are you playing, son?" she asked him. "I have it on good authority that you are on a date with Casey Walsh tonight, yet you're here demanding to see the woman you almost married two weeks ago?"

Boone pinched the bridge of his nose.

"How does news travel so—?" He shook his head. "I don't even know why I bother asking. What is there to talk about in this town if it's not everyone *else's* private business?"

Pearl narrowed her eyes at him, her arms crossed defiantly over her chest.

"I'm sorry, Pearl. Truly, I mean you no disrespect. I'm well aware that I've made quite a mess of things—tonight in particular. But you have to know it was with the best of intentions. Everything I've done in the past two weeks has been because of how I feel about Casey Walsh. Now I have less than fifteen minutes to make sure I don't undo all the progress Casey and I have made. So will you *please* tell me which room is Elizabeth's so I can make things right?"

The older woman sighed. "It's my inn, you know. I don't have to tell you anything." She raised her brows and squared her shoulders.

Boone chuckled. "Same thing you used to say to me when I'd hide out in your kitchen after closing in those early years when I didn't know where to go when everyone else was at Midtown."

Her expression softened. "Your parents were dear friends of mine, and despite what the rumor mill said…" She shook her head. "I always knew you were a good boy—or I guess I should say *man* now. How is your father these days?"

Boone blew out a shaky breath. "My parents seem really happy at the assisted living facility. Granted, they're the youngest ones there, but it's easier on my mom not having to be the sole caregiver for him. Plus they're getting really into bunco with a group of friends. My uncle foots most of the bill. Eli and I send what we can." He scrubbed a hand across his jaw. "I sent what I *could* when I had the shop, which is why I'm here. Elizabeth bought the shop, and I need to get it back."

"Room 2B," Pearl relented. "She's in 2B. Up the stairs and to the right. She's been there since this afternoon. Now get your shop back and do right by our girl Casey. And by Elizabeth too. I might not like her waltzing into town to lord your shop over your head, but the woman has to be hurting quite a bit to be doing what she's doing."

Boone nodded. He sure was good at doling out the hurt, even when it was the last thing he ever wanted to do. It was time to set it all right. For everyone.

Was this move impulsive? Yes. But he was aware of it. He'd set a timer. Even if he got carried away, he had backup.

"Thank you, Pearl!" he exclaimed, leaning over

the check-in counter and kissing her on the cheek. "You're the best!" he called over his shoulder as he headed for the stairs.

"I know!" Pearl called back. "And don't you forget it!"

He took the stairs two and three at a time so that he was at the top before the last word left Pearl's lips. And then he stood in front of 2B, fist ready to pound on the door. But he realized that might scare Elizabeth, and all he wanted to do was talk. *Listen* and talk—and get his shop back.

Instead of pounding, Boone knocked with intention.

"Elizabeth? It's Boone. I know you're in there even though you just screened my call. Nice job on the new number, by the way." He checked the timer on his phone. He had eight and a half minutes left. Could he be late getting back to the tavern? Sure. He *could*. But he'd made Casey a promise, and he was going to keep that promise and all the others he made from here on out.

"I'm sorry, Elizabeth," he added when there was no response. "I really am sorry. For hurting you. For not acknowledging how I felt earlier—to you *and* to myself. I truly cared about you. I still do. So can we please talk?"

The door opened a crack, enough that he could see one of her dark-brown eyes and half of her glossed pink lips.

"I'm not selling the shop back to you," she said coolly. "So don't waste your breath."

Boone's throat tightened. As much as this was about the shop, it was also about making things right. Maybe he wouldn't get everything he came for this evening. But an open door certainly was a start.

"Then let's not talk about the shop. Let's talk about us. Let's talk about what I can do to fix the hurt I caused you." He glanced down at his phone. "I just sort of kind of only have eight minutes. But we can pick things back up tomorrow morning if you're willing. Coffee? My treat?"

Elizabeth sighed but opened the door wide enough to invite him in.

"Let me guess," she started as he strode past her, his hand running through his hair as he tried to think of what to say next. "We're bound by one of your timers?"

He spun to face her and swallowed. Then he held up his phone. "It's how I function. You know that. If I don't write it down or—"

"Or keep track of time, you get carried away and might miss something important. I know. I almost married you, remember?" Her tone was gentle when it could have been mocking, and for that he silently thanked her. She held out her hand, and he gave her the phone. "I'll keep watch so you can say all the brilliant things you came here to tell me," she added. Okay, so maybe he deserved a tiny serving of derision. "Also, what's with the shredded tie?"

He glanced down at what was left of the tavern blender's evening snack and then shook his head. "Long story. Look, I should have done this sooner, but you said you didn't want to hear from me, and I took the easy way out and listened when I should have fought harder to let you know how truly sorry I am for hurting you and how I wish I could undo it all so you didn't have to waste your time on me."

She swallowed, glanced down at the phone and then back up at Boone. She looked so different. So vulnerable in nothing but her UC Santa Cruz hoodie and sweats. He was so used to her in her power suits and heels that the Elizabeth in front of him almost seemed like a stranger.

"So you're saying you wish *we'd* never happened?" she asked.

"No," Boone answered without hesitation. "You are an amazing woman, and I don't regret a minute I spent with you."

"But I'm not the *right* woman," she observed. "I'm not Casey Walsh."

Boone blinked. "How do you—?"

"How do I know that you were just locking lips with your high school sweetheart in a public tavern two weeks after you left me on our wedding day?"

Wow. Boone joked about Meadow Valley's gossip mill, but this took the cake—news spreading mere minutes after the kiss actually happened? That was fast even for Meadow Valley standards.

Oh.

"You were there," he said, a statement rather than a question.

Elizabeth crossed her arms and nodded. "It was quite a show. You walked right past my table on your way out, not that you noticed."

Shit. He knew how it must look from her perspective, but he didn't have time to explain his entire history with Casey to make her understand.

"The funny thing is," she started, "that all I could think was how happy you looked. How in the almost year that we were together, I don't remember you ever smiling like that at me." She blew out a breath. "I'm not a vindictive person, Boone. If you know me at all, then you know that much. I guess I just realized that I never truly knew you, did I?"

"Elizabeth," he pleaded softly, his eyes inadvertently dipping toward his phone in her hand.

She groaned and flashed the screen at him for a millisecond. "You still have more than five minutes left, so let me say my piece."

He blew out a breath. "I'm sorry," he offered. "You deserve to be heard, and I'm listening."

She leaned against the door, and he stayed rooted where he was, in between the bed and the dresser, giving her both space and attention.

"I bought your shop—well, my company

did—as insurance. I guess deep down I knew that the marriage wasn't going to happen, so I needed a plan B."

His brows furrowed. "Plan B?"

She nodded. "To keep the upper hand." She chuckled. "I told you I wasn't vindictive, but that doesn't mean I easily swallow my pride. I don't like to lose. It's as simple as that. So maybe I lost out on getting married a couple weeks ago, but now you lose something too. It only seems fair." She shrugged.

They went back and forth like this for a while, Elizabeth revealing more of herself than she ever had when they were dating, and Boone apologizing for not knowing how she really felt. They both bore the blame for how things had ended, but he couldn't get past the guilt of having hurt someone he truly cared about. *Again.*

Boone's heart sank. "I hurt you more than I realized," he said quietly. "I can't change it, and I will always be sorry for that. Tomorrow, if you'll meet me to talk some more, I'll tell you whatever you want to know about me and Casey Walsh. But the shop, Elizabeth. That place has been my life since I was barely out of high school. It's a part of me. It's the only place where I'm not the guy who's still learning how to retrain his brain to read, to remember, to focus on the moment and not risk life and love and—"

Both their heads turned toward the window that looked out onto the street—to the sound that pulled their attention in that direction.

Sirens.

Boone moved slowly toward the window, somehow already knowing what he would find.

Despite the inn being on the same side of the street as the tavern, he could still tell where the ambulance, fire truck, and sheriff's vehicle were parked. Right in front of Midtown Tavern.

"Oh my god," he whispered as he pressed his cheek to the window so he could see the person on the stretcher. He'd recognize that silver hair and the ever-present Midtown T-shirt anywhere. "I was supposed to be there. Shit, Elizabeth. I was supposed to *be* there."

"I paused the timer," she admitted from over his shoulder, her voice shaky. "I just wanted your undivided attention for a few more minutes. I don't think that was too much to ask. But I—I—"

He spun to face her. "How long have I been here?"

"Twenty-eight minutes."

There was *no* way he heard her correctly.

"What?" he asked, his voice sounding far away, like he was in a tunnel.

"Twenty-eight minutes," she said again. "*Go*," she added, handing him his phone. Boone realized he still hadn't moved. "Someone obviously needs you. I didn't mean to take advantage of—"

He pushed past her without letting her finish, his pace quickening with every step. He didn't even remember taking the stairs this time or whether Pearl was at the desk when he barreled through the door and out into the street. The whole *town* was out on the street at this point, and Boone had to elbow and shoulder his way through the crowd and up to the ambulance where Carter Bowen—fire chief and EMT—performed chest compressions on Bill Walsh while another member of his unit hoisted them into the ambulance.

"What happened?" Boone asked whoever could answer as he spun, hands tearing at his hair while he scanned the crowd for Casey.

Finally he saw her in the upstairs window—the one in her parents' kitchen that looked out onto the street. Casey was talking to her mother, who suddenly went limp, and Boone knew in that moment that whatever had happened to Casey's father, Casey had been there to witness it.

After catching her mother and settling her into a chair, Casey stared out from above, her eyes meeting his.

"Where *were* you?" she mouthed.

And that was all it took for Boone's world to crumble. Twelve years he'd spent rebuilding from the rubble, and in the span of two weeks, he'd managed to claw his way back to happiness and lose it all over again.

Boone pulled out his phone and opened his last text to his brother.

Help. It's happening. I'm losing her again.

Eli's response came instantly.

What do you need? Where should I go? Whatever it is, I'm on it.

Come pick up Casey and her mom and get them to the hospital. I think Casey's dad had a heart attack.

Already on the way.

Chapter 26

ONCE CASEY SAW THAT HER DAD WAS CONSCIOUS and cracking jokes with the emergency room staff—after having a *heart attack*—she found herself rushing for the nearest restroom, where she barely made it into a stall before dropping to her knees and emptying the contents of her stomach into the very public toilet.

Ew.

Not that she had time to analyze the situation.

"Walsh?" she heard over her shoulder, and she realized she hadn't had a chance to lock her stall.

"Please go, Boone. I don't need to be humiliated on top of everything else tonight."

Instead of feeling him leave, she sensed him move closer. Then his hand was gently rubbing her back as she heaved again.

She didn't have it in her to push him away, so she grabbed a wad of toilet paper, wiped her nose and her mouth, and collapsed onto her knees, falling back on her heels. Only when she was sure she wasn't going to heave again did she dare to speak, her back still to him.

"Where were you, Boone?" she asked, her voice

barely above a trembling whisper. "I was so busy bussing tables when I got back that for several minutes—*minutes*—I didn't know that my father was on the floor in the cooler unconscious." She braced her hands on the stall's metal partitions and pushed herself to standing. Boone gave her space to exit the stall and make her way to a sink where she could rinse out her mouth and splash some cold water on her face.

"He's okay, isn't he? Your dad's going to be okay?" Boone asked.

She dried her hands and her face, then finally turned to face him.

"He was getting in shape for their fortieth anniversary," she mused, huffing out an incredulous laugh. "Even bought tickets to take my mom to the South of France. Can you believe that? The South of France." She shook her head. "He didn't want to embarrass her at the nude beaches. So he started using the gym at the firehouse. The bike, the treadmill. Lifting weights. Never even knew he had a heart condition until he overworked it. Doctor actually said it was a blessing in disguise. Said this might have happened later in life when he wasn't healthy enough to fight it if he hadn't started exercising so vigorously. Ironic, right?" She was running on pure adrenaline now, afraid that if she stopped moving or stopped talking, she might just collapse.

Boone took a step toward her, so Casey moved one step back.

"I just want to know where you were, Boone. Where did you disappear to when we were supposed to be there for my dad?" She threw her hands in the air. "Why did I even let you carry me out of the bar like that? It was impulsive and irresponsible and—and do you know how much an ambulance ride costs? Plus the ER visit and my father having to be admitted for observation?"

Boone undid the knot of his shredded tie, gave it a long look, and then tossed it in the trash.

"Your parents have health insurance, don't they?" he asked.

Casey shrugged. "Of course. But they're a self-employed small-town business. It's not like they have some great corporate plan or anything like that. They're going to have out-of-pocket expenses they weren't expecting. And now finding out about the vacation my father already purchased? I can tell you where most of my moonlighting paychecks are going." She sniffed. "God, I'm the worst, aren't I? My father almost died tonight, and I'm playing the poor-me card, worrying about what *I'm* going to lose out of all this when I should just be grateful he's going to be okay."

"Walsh," Boone said, taking a step closer again. This time, she didn't move. She needed someone to tell her everything was going to be okay. She needed those strong arms to hold her and make her feel safe.

So she stood still, let him approach, and when he did take her into his arms, she collapsed into him and cried. For the first time in twelve years, she let herself feel what she swore she'd never feel to this extent again.

Loss.

"Casey?" he asked, but she could barely hear him over the hiccupping sobs tearing from her chest. She could barely make out the fear in his tone, the fear she knew was for both of them—for having almost found their way back but not quite.

"I saw her," Casey said into the shoulder she'd now soaked with her tears. "I saw Elizabeth in the waiting room. You were with her tonight." She didn't need to ask. All the pieces were falling into place.

"*Casey*," he said again, and she could hear the worry in his voice. So she straightened and stepped away from him, doing her best to see him through the blur of tears. To see *them* for what they were—a constant disaster waiting to happen.

She ran her forearm under her nose, then her finger under each eye.

"This was too soon. We never should have started whatever it is we're doing here. I mean, look at me. Look at us. Look at where we are again, at how much it *hurts* to still not come first for you."

"*Still?*" he asked, and this time, the worry was

replaced with something harsher, something she hadn't heard from him before—or hadn't let herself hear.

Pain.

"I know tonight was scary, but me not being there wasn't because you weren't a priority. And the same goes for when we lost—"

"Don't!" she cried. "You promised you wouldn't bring up the past. You promised we could leave it where it was and just move forward."

His hands clenched into fists at his sides. "Move *forward*? How? *How*, Casey? If you won't even talk about what happened to us, how do you expect to move on? *We* got pregnant. *We* lost the baby. And *we* suffered the consequences of you having to go through the procedure alone because my goddamn brain chemistry was working against me. I will *always* be sorry for forgetting the doctor's appointment and not knowing about this miscarriage until the ER. I will never forgive myself for not being there for you that night. But I won't ignore it. I *haven't* ignored it. Did you know that I didn't even graduate that year? The school let me walk, but I failed English. Both semesters. Finally got my GED a few years later but..." He shook his head and scratched the back of his neck. "I've been in therapy for almost a decade, thanks to my brother. I don't blame my parents. They were busy enough dealing with my father's injury and care. Eli was the first to notice that maybe what was going on with me was partially beyond my control. You want the laundry list of what you get when you sign on to be with me? Here we go: dyslexia, ADHD, anxiety..." He held up a finger for each item he rattled off his list, his light eyes darkening to a storm of blue. "I rely on calendars and alarms and reminders and—and medication to keep myself from messing up again like I did in school...like I did with *you*. And I've been so damned scared to tell you any of this, not because I'm ashamed of needing help..." He shook his head and let out a bitter laugh. "God, Eli would love to hear me come to *that* realization," he mused, staring at the ceiling rather than at her. But then he fixed his gaze on Casey again, and she barely recognized him. "I've been so scared to tell you because how could I do it without going back to that night twelve years ago? Because how did I dare ask *you* for help without making you realize I might mess up again when you needed help from me?"

"Boone," she said, her voice shaking as she took a step toward him, but he shook his head and held out his hand, halting her in her tracks.

"You want to wipe the slate clean and pretend our past never happened, and you want a version of me that doesn't exist." He scrubbed a hand across his jaw, and when he blinked, his wet lashes shone in the harsh fluorescent light. "I guess the universe *is* conspiring against us, because it shouldn't hurt so damned much to love you either, Casey. I don't think either of us wants to be the cause of that kind of pain anymore."

He stood there for a moment after echoing her own words back at her after all these years, and then he simply pivoted toward the bathroom's exit and walked out.

When the door swung open only moments later, Casey dared to let hope in. But when Ivy's eyes met hers, Casey's knees finally gave out, and she sank to the floor. Ivy was next to her in a matter of seconds, her arms around Casey's shoulders as Casey finally let out all that she'd buried for the past twelve years.

"I really lost him this time," she admitted when she was finally able to catch her breath.

"What do you mean?" Ivy asked. "Carter said your dad's going to be okay—ready to hit those South of France nude beaches in time for their anniversary trip."

Casey shook her head and straightened where the two of them sat.

"Boone," she answered with a sniffle. "I messed up, Ives. Big time. I've spent so much time building up my defenses and protecting myself from the past that I never truly gave him the chance he deserved. I never saw him—like, *truly* saw him and how much he's been hurting too. And now he's gone."

Ivy squeezed her shoulders. "What do you mean, gone? I saw him out there talking to the doctor and your mom, checking on your dad's prognosis. He's the one who told me to come in here and check on you."

Casey's heart squeezed, and her throat tightened. Because of course he could end things like that and still send Ivy in to make sure she was okay. Not that Casey believed she'd *ever* truly be okay.

"I still lost him, Ives. That's why he had you check on me. Because it just ended. *We* ended. But he's too good a man to walk out on me and leave me to my own devices." She squeezed her eyes shut and leaned on her best friend's shoulder. "I'm so tired," she said.

Ivy rubbed a hand up and down Casey's arm. "I know, honey. I know."

When she finally made it to her father's room, where he'd be staying for observation, Casey's mom was already curled up in the chair beside his bed, her hand in his as she snored softly.

"Hey, sweetheart." His head turned toward the door as Casey entered.

"Sorry, Dad. I didn't mean to wake you."

He laughed. "Like I could sleep while your mother is sawing logs over here?"

Casey meant to laugh with him, but instead silent tears started streaming down her cheeks.

"Sweetheart," he said again, then held out his open arm.

Casey rushed to him, hugging him carefully, gently, but hoping he could still feel all her love.

"I'm so sorry, baby girl," he whispered. "You must have been so scared."

She nodded against his shoulder, then rose and glanced around the room.

"Don't you want to go home and get some sleep?" her father asked as both their eyes locked on the small love seat beneath the window across from his bed.

She shook her head and kissed him on the forehead. "If you think I'm leaving you for even a *second*…" Then she made her way to the small piece of furniture. If her mother could make do on a chair, Casey could certainly make the sad excuse for a couch work. "You're not going to be able to get rid of me," she added, settling in and pulling her knees to her chest so she could stretch the skirt of her dress over her exposed skin. "I might even have to tag along on that anniversary trip too."

"Never gonna happen, darlin'," her mother chimed in, eyes still closed and voice groggy with sleep. "And I *don't* saw logs."

A second later, she was snoring again.

Casey and her father both snorted, and she realized how much of both her parents had found their way to her—her mother's silent struggle with trust, even when she knew in her heart her father couldn't love anyone more, and her father's private worry about how he might look on a nude beach in France. Casey knew she was a product of the best parts of the two people she loved most in the world. But whatever it was that kept them from wanting to burden others with their own needs had somehow found its way to her too.

Tonight she'd let them sleep—let her father's heart rest and start to heal. But when they got home, she'd tell them about the money she needed for school. But that wasn't the only factor standing in the way of her future. She'd blamed Boone for not showing up when she needed him, but the truth was that she'd been scared of losing him the second she knew the baby was gone. What if that was the only reason he'd proposed? What if he'd only stayed out of obligation? What if—what if she was an eighteen-year-old kid so scared of life not turning out like she'd planned that she turned her back on all that was good, pushing happiness away before it left her first?

She blew out a shaky breath and let the tears keep falling. She'd spent so many years afraid of vulnerability, and where had it gotten her?

In a hospital room.

Her heart broken.

Her life one big, scary question mark.

Again.

Maybe it was time for a new approach.

Sometime in the middle of the night, she woke

with a start. But her father was sleeping soundly, her mother now curled up in the tiny, one-person bed next to him.

That was when she realized she was awoken by the familiar scent—the clean, woodsy scent that could only be described as Boone. Casey glanced down to find his navy suit jacket draped over her like a blanket. And in that moment, she knew...

Even when she'd pushed him away that night he showed up in the ER after she'd already lost the baby, he'd shown back up in her room and covered the thin hospital blanket with his red sweater. With his *father's* red sweater.

She'd convinced herself that he'd walked away from her so easily, but he'd always been there, hadn't he? In the hospital. Across the street in his shop. On the road back from the wedding he never went through with just in time to save her from missing her interview—and from serious injury.

"Boone," she whispered, even though she knew he was long gone. In his own quiet way, he'd fought for her. "I'm sorry I didn't see it," she added. "I'm so sorry."

Now it was her turn to fight.

She slipped her arms through Boone's jacket and pulled it tight around her. As she did, a small piece of paper fell to the floor. No. Not paper. A business card.

Elizabeth Westfield, Real Estate Broker

Contact me for all your residential
and commercial real estate needs.

Casey slid the card back into the jacket's inside
pocket and snuggled back into the lumpy pillows
of the love seat wrapped—as best she could be—in
Boone Murphy's arms.

Chapter 27

Twelve Years Ago

THE ONLY PLACE BOONE MURPHY EVER FELT IN control was in a horse's saddle or on the back of his bike. But the stable wasn't an option this afternoon, not unless he wanted to help his younger brother, Ash, muck out the stalls before he had the chance to ride. Nope. Not today. Not with the letter from school burning a hole in his pocket.

Dear Mr. and Mrs. Murphy,

I'm Boone's English teacher. This is my first year at Meadow Valley High School and my first year teaching in general, which means I'm still in that eager-to-reach-each-and-every-student   phase, and I'm still trying to reach Boone. I know your family has been through a lot this year with Mr. Murphy's accident, and while I have done my best to give Boone some leeway to get his academics back on track following the upheaval at home, I wanted to let you know that he is failing the first semester of senior English, a class that is a graduation requirement. I have tried to reach you via phone and email but have not received any response. I hope this letter reaches you and that we can get Boone the help he needs to graduate in the spring. I've spoken to Boone myself about coming to see me during office hours for extra help, but he has yet to take me up on the offer. He's a great kid with lots of potential. In fact, I hear he's a natural in his autos class and seems to be a very promising mechanic. But he is at a crossroads that can and will affect his future if we don't intervene. Please contact me at your earliest convenience so we can discuss next steps.

Sincerely,
Isaac Navarro

Next steps. How could Boone focus on next steps when there were so many steps that needed to be taken in all aspects of his life?

Did he need to graduate? Of course.

Did he need to figure out how to be a good husband and father if he and Casey kept the baby? Absolutely.

Did he worry about what would happen to them if they decided *not* to keep it? Every. Single. Day.

And what *about* his future? Did he even have a choice? He and his brothers had already taken over the farm and family business. Was a piece of paper saying he somehow managed to *not* fail senior English going to change that? No. It wasn't.

Boone needed to shut out all the noise, to silence the questions he didn't want to answer. So he hopped on the back of his bike, took it out to the quiet country road that eventually connected Meadow Valley to freeways and civilization. But right here, in his small pocket of the universe, *he* was in charge.

He paused for one final moment to clear his head and then took off down the deserted road, opening the throttle and soaring as far as he could from reality. The trip didn't last as long as he'd anticipated.

He took the first turn on the winding road with ease. Again with the second and then the third. The next one was sharper. He remembered that much and eased up on the bike's power, but the herd of cows crossing the road hadn't gotten the memo that Boone was approaching, nor had Boone counted on anyone or any*thing* interrupting his ride.

Of course he panicked. He was a good rider but still new. He had the wherewithal to ease up on the throttle, but a hard pull on the front brake with nothing on the rear launched him headfirst over the handlebars—and straight into the herd.

"Those cows saved your life," the emergency room doctor told him, which—in the physical sense—was true. They'd broken his fall and saved him from the road rash, leaving him with nothing but a concussion, a few stitches, and a pretty banged-up bike. He was for all intents and purposes lucky. But it was seeing Casey's parents in the waiting room upon his discharge that told him quite the opposite was true.

"Shit. The doctor's appointment." He scrambled past Eli, who was still asking the doctor questions about Boone's aftercare. "Mr. Walsh! Mr. Walsh!" he called as he approached the two people who'd been like surrogate parents to him, especially this year when Boone's family had been through so much. "What happened? Where's Casey?"

Casey's mother swiped at a tear under her eye while Mr. Walsh looked at Boone with what he knew was a mixture of sadness and disappointment.

"Were you two going to tell us? About the baby?" Mr. Walsh asked.

Boone opened his mouth to speak, but the words wouldn't come.

"She was at the doctor's office by herself. Said she was waiting for you to go in," Mrs. Walsh added. "But she started bleeding and—and we couldn't get there before they put her in an ambulance and sent her here."

Despite the local anesthetic for the stitches, the recently closed gash that ran through his eyebrow stung, and his head throbbed. But it was all nothing compared to the tightness in his chest, the feeling of his stomach plummeting to unimaginable depths.

"Can I see her?" he asked, his voice growing frantic. "Where is she? I need to see her!" A hand landed on his shoulder, and Boone spun, knocking his assailant's arm free and the young man attached to the arm to the ground.

Eli.

Before he could apologize or help his brother up, a security officer had Boone's wrist in his grasp, wrenching Boone's arm behind his back as he struggled to free himself to get to Eli or Casey or anyone who could tell him that everything was going to be okay, even though he knew it wasn't.

"It's okay!" Eli called, quickly climbing to his feet. "He's my brother, and he was just in an accident." Eli's brows furrowed. "Jeremiah? That you?"

The man ready to snap Boone's arm off suddenly loosened his grip and stepped to Boone's side.

"Eli!" he said over Boone's shoulder, then glanced at Boone. "And the middle Murphy child is still keeping it interesting, I see?"

Eli laughed, then brushed his palms off on his jeans. "Didn't realize you were working security these days."

Jeremiah Thompson—who Boone remembered had graduated with Eli a few years before—shrugged. "It pays the bills while I'm in school part-time. Also good to have on my résumé when I apply to be deputy sheriff after I complete my degree."

Boone jerked his arm, which only made Jeremiah grip his wrist tighter.

"Do you think you two can have this reunion on your own while I go find Casey?"

It was only then that Eli seemed to notice Mr. and Mrs. Walsh standing ten feet away.

"Wait…what happened to Casey?" Eli asked.

Boone glanced from the Walshes to his brother to the guy still restraining him and let out a long breath, forcing himself to stay calm so that maybe, *hopefully*, someone would tell him where Casey was and how he could get to her.

"I missed our appointment today, and something went wrong. I should be there, Eli. *Please*," Boone pleaded.

"Missed what appointment?" his brother asked, confused.

Mr. Walsh finally stepped forward and entered the fray.

"It seems that…uh…Boone and Casey were going to have a baby, but Casey lost it and had to have a small procedure to…" He cleared his throat. "To finalize things and stop the bleeding. She'll be okay but…" Mr. Walsh squeezed Boone's shoulder. "I'm sorry you had to find out this way. Sorry any of us did."

Boone's throat tightened. This man should *hate*

him, should be screaming at him for putting Casey in this situation in the first place. But Casey came from better stock than that.

"I don't deserve your compassion," Boone admitted to Casey's father. "But I'd really like to see her."

The older man nodded. "We *all* deserve compassion, son. That doesn't mean we're not going to have some words about this later, but my daughter needs you right now, and I'm betting you need her too."

"Eli?" Boone said to his brother, then looked at Jeremiah Thompson, still holding Boone in place.

Eli nodded, and Jeremiah let him go so he could follow the Walshes to wherever Casey would be after her procedure was over.

The fourth-floor waiting room—the maternity floor—bustled with excitement as family members awaited happy announcements.

"We can get your daughter a private room," a nurse had told Casey's parents. "But it's located on the maternity floor. We can place her somewhere else if you'd like, but she'll have to share a room if we do. I understand this isn't the optimal situation, but the room is at the end of the hallway, nowhere near the waiting area. It's pretty quiet, actually."

So they'd opted for the private room, especially since it was available and they could wait there until Casey arrived.

Mr. and Mrs. Walsh sat hand in hand on the small couch while Boone sat in the chair on the opposite wall. They all stared at the empty bed for what felt like hours. Maybe it was because by the time Casey was wheeled in, Boone had lost all concept of time.

He struggled to keep from bursting out of his chair, allowing Casey's parents to be the first to greet their daughter, who they were told was still groggy from the anesthesia.

"She's going to be fine," the doctor assured them as Boone listened from where he sat. "These things happen. The amount of bleeding, though, while not highly out of the ordinary, is a bit concerning for someone so young and healthy. She's also running a fever, so we'd like to keep her overnight and administer antibiotics for what looks like a mild infection. If it's okay with the two of you, we'd also like her to speak to one of our on-call psychologists before we discharge her. This is a lot for an eighteen-year-old to handle in general. But on top of that, miscarriages do a number on the hormones, and Casey may experience some postpartum depression or anxiety. Or she may not. We just want her to be equipped with the help she needs to recover both physically and otherwise."

Casey's parents nodded along to everything the doctor explained while Boone felt every word like a punch to his gut. *He* was just as responsible as Casey was for her being in this situation, yet *she* had to weather the physical and emotional fallout. How was that fair?

"There's a cup of ice water on the table for when she wakes up. If she can keep that down, then we'll move on to a clear liquid diet and hopefully progress to solids by morning."

Finally, after the doctor left, Mr. and Mrs. Walsh both hugged and kissed their sleeping daughter before nodding at Boone.

"We'll give you some time alone with her," Mr. Walsh offered, his jaw tight. Despite what Boone could tell were conflicted feelings about the offer, it was a kindness—along with compassion—that Boone didn't feel he deserved.

Boone nodded, then swallowed the lump in his throat before pushing himself to his feet and approaching Casey's bed.

She looked so small, so vulnerable.

"Even Supergirl gets knocked down a time or two," he said quietly, skimming his fingers softly across her long blond bangs. "It's okay, you know. You can lean on me, because I swear on—on—I don't know, Walsh. Whatever you want me to swear on, I'll do it. I'll figure out how to be better at this, how to make sure you can count on me so you never have to go through anything like this alone again."

He swiped at the wetness pooling under his eyes and sniffed.

"Murph?" Casey's voice was groggy and weak. Her eyes were still shut, but he felt the tips of her fingers brush the hand he rested next to hers.

"There's my Supergirl," he whispered.

Casey's eyes fluttered open, then closed. Then she opened them again.

"I was so scared," she told him. "I didn't know where you were and—" She stopped short, and the hand free from the IV reached for the bandaged wound over his eye. "What...?" She swallowed, then licked her lips.

"Are you thirsty?" he asked, grateful for the temporary reprieve of having to tell her where he'd been.

She nodded.

Boone pulled the small rolling table over to the bedside and held the plastic cup and straw for her while she leaned up on her elbows and took in a few large sips.

"Careful," he said. "Doc told your parents you might be a little queasy, so go slow."

Her eyes widened and seemed to lock into focus. "My parents are here? And they know? They know about the baby and us and..." Tears leaked out of the corners of her eyes as Boone nodded.

"I'm so sorry I wasn't there, Walsh. You have no idea how sorry I am that you had to go through this alone. I don't know..." He scrubbed a hand across his face. "I don't know why I do these things, Case.

I don't know why I forget or get lost in my thoughts or on the bike when I try to outrun them. I don't—"

"You were on your bike?" she interrupted, voice trembling.

Boone set the water back on the table, then clasped her hand in his.

"I just needed to clear my head. I needed to get away from all the noise. I remembered the appointment. I swear I did. But then I took a turn too fast, and there was a herd of cows—"

"You were on your *bike*," she said again, this time an emphatic accusation rather than a question. "You were risking your life on your bike while I was waiting for you because *you* needed to clear your head."

"Casey," he pleaded, but she shook her head. Then she pushed herself to sitting, wincing as she did. "Does it hurt?" he asked. "Of course it hurts. Don't answer that. Shit, Casey. I don't know what to say to make you understand that this is killing me."

She reached for his face and ran the tips of her fingers over the surgical tape above his wound.

"You could have killed yourself today, Boone. We never even had the chance to figure out what we wanted, but I could have lost the baby *and* you all in one day. Yes, Boone. It hurts." She pressed a hand to her chest. "Loving a boy like you hurts *too* much. And I—I don't want to hurt like this ever again."

Present Day

Once they were parked in front of the vet clinic, Eli stared at him for several long moments and then sighed.

"Why did it take you more than a decade to tell me the whole story?" Boone's brother asked.

Boone shrugged. "I told Dr. Sharon. And the knitting group."

Eli's eyes widened. "I'm sorry, what? The knitting group?" Then he looked Boone up and down. "Where's my tie...and my jacket?"

Boone sighed. "Can we focus on the big picture here, which is that I have basically irreparably hurt the woman I love—again—*and* that I needed to call my big brother to help clean up my mess? *Again.*"

Eli shook his head. "Not irreparably."

"You weren't there, Eli. You didn't see the hurt in her eyes twelve years ago and again today," Boone told him.

This time, his brother shrugged. "You're still wrong."

"And you're starting to annoy me, even though you came through for me in so many ways tonight and I should probably thank you, especially for the free suit that you don't expect me to return." Boone winced, yet talking to his brother like this—no matter how wrong the guy was—somehow made the weight pressing down on his chest feel a little lighter, a little less suffocating.

Eli turned as best he could in the driver's seat to better face him. "If the damage you did when you were a scared kid who didn't know he was self-medicating with some semi-reckless behavior was *actually* irreparable, Casey never would have given you a second chance. If you two were able to find your way back to each other after all those years, then maybe there's a chance that tonight wasn't the end."

Boone opened his mouth to argue with his brother but then realized the guy had a point. "Okay," he said, finally giving in as he realized he'd missed one tiny detail. "But there's one more thing."

Eli rubbed a hand across his cleanly shaved jaw, and Boone chuckled softly. They were so alike—the two of them—but worlds apart in how they lived their lives. Yet neither of them, Boone guessed, was happy.

"Lay it on me," Eli said with resignation.

Boone blew out a shaky breath. "I sort of let her have it. Like everything that had been building in me for the past decade. Her one condition on us getting back together was that we left the past in the past, and I couldn't do it, Eli. I couldn't, not when everything I am today—the good, the bad, and everything in between that I'm damn proud to be, by the way—is because of who I was then. Really, the man I am today is...um...all thanks to you." His throat tightened, and he cleared it as Eli's eyes widened. Boone waved him off. "I'm not good at this stuff, so just let me get it all out there. I promise not to just walk away like I did with Casey."

Eli winced. "You walked out on her? At the hospital? Yikes."

"I know," Boone agreed. "Look, I was a mess back then. You had your hands full going to school and keeping the horse ranch up and running, but somehow you also found time to look after me and Ash. If you hadn't come to the ER that day and found the letter from Mr. Navarro?" Boone shook his head. "I'd probably still be pretty damned lost. But you took me to the doctor. You got me tested for *all* the possible learning disorders, and thanks to you, I'm a mostly functioning adult today."

Eli laughed, then cleared his own throat. Boone knew they were reaching some emotional territory, which Eli handled about as well as Boone did, so he brought it back to the present.

"I love her, Eli. I truly do. But it shouldn't hurt this much, should it?" he finally asked.

Eli clapped a hand on Boone's shoulder and squeezed. "Things weren't always perfect with Tess," he said, and Boone held his breath as his brother continued with a subject he rarely broached—his late wife. "But I would relive every fight, every time we hurt each other with the mistakes we made, if it meant having her back here with me. There will always be lows to go with the highs, Little Brother. That's how you know the good times are good. You just have to ask yourself if those peaks are worth a few valleys every now and then."

Boone nodded. "Make sure she loves me at my best but can also still find that hidden ray of light when I'm at my worst and vice versa?"

"Yeah," Eli noted, brows furrowed. "That's some damned good advice. Who said that?"

Boone grinned. "You did, Brother. *You* did."

Chapter 28

CASEY PROPPED A COUPLE OF THROW PILLOWS on her father's old but trusty brown leather recliner.

"Take it easy," she said, motioning for him to finally sit down. "No need to rush. The chair's not going anywhere."

"It is if *I* have anything to say about it!" Casey's mother called from where she was still loading in casserole dishes and cooler bags that had been left outside the apartment door, the whole town rallying to take care of the family who took care of them every afternoon and evening.

Casey's dad lowered himself into the chair and let out a contented sigh. "If you *ever* see your mother dragging this beauty out of the apartment door, call Sheriff Thompson, because I've obviously been murdered."

Casey snorted and swatted him playfully on the shoulder.

"Hey there," he said. "I thought you were supposed to be taking care of the patient, not abusing him."

Casey's mom breezed past them with cooler bags hanging over each arm and a stack of casseroles in her hands. "Your daughter has *lived* in that hospital room with you all week while I tended to the tavern. I think she's more than done her part of taking care of you, Mr. Nude Beach."

Her mother chuckled, and Casey winced. "Can there please be *no* mention of nude beaches while I'm around?" she begged. "But also, now that we're home and I *am* around, I need to talk to you two about some things. But only if you're feeling up to it, Dad."

It had been a whirlwind of a week—Casey coordinating all her father's care both at the hospital and for after he was released while her mother kept the family business afloat. She'd barely had a chance to breathe, let alone figure out next steps—if there *were* next steps to take—with Boone. Granted, she hadn't contacted him yet, but he hadn't reached out either. Though telling her it hurt too much to love her and then walking out the door didn't require much reaching out after, did it?

"This sounds serious. Is it serious? Remember I have a weak heart," her father teased as her mother strolled back from the kitchen and took a seat on the couch.

Casey dragged a chair from the kitchen table into the living room and sat facing her mom so they were all in a small circle or triangle of sorts. Then she crossed her arms and gave her dad a pointed look.

"I appreciate you cracking jokes, Dad, but you scared the hell out of me the other night, and I'm gonna be traumatized likely for the rest of my life, so think about that the next time you worry about what Mom or everyone else in the South of France is going to think when they see you naked." She winced at her own mention of the nude beach situation.

Her father leaned forward and rested a hand on her knee. "I am so sorry for scaring you, sweetheart. You know I am. This is just how we Walshes do things, right? We laugh. We put on a brave face. We don't let our fears get the best of us."

Casey let out a long sigh. "Yeah, see, *why* do we do things like that?" Her father opened his mouth to respond, but Casey held up a finger. "Just wait. That was sort of rhetorical, and I'm just kind of working this out as I go. Here's the thing. I love you two, *so* much. But I'm not sure I really *know* you or that you really know me. We are all so good at the humor and the brave-face thing that I think we might have missed out on learning a hell of a lot more about each other than we know. You know? I don't know." She let out a nervous laugh as her parents simply stared at her. "Okay, here goes," she continued, taking a steadying breath. "I *love* Boone Murphy. I think I have for most of my life, even the years we weren't together. But I was so devastated at what happened to us. I needed someone to blame, some way to avoid the prospect of losing him in a way I couldn't control, so I pushed him away before he had the chance to do the same to me—before I had the chance to get to truly know him and all the stuff I didn't even know he was dealing with because I was so focused on dealing with *me*. I was protecting *my* heart and trying to leave the past in the past. But all that did was cause me more hurt in the long run. I don't want that to be me anymore."

"Oh, honey," her mother sighed, leaning forward and pressing a hand to Casey's cheek. "We never meant to teach you to hide yourself away like that." A tear streamed down the other woman's cheek. "We just wanted you to be happy. But maybe we went too far in the other direction." Her mother turned to face her father. "I should have *asked* you about sneaking out in the mornings rather than just accusing you and walking out that night."

Her father nodded. "And I should have told you up front what I was doing. I still could have kept the trip a secret if I had, but I guess part of me was embarrassed about trying so hard to impress you after all these years. But the truth is that I still can't believe you picked *me*. It's why I thank you every night and hope I do my best to deserve you for yet another day."

Casey swiped at a tear under her eye and sniffled. "Well, I guess the dam is broken now." She let out a combination of a laugh and a sob. "Haven't let myself do this for more than a decade, so it looks like I'm making up for lost time."

Both Casey and her mom, as if choreographed, left their seats to kneel next to the recliner as they all wrapped each other in a much-needed, tear-soaked group hug.

When she was finally back in her chair, Casey blew out a long, shaky breath before breaking the news. "I'm not going to go finish cosmetology school," she said. "At least not this year. The tuition is more than I was expecting, and you two are going to need help both at the tavern and with the medical bills, so I'm putting things on hold for one more year."

Her mother shook her head as her father pressed a hand over his heart, and Casey's stomach sank.

"Are you okay, Dad? Should I call the doctor? Dammit, I should have waited another day or week or something before saying anything."

"No, sweetheart," he began. "It's not that kind of pain. My heart just breaks to think of how much you've given up all these years, and here you are having to put your dreams on the back burner again because of me."

Casey grabbed a box of tissues from the end table next to the couch and passed one out to each of her parents before grabbing one herself. They collectively sniffled, blew noses, and dried tears, which brought unexpected joy to Casey's heart.

She laughed at the realization. "Name one person in this town whose hair I don't cut or color on occasion."

Her parents stared at her blankly, but neither said a word.

"How many wedding updos have I done? Or—or wedding makeup? How many men let me take a straight razor to their beards? Okay, that last number is probably really small because I don't have a ton of experience there. All I'm saying is that I've been living my dream for years. I'm just maybe missing that piece of paper that says I'm actually licensed to do what I'm doing, say, in an official salon-type capacity. But I know now that I *can* get back into school on my own merit, and someday I will. But for now, my dream is making sure you two are safe and healthy and that we fix whatever it is that has kept us from truly getting to know one another."

And Boone. The last piece of the puzzle that was her misshapen-yet-perfect-in-its-own-way dream was *Boone*.

"I'll start," her mother offered. "Breaking down the walls. I—I'm very excited for our trip, Bill, but there's one thing I've always wanted to do right here at home that I thought you might find a bit silly, seeing as how I've never shown an interest in it before now."

Her father's brows furrowed, but Casey smiled warmly at her mom, urging her to continue.

"I want to become an equestrian. Like, do the whole horse show thing. I know I can take lessons at the ranch, but I want to actually enter a horse show and compete. After I learn of course."

Casey's eyes widened. "*Mom!* This is amazing. And also brand-new information. I always thought you didn't like horses. You never stayed to watch my lessons at the Murphys' ranch."

Her mom smiled sheepishly. "It's because I was a little envious of how good you were—and ashamed that I grew up in a ranching town but never learned how to ride."

"I want to take my wife to a nude beach in the South of France," her father declared. "But I think you both already knew that."

Casey laughed. "Yes. Yes. We know, but I have placed a moratorium on that subject until I am out of earshot, okay?"

Her father laughed. "And what about you, sweetheart? Which one of your walls will you let down?"

She smiled at both her parents. Sure, they all had parts of themselves to work on to grow into the people they all wanted to be, but that didn't knock them off the pedestal she'd put them on. Their love and their relationship were still what she aspired to. The only thing that had changed was that now she knew they were human and flawed. They all were. Which meant there was hope for a flawed human like herself and the man it might hurt sometimes to love, but it hurt so much more not to have him by her side.

"I'm going to marry Boone Murphy," she said. "He just doesn't know it yet."

———————

When Casey arrived at the Meadow Valley Ranch, Delaney Callahan scrambled out from behind the check-in desk in the small registration building while her toddler daughter, Nolan, wrestled with Scout, their boxer, and their three-legged cat Butch Catsidy. The scene before them was both adorable and utterly chaotic.

"Nolan, honey, don't sit on the puppy, okay! Don't…" She lifted her daughter up, and the child proceeded to go boneless so that Delaney almost dropped her right back on the dog that was definitely *not* a puppy.

"Do you need help?" Casey asked, catching Nolan by the legs before Delaney could answer.

"Thank *you*!" Delaney exclaimed as she got a better grip on the squealing girl. "Sam? Honey? Love of my freaking life? Are you done in the office? Because I could use a hand out here with the animals or your daughter or both."

A door behind the registration desk flew open, and Sam, Ben, and Colt poured out of what Casey knew was not the largest room to contain three strapping cowboys such as the three men standing before her.

"Who wants to come to the barn with Uncle Colt?" Colt asked, holding his arms open as Nolan wriggled in Delaney's arms.

"She's all yours," Delaney said with a relieved sigh, handing her daughter over.

"If you want, Jenna and I can babysit tonight since you and Sam are both off. We'd love to have Nolan for a sleepover. Maybe let you two have a date night?" Colt offered.

Delaney gave Sam a knowing look, and he gave her the same look right back.

"Order in and put on some Netflix?" Sam asked.

Delaney raised her brows. "And maybe some chill?"

"All right, you two," Casey finally chimed in. "Remember me? I came through the door where guests are usually welcomed, taken care of, stuff like that?"

Delaney laughed and waved her off. "You're not a guest. You're family. Family doesn't get special treatment." She waggled her brows. "Unless that family is my husband on an unexpected quiet night in."

Ben pretended to gag while Colt blew raspberries on a giggling Nolan's belly.

Casey bore no blood relation to anyone in the

room, yet Delaney had been right. These people,- this town—all of them were her family, and she couldn't believe she'd ever mourned the fact that she hadn't left, because everything and everyone who made her happy was here.

"Is Boone at the stables?" she asked nervously. "Maybe leading a trail ride? I checked the barn garage and found Adeline looking much better than she did a couple of weeks ago but no Boone."

Delaney's brows furrowed. "Adeline?"

Casey nodded. "My car. She was a gift from my late great-grandmother, tough as nails just like she was, so I named her for my gran."

Delaney grinned. "Mine's Millie. My car, I mean. We should get her and Adeline together some day. I bet they'd hit it off."

Casey laughed, but she sensed a hint of worry behind Delaney's smile. Also, she could feel *every* person in the room looking at her—toddler, dog, and cat included.

"Um…am I missing something?" she asked.

Sam cleared his throat. "It's okay, Delaney. I'll tell her." He turned his attention to Casey, and her stomach sank straight through the floor when she saw the concern in his crisp blue eyes.

"Okay, now you're scaring me, Sam," Casey said with a nervous laugh. "Just say whatever it is you need to say."

He scratched the back of his neck and looked

away for a brief moment before meeting her gaze again.

"Boone's gone," Sam told her. "For now, at least. Said something about business he needed to take care of out of town, that he didn't expect me to hold his job for him but that if it was still here when he got back, he'd be mighty grateful."

Casey's eyes burned, and her palms began to sweat. The room felt like it was tilting too, which was a little weird considering rooms weren't supposed to do that.

"Casey, are you okay?" Delaney asked, but her voice sounded so far away.

"I...um...no," Casey sputtered, because she was done putting on a brave face when life decided to kick her in the teeth. "No," she said again, planting her feet firmly on the ground and forcing the room to stand still. "I'm not okay. But I think I know a way I can be." She pulled out the business card from her pocket—the one she'd pilfered from Boone's suit jacket. "Do you know if Elizabeth Westfield is still in town? Also, how does one go about selling a car?"

Chapter 29

IVY STARED AT CASEY OVER THE FRAMES OF HER oversize sunglasses.

"How do you know this…contraption…is safe to drive?"

Casey's jaw dropped, and she gave her steering wheel a soothing caress. "Don't listen to her, Addy. *I* know you won't let me down." Then she turned her attention to her best friend. "It was in Boone's garage. Or barn. Or whatever you want to call it. And it looked a hell of a lot better than it did when we left it on the side of the road a few weeks ago. Also…" She worried her bottom lip between her teeth and kept her eyes on the road ahead of her, since moving forward was all she could do now. "He left a note on the dashboard."

She hadn't seen it when she'd first gone looking for him the day before, but once Casey realized that Boone was gone and Elizabeth was back in Carson City, she needed to take matters into her own hands, even if it meant having the car towed from the barn to whoever might be willing to give her *something* for it.

"Um, hand it over, darlin', especially if it means the

security of knowing I'm not riding in a death trap. I'd kind of like to spend Christmas with my fiancé and also maybe, possibly make it to the wedding."

Casey rolled her eyes behind her own sunglasses, then gave a quick nod toward the back seat where her bag sat on the floor. "It's in the front pocket. Just promise me you're not going to—"

"Oh, I'm one hundred percent reading it aloud so we can dissect Mr. Murphy's every word," Ivy interrupted before contorting her body so she could reach into the back seat and retrieve the letter. "Also, I cannot believe you saved this very important information until now. How did you not call me the second you found it?"

Casey sighed. "I'm trying this new thing," she explained, "where I marinate in my feelings for a bit before reacting. Also, it gave me time to work on the new hair color. I guess my hair and I needed to marinate alone for a while."

Ivy placed a hand on Casey's forearm and gave her a soft squeeze. "I'm proud of you—of how strong you are. You know that, don't you?"

"I'm proud of me too," Casey admitted with a sad smile. Maybe she hadn't figured out the key to everlasting happiness or what the right next step was as far as her future with her career or with Boone—if they even had one—but for the first time in too many years to count, Casey Walsh felt comfortable in her own skin, in acknowledging her past and how it still shaped her present. The future, though, that was all hers to determine, and it started with Adeline.

"Okay," she said to Ivy. "Let's hear it." Casey had already committed almost every word to memory, so she guessed it didn't matter if she heard it one more time.

Ivy unfolded the paper—stamped with Boone's telltale mechanic fingerprints—and read.

Dear Supergirl,

I'm not sure if this is brave or the coward's way out, putting my thoughts down on paper instead of saying them out loud to you face-to-face, but here we are. First, if you found this note, that means you came looking for Adeline, and let me assure you that she is finished and good to go. Aside from repairing the damage from the accident, she's got brand-new tires fit for Nor Cal winters. Keys are in the glove box. Second, I was an ass for walking out on you the other night right after what happened with your dad. It was shit timing, and I own that. I've wanted for so long to tell you all the things you don't know about me, all the things I've done to get my life under control—things I'm proud of and that I work at every single day—but instead it came out like a weapon used to hurt you, because I was hurting too. I don't want to hurt you anymore, Walsh. I only ever wanted to make you happy—from the time I was nine years old. When I left Meadow Valley a few weeks ago, I thought it was to move on with my life, but I realize now it was because I was running from it—running from how I felt about you. While I know it doesn't make sense, please trust me that my leaving now is for you. To make you happy the only way I know how, even if we aren't together.

I have only ever loved one person outside my family, Casey Walsh, and that's you. Wherever life takes us from here on out, I want you to at least know that much.

Love,
Boone

Casey mouthed the last lines along with Ivy as her friend read them with a tremble in her voice.

"Are you okay, Ives?" Casey asked.

"What? Yes. I'm not crying, *you're* crying," Ivy bellowed as her eyes leaked evidence to the contrary.

Casey did cry the first time she read the letter and maybe the second and third time as well. But now she could hear his words with the confidence that no matter what happened next, they'd both be okay. And just because Boone was gone didn't mean all was lost. She could still show him in the best way she knew how that she loved him—the boy he was and the man he'd become—too.

When they finally made it to the vintage car buyer's lot in Carson City, Casey was ready to take one last look at her past and then finally let it go.

"Are you sure you want to do this?" Ivy asked as they rolled to a stop.

Casey nodded. "And Carter will be here to take us to the meeting with Elizabeth?"

Ivy checked her phone and nodded. "He's about a half hour behind us, which should be perfect timing."

Casey blew out a breath and then hugged her steering wheel.

"Thank you, Gran," she whispered. "Even though you've been gone for years, you shaped my life in so many ways, and for that I will always be grateful. But I need to let go of who I was and figure out who I'm going to be moving forward. Love you."

She turned the car off, pulled the key from the ignition, squared her shoulders, and opened the driver's side door. Then she tried to coolly exit the vehicle, only to be snapped back into place.

"Seat belt," Ivy whispered with a giggle.

"Right," Casey said, biting back a grin. She unfastened her seat belt and gave the vehicle's interior one last look before hoisting her bag onto her shoulder and finally breaking free.

"What do you mean, you already sold it?" Boone asked, pacing the floor in Elizabeth's Carson City office, which was half packed up and ready to be moved to her new place in Los Angeles.

She shrugged. "Well, I didn't actually *sell* it. I leased it. For six months. The tenant didn't have enough collateral to purchase the property outright, but they had quite the compelling argument to convince me to maintain ownership and let them lease it with the option to buy later on down the road once their business was under way."

Boone stopped pacing long enough to pinch the bridge of his nose in an attempt to ward off a full and complete meltdown.

"I had to spend the last three days in LA negotiating with three different buyers before getting the price I wanted for my bike, the price that would give me enough to make a down payment on the shop and…" He trailed off. What he actually meant to do with the shop once it was back in his hands had nothing to do with Elizabeth. What mattered was that he was here, ready to do what needed to be done to make the grandest of grand gestures, and she had gone and sold the place out from under him. "We had a deal," he finally added.

Elizabeth shrugged. "It was a verbal agreement to meet and *discuss* a deal. It wasn't a promise."

He finally sat down in the chair opposite her desk and let out a sigh. "I thought after that night last week that we were okay. Did I miss something in the last handful of days that said otherwise?"

Elizabeth folded her hands and set them on top of her desk.

"We *are* okay, Boone. We're better than okay. At least I am," she admitted. "I realized that night how much your life and your heart belong to Meadow Valley and the people in that town. I also realized it was wrong of me to take advantage of and manipulate you just to get a few extra minutes of your time. You're a good man, Boone Murphy. I want you to be happy. But I also want *me* to be happy too, and if that means leasing your shop for a worthy six-month contract, then so be it. Someday you'll understand. Heck, you might even thank me."

Thank her? How could he thank her for taking away his last shot at making things right?

An alarm sounded on his phone, and Boone pulled it out of his pocket to see the reminder that the next bus back to Meadow Valley left in fifteen minutes.

"I...um...I have to go," he stammered.

Elizabeth stood and brushed nonexistent wrinkles from her skirt. Then she held out her right hand over her desk.

Boone shook it absently.

"It was a pleasure doing business with you,

Mr. Murphy," she said with a warm smile. "Truly it was, Boone. I really do wish you all the best."

He swallowed, then nodded. "Yeah. You too, Elizabeth. I hope you find the happiness you deserve."

She dropped his hand, stepped around the desk, and placed her hands on his shoulders. "You too." She kissed him on the cheek. "Sometimes I think you just need to stop looking so hard, though, and let the happiness find you."

Let the happiness find you.

What the hell did she mean? Boone spent the entire bus ride back to Meadow Valley trying to reconcile Elizabeth's change of heart as far as selling him back the shop with her oddly vague advice.

He pulled out his phone and opened up his banking app, checking his balance to see that the transaction for the bike had cleared. There it was, a pile of money sitting in his account with no shop and no future to show for it—at least not the future he'd intended.

Maybe this was the universe's way of calling him selfish for trying to keep Casey in Meadow Valley after she finished school without even asking her if she wanted to stay. She deserved to sow her career-related oats however she wanted, to gain the experience she'd always told him she needed before settling down in a shop of her own.

Then the answer hit him. It was like he'd been

struck on the back of the head with a frying pan, not in the *Oh my god, an intruder* kind of way but instead the *Wake up, Murphy, and focus on the obvious piece of the puzzle you somehow missed* way.

Boone chalked the missed opportunity up to the change in his life's routine and all the thoughts swirling around in his head. He realized he'd been focusing on the *wrong* piece of the puzzle. It didn't matter what Elizabeth said or did to throw him off-kilter. He had the answer now, and all it would take—he hoped—was a quick phone call to set it all in place.

Chapter 30

CASEY COULD BARELY SEE OUT OF HER APART-
ment window through the thick flakes of snow,
but now that the sun had set and shop owners
had turned on their constantly growing holiday
light displays thanks to the upcoming contest—a
Meadow Valley tradition—she could at least
make out the dark window of Boone's old shop
and the untouched snow on the sidewalk in front
of the window.

"He's not there yet," Casey revealed as she
pointed her phone across the street so Ivy could
corroborate the evidence.

"Okay," Ivy said. "But why are you still in your
apartment?"

Casey blew out a shaky breath. "I don't know.
Maybe because Boone's been back in town for days
and hasn't contacted me. Just because he agreed to
meet me outside the shop doesn't mean he's actually
going to show."

She brought the phone's screen back into view
to see Ivy's annoyed glare.

"I'm doing the lights whether you're here or not,
Case. The second I see a tall, dark, and bearded

figure on the sidewalk—and I mean one *not* in a Santa suit—all bets are off. I'm flipping the switch for all to see, so you better bundle your ass up and get down there."

Casey opened her mouth to say something, but Ivy apparently was only pausing for a breath.

"I'm not finished," her friend sighed. "I know you're scared, honey. Putting yourself out there like this is *huge*. But he loves you, and you love him, and to me that means there is always a chance. Plus, you're the girl who doesn't hide her feelings any-more, right? So get out there and *feel* all of them and get your man back!"

Casey nodded, made sure her coat was zipped and her hat pulled down over her ears. "Okay. You're right. I'm headed down. Do *not* do anything without me there. Promise?"

Ivy held up her pinky. "Promise. But it's getting pretty cold in this back office. Maybe in addition to the electricity, you could have paid the first month's gas bill too? I can't promise that Carter and I won't take measures into our own hands and use the skin-to-skin technique in order to stay warm."

"Hey, Casey," Carter said, waving from over Ivy's shoulder.

Casey wagged a scolding finger at her friend. "No hanky-panky in the shop, you two. This is *our* moment, okay? Not yours."

Ivy snorted, and Casey blew her friend a kiss, then ended the call.

She dropped her phone in her coat pocket, then patted it to make sure the other item was there as well. Then she tugged on her mittens and headed for her apartment door just in time to hear a knock.

Her stomach tightened, and her heart squeezed. It wasn't... He wouldn't just...

She threw open the door, her heart hammering in her chest, to find her mother with a stack of mail.

"Oh!" her mother cried with a start. "I didn't realize you were going out tonight."

Casey gave her mom a pointed look. "It's *tonight*," she simply said, and the other woman's eyes widened.

"Is it *tonight*? I thought you were going to put things on hold because of the storm."

Casey shook her head. "I was afraid we might lose power, but we didn't, so I'm...um...I'm going through with it. If he shows."

"Oh, sweetheart. He told you he'll show, right?"

"Well, yeah," Casey noted with a shrug. "I said we needed to talk and he said okay, but that doesn't mean..." Nope. She was *not* going to focus on the *What if he says no?* when she could just as easily focus on *What if he says yes?* But because the latter still felt like a long shot, she decided not to focus on anything other than putting one foot in front of the other and walking across the damned street. *That* much she could do.

"Anyway," Casey continued, "I should go, so…"

"Right," her mother agreed. "Just wanted to drop these off since the mail carrier put all your stuff in our box again. I'm guessing you haven't emptied yours in a while?"

Casey winced. "Guilty." She grabbed the stack from her mom and thanked her, intending to toss the pile on the breakfast bar when she noted the return address of one of the envelopes poking out of the pile.

The Salon and Cosmetology Institute in Reno, Nevada.

Her brows furrowed as she stared at the bold-faced type. She hadn't yet contacted the school to ask if they would wait-list or defer her readmittance for another year or two. Maybe they'd already decided that since they hadn't heard back from her in a few weeks, they were going to cancel the offer altogether.

She dropped the rest of the mail where she'd intended but held the ominous envelope in her mittens.

"Do you want me to open it?" her mother asked.

Casey nodded, then shook her head. "I thought I was ready to put this aside, but now that it's real, I'm scared. What if this was my only chance to finish what I started? To make it official, you know?"

Her mom placed a warm palm on Casey's cheek. "This envelope doesn't change anything you've already accomplished or *will* accomplish in the future. Remember that. And when your father and I are back on our financial feet, we're going to make sure that you get that certificate, if that's what you want."

Casey nodded again, then handed her mom the envelope.

Her mother paused for a moment before tearing the seal and pulling out a sheaf of papers. Her mouth fell open as she read the first page silently to herself, then handed it with a shaking hand to Casey.

Dear Ms. Walsh,

We have received your deposit and the first half of your tuition payment for the final semester of your degree and are pleased to welcome you back to Reno's Salon and Cosmetology Institute. We know you'll be an asset to our current student body and are looking forward to seeing what you'll achieve at the institute and beyond your degree.

There were more welcoming remarks and logistical information about where and when her classes would meet, but all she could do was keep reading that first line over and over again.

We have received your deposit and the first half of your tuition payment for the final semester of your degree…

And she knew.

"I have to go, Mom!"

She didn't wait for the other woman to react before brushing past her and out the door.

Casey had zero recollection of running down the stairs and out into the street. She panted as she somehow made it to the other side and onto the walkway in front of the dark storefront. Snow fell on her eyelashes, blurring her vision so that she didn't see him until he was right in front of her.

"You bought my shop," he said just as she blurted, "You paid my tuition."

"I wanted to—" they both began.

"I should have—" they sputtered in unison again.

"You first, Supergirl," he insisted, and Casey's knees threatened to give out just at the sound of her nickname on his lips. But it wasn't time yet.

"I didn't buy it," she said. "Just leased it for the first half of the year. In a roundabout way, you sold and lost your dream because of me. And no matter what happens with us, I wanted to give you that dream back." She sniffed back the threat of tears. "I don't want to look out the tavern window and see anything other than Murphy's Auto Shop, which has been a Meadow Valley staple for most of my adult life. You belong there, Boone. You belong here in Meadow Valley. I don't want to be the reason you leave or the reason you lose what was always meant to be yours. Also, how did you know it was me?"

She blew out a trembling breath.

"Is it my turn now?" he asked.

White snowflakes peppered his hair and beard, and despite knowing he was likely getting wetter and colder by the minute, Casey wanted to keep him here for as long as she could.

She nodded.

"When I saw you took the car and that it wasn't in your usual parking spot behind the tavern, I had my suspicions. Then Ivy cracked the second I asked her," he said with a soft laugh.

Casey narrowed her eyes and glared at the dark window of the shop, but she wouldn't interrupt him.

"I can work on cars anywhere," he noted. "As evidenced by the little shop I set up at the ranch. But here's the thing. Despite the *multiple*—and I might add pretty damned painful—injuries I've sustained in the past few weeks due to ranch working, the time I've spent getting to know and help rehabilitate Cirrus has been some of the most meaningful work I've done in a long time. I still need to hammer things out with Eli, but I want to reopen our place, not for training horses but for rehabbing ones like Cirrus who've had a rough go of it." He brushed a hand over his head, causing a flurry of snowflakes to land on the shoulders of his jacket. "Work is work," he said. "And while I want to do something that's meaningful—whether it's cars or horses or both—my dream, Casey Walsh, is *you*."

Her knees wobbled, but she did her best to plant her feet firmly on the ground, if only for a few minutes more.

"But how did you get the money?" she started. "My—my tuition…" She couldn't form a coherent sentence.

"Sold my bike," he replied, and she sucked in a sharp breath. "It's not like I have very far to go when everything I want—everything I *need*—is right here in Meadow Valley."

Casey's eyes burned, and her throat grew tight. "But the shop. What are we going to do if you don't—"

Boone pulled his phone from his pocket and—no, not a phone but what looked like Carter's walkie-talkie. "Now, Ivy," he said, and the auto shop storefront lit up *not* with MARRY ME, BOONE MURPHY like she and Ivy had planned but instead with fairy lights curved into letters that read CASEY'S SALON.

Casey's knees finally gave out, and she dropped down into the wet snow, quickly managing to plant one of her booted feet back on the ground so that she was in proper position.

Before Boone could pull her to her feet, she had the small box in her hand, opening it to reveal the simple silver band.

"Marry me, Boone Murphy," she said.

Boone lowered himself to his knees right in front of her, clasping her cold cheeks in his gloved hands.

"And here I thought we'd been engaged for the past twelve years," he said, his deep voice cracking on something that sounded like a laugh but that Casey knew was something much more.

She gave him a tearful laugh of her own. "I think we've waited long enough, don't you?"

His brows furrowed, and then he tugged her hat off her head.

"Blond," he noted with a smile so full of love that Casey took a mental photograph, hoping never to forget this moment. "*There's* my Supergirl. And hell yes, we've waited long enough."

He finally kissed her, and she could taste the salt of their mingled tears. But these were happy tears because *they* were happy, and Casey knew that whatever they faced from here on out, they'd face it together.

"Thank you," he whispered against her mouth, then kissed her again.

"For what?" she asked.

"Choosing me," he answered.

Her breath caught in her throat as she nodded against him.

"Always," she said. "Every single day from here on out. You're my dream too, Boone Murphy. So prepare to be stuck with me for the rest of your days, because I'm not going anywhere unless you're with me too."

They might have been cold and wet and kissing there on the lighted pavement for all to see, but it didn't matter. Casey Walsh was done chasing the happiness that had eluded her for so long, because it had always been there. Right across the street. Waiting for her to grab on to it and never let it go again..

Chapter 31

New Year's Eve

BOONE APPROACHED THE SOLE OCCUPIED STALL in the stable that had stood empty for far too long, despite part of it serving as a coop for Jenna's chickens. The Murphy Horse Ranch and Egg Farm didn't quite have the ring to it he was hoping for, but just the fact that Eli had agreed to Boone's idea was enough for now.

Before he reached the stall door, a loud, definitive squawk sounded from inside, and Boone was certain that the last time he'd checked, Cirrus had been a horse and not a hen.

"Lucy?" he called, drawing out the hen's name.

She squawked in response, and he couldn't tell if the sound was distressed or annoyed.

"Cirrus," he cursed under his breath as he unlocked the stall door. "Please tell me you're not about to eat Jenna's supposedly psychic chicken."

The bird no longer produced eggs but was more Jenna Owens's pet than anything else, and Jenna claimed the hen had a knack for intuition when it came to matters of the heart. Boone, though, had yet to see her in action.

He threw open the door, bracing himself for the worst, only to find Cirrus dipping his head and brushing his nose against Lucy's beak.

"You've got to be kidding me," he said with a laugh. "Are you hitting on a chicken?"

"I'm sure it's purely platonic," a voice called from over his shoulder, and despite the bite in the air, a warm glow spread through Boone's body as he spun to find his fiancée approaching, her riding boots picking up pace with every step.

She wrapped her arms around his neck and stood up on her toes to kiss him.

"Are you ready?" she asked.

He nodded. "Been ready for more than twenty years of my life, Supergirl. You sure you feel safe with Cirrus?"

"Of course," she replied without hesitation. "He's taken to the move so well, and he hasn't knocked you on your ass in at least a few weeks. What could possibly go wrong?"

Boone covered her mouth with his palm. "It's like you're *asking* for the universe to mess with us. Don't you think we should try flying under the radar this once?"

She crossed her arms. "Look at what happened when we both tried flying under the radar to buy your shop," she said.

He laughed. "I guess even when it messes with us, we still come out on top."

"So? Let's get on top of that horse and go get hitched." She raised her brows. "Am I punny or what?"

She unzipped her coat to quickly show him her *bridal* wear—the white sweater on which Ivy had embroidered *Mrs. Murphy* in gold stitching.

Boone grinned, unzipping his vest and pulling open the denim jacket underneath to reveal a similar sweater—his black—with embroidery that read *Mr. Mrs. Murphy*.

Casey snorted, and Boone raised his brows.

"You're missing one tiny detail," he noted. Then, like a clown pulling colored handkerchiefs out of his sleeve, Boone pulled from his pocket a long blue knitted *something*. Because even he knew it wasn't wide enough to be a scarf yet was entirely too long to be a belt.

He wrapped it carefully but loosely around her neck several times to lessen the length.

"Um, what *is* it?" she asked.

He bit his lip and then laughed. "It's the product of me going on and on about you to the boys at our Saturday morning club. You're the one who told me I should take up knitting or something to help me relax. You didn't say I had to be good at it. But aren't you supposed to have something old, something new, something borrowed, and something blue? That's what Ivy told me. So the yarn is both old and new. It's been sitting on the shelf in Trudy's knitting nook for months, but it's also new because I'm the first one to use it. It's borrowed because I technically haven't paid for it yet, but I plan to take care of that after the wedding. And, well, it's blue."

Casey burrowed her chin into the soft not-a-belt-yet-not-a-scarf and grinned. "I love it," she said and beamed. "It's perfect."

Cirrus whinnied, reminding them that it was time to go, so Casey climbed into the stirrups, and then Boone climbed on behind her.

Lucy squawked and then backed out of the way so Cirrus could exit the stall.

"See?" Casey said. "She knows two crazy kids in love when she sees them."

Boone laughed and then kissed her on the neck. "I guess I can't argue with that."

They rode out into the crisp evening air, the arena adorned with twinkling white lights and their small congregation of guests—Casey's parents, Eli, Boone's parents, the Callahan crew, Jenna and Colt, and, of course, Ivy and Carter. Mayor Cooper stood at the center of the arena, ready to officiate.

"You're doing great," Boone crooned softly.

"Thanks," Casey said. "You too."

He laughed. "I was talking to Cirrus, but I guess you get some credit too."

They rode slowly toward their destination while

everyone pulled out their phones and started snapping photos.

Boone had made the specific request ahead of time that everyone turn off any clicking sound their phone cameras might make as well as their flashes. "We'll have to make do with the arena lighting," he'd said. "We don't want to spook the horse."

But someone either hadn't gotten the memo or had forgotten. It didn't matter. The second the flash went off, Cirrus stopped dead in his tracks, and Boone could feel in his bones that the horse was getting ready to buck.

A collective gasp rose from their guests as Cirrus rocked forward onto his front feet.

Before Boone could react, he heard Casey's voice.

"It's okay, boy," she cooed softly, leaning down toward Cirrus's ear. "You're safe, Cirrus. You're safe, and you're loved, and you deserve to have everything you thought wasn't for you. So just trust us, okay?" she pleaded. "Trust that no matter what happened before you got here, there are only good things for you from here on out. You're home now, Cirrus. Okay?"

Boone's throat tightened as he felt the tension leave the horse's body as Cirrus's weight fell back onto his hind legs. He knew Casey wasn't only talking to the horse. For all the times Boone had questioned if the mistakes he'd made—whether or not they were out of his control—meant he didn't deserve a second chance, all he needed was to hear Casey say those few simple words.

You're safe.

You're loved.

You're home.

She straightened and looked back at him over her shoulder.

"Crisis averted, cowboy. Are you ready for me to claim you as mine for the rest of our days?"

"I am," he told her, squeezing his arms around her waist. "For the rest of our days." And he'd spend each and every one of them making sure she knew she was safe and loved and home.

Epilogue

"I DON'T FEEL VERY SAFE," BOONE ADMITTED, HIS head resting and reclined on the leather salon chair, fifteen months after their wedding.

Casey crossed her arms and stared down at her husband's shaving cream–covered face and glared at him. "I am fully licensed to do this. You saw me graduate. It's not like it's my first time, and you *said* you wanted to lose the beard before Ivy and Carter's wedding. The wedding is tomorrow."

Boone cleared his throat. "Yeah, but if you slit my throat, I won't *be* at the wedding tomorrow."

She groaned, then decided to change her approach. "Murph," she teased softly. "I know you're scared, but *you* know I would never put you in harm's way. Can I just do the first shave—just one little line—and if I so much as nick you, I'll stop and let you take care of business with your cheap store-bought razor that will leave you all scabbed for tomorrow's festivities."

He sighed and closed his eyes. "Okay. I trust you. I'm ready."

She glided the razor through the foam and over the beard she'd already trimmed with the electric shaver.

"Am I dead?" he asked when she stepped away to grab the handheld mirror.

"Not *yet*," she teased, showing him the clean line and lack of blood on his cheek.

He raised his brows. "Okay, wow. That looks really good." He settled back into his chair and closed his eyes again, his shoulders finally relaxing. "I trust you, Supergirl," he told her again, and most—if not all—of her annoyance melted away. She still had one ace up her sleeve, but she had to wait until the final shave to show her hand.

"Okay," Casey said when she was ready for the last glide of the blade. "You did great, Murph. It's really a dance between the barber and the client, you know? A steady hand plus a calm and controlled man in the chair. If either one of us loses our cool, it's going to get all Sweeney Todd up in here, you know what I mean? So now's where you show me just how you can maintain your cool, because this is the final shave, and I'm going to tell you something really important while I do it, but you can't react until the blade leaves your skin or you will ruin Ivy and Carter's pictures tomorrow."

He remained still, but his shaky exhale told her she was on borrowed time. So because she loved this man and did not want to kill or maim him, she slid the blade across the last patch of beard, set it on the counter, and *then* whispered in his ear.

"I'm pregnant, Murph. You're going to be a daddy."

His knuckles turned white as he gripped the arms of the salon chair, holding himself as still as a statue.

Casey laughed. "I already finished. Blade's out of my hand, I swear."

He opened his eyes, his lashes already damp.

"What did you just say?" he asked.

She climbed over him, straddling him in the chair. He looked so young without the beard, like the boy she fell in love with all those years ago.

"Our family of two is going to be a family of three late this summer," she gushed.

Boone cleared his throat. "I will not tell Cirrus you just forgot to include him in our family count and also..." He lifted her T-shirt to expose her belly, then pressed his lips to her soft skin. "Thank you, baby Murphy, for choosing me as your daddy and this amazing woman as your mama." Then he looked up at Casey. "I can't *believe* you were going to tell me that with a blade to my throat."

"I didn't. I swear!" she cried, holding her hands up in surrender. "And I already went to the doctor just to make sure... I mean, I didn't want to tell you just in case anything happened like last time, but she said I'm already twelve weeks along and that everything looks good. We can go back tomorrow and listen to the heartbeat if you want. I didn't want to do that without you."

Boone sat up straight and cradled her cheeks in his palms.

"I'm putting every damned one of those appointments in my calendar with every loud, annoying reminder I can think of. I'm not going to miss a second of *any* of this."

She let out a tearful laugh. "But if you do, I'll understand, Murph. Some things are beyond our control, and we all make mistakes. I am *not* going to put that kind of expectation on you again. I love you and trust you no matter what, okay?"

He nodded, then pressed his lips to hers. His kisses were tentative and soft at first, but soon they were both a mess of swollen lips and tearful, wonderful joy.

"You will always see that hidden ray of light in me, won't you, Supergirl?" he asked.

Her brows furrowed, and she felt like he was letting her in on a conversation he'd been having with himself in his head. But she nodded anyway.

"Always, Murph," she insisted, then kissed him again. "Every. Single. Day."

Acknowledgments

None of what I do would be possible without you, the reader. So first and foremost, I want to thank you for falling in love with Meadow Valley and all the characters who make up my little ranching town, from psychic chickens, to three-legged cats, to the heroes and heroines who do their best to make you swoon.

To my agent, Emily, thank you for championing my work and always wanting the best for me. It has been quite the ride so far, and I wouldn't want to do it with anyone else.

Deb Werksman, editor extraordinaire, I'm so thrilled to be the recipient of your guidance and creativity. This is just the beginning!

Jen, Chanel, and Lea, I wouldn't survive without your big unicorn energy.

Lea and Megan, my hubaes, thank you for the shared joy of all things K-drama and K-pop as it's instilled a whole new level of love and appreciation for writing romance.

And always, thank you to S and C for supporting your mama's dreams the same way I hope you know I support yours. To Mom for reading every word I write and Dad for buying every book and keeping them closed. Love you all.

About the Author

A corporate trainer by day and *USA Today* bestselling author by night, A.J. Pine can't seem to escape the world of fiction, and she wouldn't have it any other way. When she finds that twenty-fifth hour in the day, she might indulge in a tiny bit of TV to nourish her undying love of K-dramas, superheroes, and everything romance. She hails from the far-off galaxy of the Chicago suburbs.

Find her online at ajpine.com, facebook.com/ajpineauthor, Instagram @aj_pine, Twitter @AJ_Pine, and TikTok @aj_pine.

LOVE DRUNK COWBOY

Was it her blue eyes...or was it the watermelon wine?

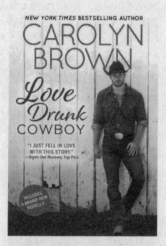

After high school, Austin Lanier left Oklahoma as fast as her feet could carry her. Years later, when she learns she's inherited her grandmother's watermelon farm, she just wants to sell the place, slip on her stilettos, and run back to corporate America. That is, until drop-dead-sexy cowboy Rye O'Donnell shows up next door and tempts Austin to trade her heels for cowboy boots…

"Fresh, funny, and sexy...filled with likable, down-to-earth characters."
—*Booklist*

For more info about Sourcebooks's books and authors, visit:
sourcebooks.com

NEVER ENOUGH COWBOY

This single mom may have her hands full,
but there's always room for a cowboy.

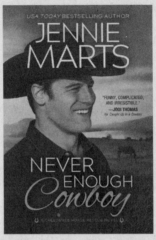

Jillian Bennett barely has a moment to herself between raising
her ten-year-old son, volunteering at the horse rescue ranch, and
working her new job as head librarian of Creedence, Colorado. She
doesn't have time for romance either, even though she and the cute
deputy, Ethan Rayburn, have been doing a lot of flirting the last few
weeks. But when he also forms a bond with her son, Milo, Jillian
falls hard, and Ethan soon realizes he would do anything for the
feisty librarian who's won his heart.

**"*Never Enough Cowboy* is the definition of
a swoon-worthy, must-read romance."**
—Sara Richardson, national bestselling author

For more info about Sourcebooks's books and authors, visit:
sourcebooks.com

COWBOY TOUGH

Sparks fly in this opposites attract cowboy romance
from bestselling author Joanne Kennedy.

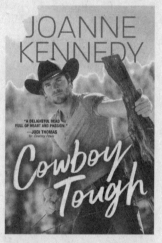

Mack Boyd might be able to ride a wild stallion to a standstill, but
he won't ever say no to his family. When his mother asks him to
help manage the family ranch, Mack arrives just in time to prepare
for an upcoming artists' retreat and to meet Cat Crandall, a passionate art teacher who can't be more different from him. But when
the ranch is threatened financially, can Mack and Cat set aside their
differences and work together?

"Full of heart and passion."
—Jodi Thomas, *New York Times* bestselling author, for
Cowboy Fever

For more info about Sourcebooks's books and authors, visit:
sourcebooks.com

CHARMING TEXAS COWBOY

At Big Chance Dog Rescue, you can always count on a cowboy to teach you a thing or two about life and love...

After an embarrassing blunder on her web show, lifestyle influencer Jen Greene attempts to outwait her notoriety by homesteading in Chance County, Texas. Jen has never lived this remotely before, but she doesn't want—though she might just need—help from Tanner Beauchamp, the handsome cowboy army veteran who lives down the road.

"A real page turner with a sexy cowboy you can root for."
—Carolyn Brown, *New York Times* bestselling author, for *Big Chance Cowboy*

For more info about Sourcebooks's books and authors, visit:
sourcebooks.com

COWBOY HEAT WAVE

Love is catching fire in Kim Redford's
Smokin' Hot Cowboys series

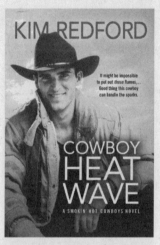

When Audrey Oakes witnesses a mustang herd theft, she looks to
hunky cowboy firefighter Cole Murphy for help. Cole is out to protect the last of his mustang herd, and he isn't sure that Audrey is an
innocent bystander. But he does know two things—that Audrey is
hiding why she's really in Wildcat Bluff County. And, that there's a
red-hot connection between them...

**"Scorching attraction flavored with just
a hint of sweet innocence."**
—*Publishers Weekly* Starred Review for
A Cowboy Firefighter for Christmas

For more info about Sourcebooks's books and authors, visit:
sourcebooks.com